PERFORATING

Pierre

Books by Pamela Burford

Jane Delaney Mysteries
Undertaking Irene
Uprooting Ernie
Perforating Pierre
Icing Allison
Preserving Peaches
Simmering Stu
Liquidating Larry
Scrapping Scarlett
Jane Delaney Humorous Mystery Series: Books 1-3 Box Set

Romantic Suspense
Snatched
Going Commando
Storming Meg
A Case of You
Twice Burned (Double Dare book 2)

Contemporary Romance
Rags to Bitches
In the Dark
Snowed
Too Darn Hot
The Boss's Runaway Bride (a novella)

The Wedding Ring matchmaking series:
Love's Funny That Way
I Do, But Here's the Catch
One Eager Bride To Go
Fiancé for Hire
*The Wedding Ring Matchmaker Series: Complete Four-Book
Romantic Comedy Box Set*

PERFORATING
Pierre

A Jane Delaney Mystery
Book 3

Pamela Burford

RADICAL POODLE
PRESS

Paperback edition published 2018 by Radical Poodle Press
Copyright © 2016 by Pamela Burford

ISBN 978-1-939215-77-2
Ebook ISBN 978-1-939215-99-4

Interior design by BB eBooks
Cover design copyright © 2016 Patricia Ryan
Author photograph copyright © Jeff Loeser

www.pamelaburford.com

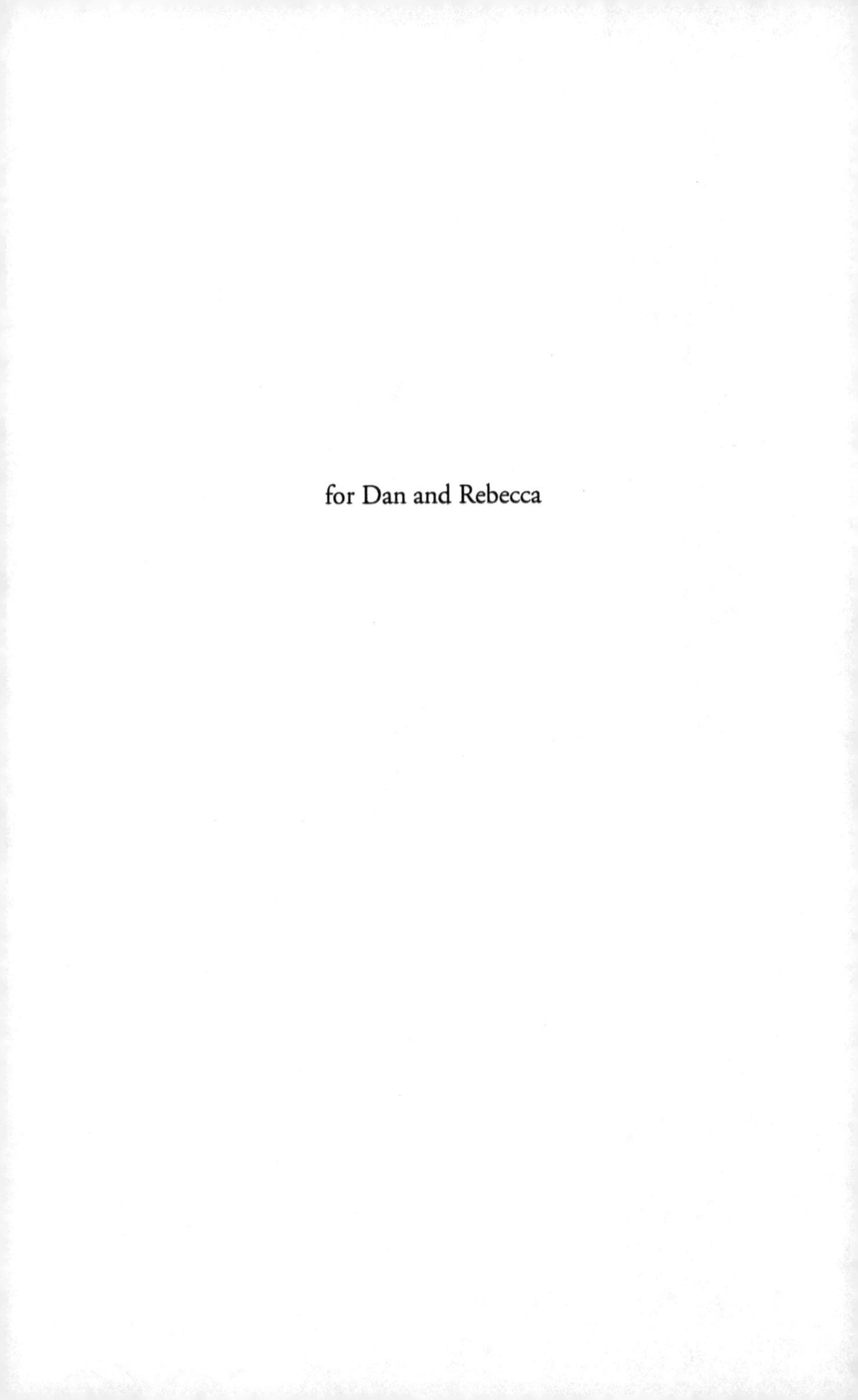

for Dan and Rebecca

1

It Ain't Got That Swing

I SHOULD HAVE guessed something was wrong from the way Sexy Beast was behaving. Well, not while we were still outside the restaurant, knocking. After standing there in a fine September drizzle for a couple of minutes wearing out my knuckles, I finally decided to try the door handle. What do you know? Swing had left it unlocked for me.

I experienced a naughty thrill as I pulled open the heavy door with its prominent CLOSED sign and ushered Sexy Beast into the dim interior. Not only was the restaurant closed on Mondays, but it was ten-thirty in the morning, too early to be open in any event. During regular business hours my little apricot poodle wouldn't be welcome in this fancy eatery—well, unless I bought a tiny "working dog" harness for him and tried to pass him off as a service animal. *Yeah, that's right, I rely on Sexy Beast to keep me from eating more than my daily allotted portion of escargot.*

Not that Swing offered anything as predictably French as snails in herb butter at Dewatre, his eponymous four-star restaurant in snooty Crystal Harbor, Long Island. Despite being French himself, he preferred experimenting with, and riffing on, the American culinary traditions. My favorite dish at

Dewatre (and Sexy Beast's favorite leftovers) was Swing's melt-in-your-mouth Dixie Brisket in sweet-and-sour sauce. All I can say is, this is not your mama's pot roast.

Once inside the restaurant, Sexy Beast and I made our way through the dining room, now stripped bare of linen and crystal, the chairs upended on tables. The scents of last night's dinner service lingered in the air, as well as the faint whiff of cleaning products. I wasn't surprised that Sexy Beast's sniffer was working nonstop. I was surprised when he began whining. Subtly at first, a barely audible thread of sound from deep in his throat. I ignored it. If I got myself worked up every time that needy little pooch got *himself* worked up, I'd be a gibbering idiot in no time.

I know you're wondering how Crystal Harbor's most renowned chef and restaurateur ended up with the moniker Swing. It's because of his surname, Dewatre. I suppose in France they give it a Frenchier spin, but on this side of the pond we pronounce it "doo-wat." Which naturally puts one in mind of Duke Ellington and his whole damn orchestra. After all, "It Don't Mean a Thing If It Ain't Got That Swing." *Everybody now!* "Doo-wat doo-wat, doo-wat doo-wat, doo-wat doo-wat…"

But to get back to Sexy Beast… and listen, you might as well call him SB, everyone does. I take the seven-pound troublemaker almost everywhere. I have a straw tote that he's turned into a comfy portable nest, complete with an old sweater for a lining and pockets for plastic poop-scooping bags and his favorite snacks. He lets me keep my wallet and keys in there too. Does this mean he's a purse dog? Or more disturbing still, that I'm one of those ditzes who carries a purse dog everywhere I go?

Okay, you know what? Let's just drop it.

Anyway, SB wasn't in his tote as we wove around tables toward the restaurant kitchen, he was on a leash. And it was all right because Swing actually liked my dog. By which I mean he liked to pet my dog and sneak him yummy scraps, not that he liked to imagine my dog arranged on a platter with a nice béarnaise sauce.

Which might seem like a creepy distinction to make if you didn't know that Swing had a reputation. I'm not sure how the rumor got started, but in this town that's like saying I'm not sure how the sun rose in the east. If gossip were a marketable commodity, Crystal Harbor would be the wealthiest town on the Island. Instead of, well, one of the wealthiest. Oh, you get my point.

A militant international organization called the Society for Endangered Animal Rights, or SEAR for short, had accused Swing of cooking and serving endangered species. Not to the general public, mind you, but to hand-picked, superwealthy individuals at private dinners during Dewatre's off hours. It was said that Swing fricasseed black rhinos and pan-seared Sumatran tigers. It was said that people from all over the world paid upwards of a hundred grand a plate for the privilege. It was said that they wore elaborate masks to conceal their identity from one another.

A lot of things were said, and a lot of folks in Crystal Harbor seemed to know someone who knew someone who knew… well, you know how the rest of that goes. But I'd never come across anyone who'd actually claimed to have enjoyed a nice, steaming bowl of loggerhead turtle soup at Dewatre.

Swing never took SEAR or any of his other critics seriously. If anything, he welcomed the publicity. We weren't best buds, but I'd known the guy for three years and counted him as a friend. Until I had solid evidence otherwise, I was giving him the benefit of the doubt. Plus I had recurring sex dreams about that brisket, and the idea of going cold turkey made me weep a little.

The hairs on my nape prickled as we passed through the dim, quiet dining room, a space I normally associated with activity and conversation, the clink of flatware and crystal, and the heavenly aromas of good food and wine. That alone shouldn't have creeped me out. It was the dog, I reasoned. SB's strange whining had ratcheted up in volume and it was beginning to get to me.

"Man up, SB," I said. "You're not turning into one of those neurotic little lap dogs, are you?" I said this just to make him feel better about himself. The poor guy had been a neurotic little lap dog from day one. There was no fighting it at this point.

In case you're wondering what I was doing there during off hours, I had an appointment to discuss a catering job with Swing. Veronica Sheffield's favorite aunt had just kicked the bucket, and only the best would do for her funeral reception. Veronica was one of my steadiest clients and she had boatloads of money, enough to sway even a world-renowned chef like Swing.

Right now you're probably thinking I'm some kind of funeral planner—like a wedding planner, only more depressing. And today you'd be right. That's kind of what I was doing for Veronica, taking care of all the funeral details. Yesterday, however, you would have found me at the Leonard T. Ahearn and Sons Funeral Home overseeing the casting of a death mask on behalf of a grieving widow. What did she intend to do with it? you ask. Why, place it on his pillow, of course, so she could continue to wake up next to him every morning. Yeah, I know, but hey, it's legal, and trust me, it's nowhere near the weirdest thing I've been hired to do. Tomorrow's job was a little more normal. I was scheduled to sort through a recently deceased surgeon's extensive collection of antique medical instruments at the request of his kids, research each piece online, and put them all up on eBay.

What's that? You sense a theme running through these various assignments? Then give yourself a gold star. My name is Jane Delaney and I'm the Death Diva. If you want something done to, or on behalf of, a dearly departed loved one, I'm your girl. Hey, it's not such an icky way to make a living. I saw a need and I filled it. The American dream in action.

"Swing?" I called, expecting an answer from the vicinity of the kitchen. Nada.

SB's whining had taken on a high, keening quality that skewered my cranium and threatened to scramble the contents. If he kept this up, Swing would regret having granted permission for me to bring him. "Come on, little man," I said, "knock it off. If you behave, you'll get a Vienna sausage when we get home."

Not even the promise of his favorite treat had the desired effect. Rather than lead the way in what should have been an intriguing new space, he stuck close to my side as I headed for the double doors to the kitchen. Light shone through the windows set in the doors. That and the unlocked front door told me the chef hadn't forgotten our meeting.

Not that he'd made a special trip. Swing routinely spent Mondays alone in his kitchen testing new recipes, planning the week's specials, and deciding which dishes would make the transition to the small screen and the cooking demos he regularly did on the morning news programs and other shows. This was in addition to his participation in those Food Network shows that pit chefs against one another.

I had it on the QT that the network was considering Swing for his own food show, maybe something that involved travel and adventure. And why not? The guy was telegenic, no doubt about it, and he knew how to address the camera so the viewer felt as if Swing were speaking directly to her. Yeah, *her*. We're talking serious sex appeal here. As in six-plus feet of craggily handsome, nicely arranged, French-accented USDA prime male on the hoof. I judged him to be in his early forties—his wavy, brown hair was just beginning to sport a few threads of silver at the temples—so he had the possibility of a long, lucrative TV career ahead of him.

I called his name again as I pushed through the double doors into the big commercial kitchen. Utensils and ingredients cluttered the U-shaped central work station. Shallots and parsley. Bottles of olive oil and Madeira. Breaded filets of meat—who knew what kind? I thought again of that stupid rumor. This meat didn't look like chicken. Veal, probably. Yeah, I was going with veal. I forced the image of an adorable giant panda out of my head and substituted an adorable calf with luxurious eyelashes. Yeah, big improvement.

Maybe my ex-husband, Dom, was on to something with his vegetarianism. He'd always tried to convert me and I'd always dismissed the possibility. I could give it a try. Then I thought of Swing's Dixie Brisket. Not to mention porterhouse steak, Peking duck, and charred hot dogs fresh off the grill, slathered with gobs of bright yellow French's mustard. To say nothing of the perennial deal-breaker. Oh, you know the one. It starts with *b* and it ends with *n*, and the whole middle part is filled with crispy, smoky *a*, *c*, and *o*.

Yeah, I *might* give up bacon. Who was I kidding?

And where was Swing, anyway? He must have stepped out to the john. Maybe he was in his office. SB's whining had increased in volume and he was attempting to climb me. Sighing, I picked him up, then jumped in surprise when music suddenly started. It emanated from the chef's cell phone lying on a steel counter across the room. I recognized the first few bars of "It Don't Mean a Thing" and smiled.

I found myself moving around the work station, intending to peek at the screen and see who was trying to phone Swing. As I rounded the far end, I nearly tripped over something on the floor. I looked down. A shoe. The shoe was attached to a foot.

He lay sprawled on his back. One could almost believe he was napping with his eyes open, were it not for the serving platter positioned under his handsome head. And the sprigs of parsley tucked behind his ears. And the great big cooking knife protruding from his white chef's jacket.

And the blood.

On the tile floor above his head, the initials SEAR had been written in squirts of dark liquid. A squeeze bottle of balsamic syrup lay nearby.

Sexy Beast and I whined in unison as I came face-to-face with what the dog's turbocharged nose had informed him the instant we'd entered the restaurant.

The phone was still doo-watting its little heart out. Numbly I glanced at the screen and saw a picture of a youngish, redheaded woman and the word *Chloe*. I slid to the floor, still clutching my dog, and sat staring at the thing that used to be Chef Pierre "Swing" Dewatre.

"They got him," I whispered. "Those wackos finally got him."

2

Ex–Husband of Interest

"WE'RE A BUNCH of wackos and we finally got him!" the man shouted from my TV screen. "That's what you're implying. Why don't you just come out and say it?"

The other talk-show guest remained calm, or as calm as she could, considering she had indeed just intimated that her fellow news-show guest was a coldblooded murderer. I recognized her from the image I'd seen on Swing's phone: an attractive redhead in her mid-thirties. It turned out her name was Chloe Sleeper and she was Swing's agent, the person who got him bookings on TV shows and public appearances. "Are you going to deny that you and your organization have been harassing him, defaming—"

"That's the least of what criminals like Pierre Dewatre deserve," the man shot back. "We performed a public service, bringing his crimes out in the open." The caption under his image identified him as Romulus Tooley, spokesman for the Society for Endangered Animal Rights. Romulus appeared to be pushing fifty, with graying blond hair, brown eyes, and a long, craggy face.

"You and your organization are the criminals," Chloe said. "You people set fires, bomb buildings. Your modus operandi is threats and intimidation. No one has ever proved that Swing did any of the things you've accused him of. You based your campaign against him on nothing more than rumor and gossip, and look what it's come to. If you didn't pull the trigger yourself, you might as well have."

"'Pull the trigger'?" Romulus scoffed. "I thought that arrogant mass murderer was stabbed through his cold, unfeeling heart."

"You know what I mean." Chloe made a conspicuous effort to keep her responses calm and reasoned. "One way or the other, you and your horrible organization are responsible."

Miranda Daniels, the show's pugnacious blond host, sat between her two guests. *Ramrod News* bills itself as a cutting-edge news program that gets to the heart of every story it tackles, but it's nothing more than sensationalist drivel. Which, I'm sad to say, is why millions of viewers tune in every weekday evening at six to watch it. The show's host lives to stir up controversy and boost ratings. I had my own mortifying history with Miranda and *Ramrod News*, one I'd be happy to permanently expunge from my memory banks.

"Mass murderer, Romulus?" Miranda said, with her Wicked Witch smile. "Do you know something about Chef Dewatre that the rest of us don't?"

"I know he was responsible for the death and mutilation of countless innocent animals, many of them critically endangered—"

Chloe interrupted. "You have no proof!"

"—and that whoever took him out should be hailed as a savior of vulnerable creatures everywhere!" He pumped his fist.

I didn't catch Chloe's response because just then the doorbell rang, prompting Sexy Beast to hurl himself off the sofa and run barking out of the game room. I still thought of it as the game room, even though the poker-loving woman I'd inherited my big house from had been gone for five months and I did little in this room except eat in front of the TV. Maybe it was time to start calling it the family room. Now all I needed was a family to install in it.

I turned off the TV and followed SB through the adjoining living room and into the foyer, where he stood scolding the big double doors and keeping his alpha female safe from whatever dire menace lurked on the other side. His diligence was proven effective with satisfying regularity. The UPS guy came. Sexy Beast barked like a maniac. The UPS guy went away. What more evidence did his walnut-size brain need?

I nudged him out of the way and opened the door. The man standing on my porch appeared to be in his late forties, of medium height and wearing an impassive expression. Everything about him was gray, from his close-cropped hair to his cheap-looking suit to the Impala parked in the circular cobblestone courtyard.

He said, "Are you Jane Angela Delaney?"

"Um, yes." I picked up SB and tried to hush him. "Can I help—"

He flashed an ID wallet with a gold shield. "Detective Paul Cullen with the Crystal Harbor Police Department, ma'am. Can I have a few words?"

"Oh." I'd heard the name once or twice but had never met him in person. "Is this about Swing?"

You know how they say there are no dumb questions? They lie.

"Yes, ma'am. Can I come in?"

"Um, well, sure." I stepped aside and set down the dog,

admonishing him to behave. As soon as the detective crossed the threshold, SB gave his shoes and pant cuffs a thorough sniff. Most people who meet my dog for the first time are charmed, or at least pretend to be. They reach down and give him scritches, coo at him a little. Not Detective Cullen.

He pulled a small notebook out of his pocket, looking around the foyer with its high, vaulted ceiling, curved staircase, and obscenely expensive macassar ebony floor. "Where do you wanna do this?" he asked. "It shouldn't take long."

I ushered him into the adjoining living room. Here the ebony floor was partially covered with a mosaic-patterned silk rug lovingly hand-crafted by a secret order of nimble-fingered French nuns. Or something like that. Hand-woven silk drapes adorned the towering Palladian window. More silk, in the palest yellow, covered the walls, on which hung a genuine Edward Hopper, a genuine Marc Chagall, and a genuine Henri Matisse—modern masterpieces that triggered not the slightest blip in Detective Cullen's bored gaze. I motioned to a pair of armchairs upholstered in ivory linen and arranged, along with a matching oversize sofa, around a glass-topped coffee table with a burl-wood cube base.

Okay, for the record, five months earlier I was living in a dank little basement apartment in a working-class town far, far away from this rarefied burg. Then my friend and best client, Irene McAuliffe died—well, she had help with the dying, but that's another story—and left me this mini mansion on five acres, this dog, and enough money to maintain them both. Actually, to be precise, Sexy Beast owns the house during his lifetime. I'm just taking care of it for him.

Stop snickering, it's just a legal, you know, technicality.

I offered the detective a cold drink. He declined and I

perched on the other chair, holding Sexy Beast to keep him from making a nuisance of himself.

"I don't know what more I can tell you that I didn't tell Bonnie this morning at Dewatre," I said.

"Detective Hernandez took herself off the case." Cullen's notebook was tiny, perhaps three by five inches, spiral-bound at the top. He flipped to a clean page. "Conflict of interest."

I frowned. Bonnie Hernandez had materialized at the restaurant that morning shortly after the responding cops had determined that yes indeed, there was a corpse lying there with a big old knife sticking out of its chest. She'd done what police detectives do, questioning me, looking for evidence, and bringing in the crime-scene specialists and ME. What kind of conflict of interest could she have, unless...?

Oh. For real? Swing and Bonnie? It wasn't inconceivable. I recalled that the chef's reputation wasn't limited to serving up endangered critters. He'd been quite the ladies' man. Had he done his love-'em-and-leave-'em thing with the beauteous Detective Hernandez? If so, I could only assume it had happened before she'd met Dominic Faso, my ex. She and Dom had been engaged now for eight months if you didn't count a three-month break this past spring and summer when Dom had tried to convince me to remarry him.

He'd only been the love of my life since eighth grade, and I'd only regretted our divorce during the entire seventeen and a half years since it had occurred, and he was only tall, handsome, and rich. Really rich. So why should I say yes when he begs for a redo? You don't want to jump into these things too quickly. Best to give yourself a chance to think about it long and hard so that said love of your life—he who you know darn well can't go for long without a significant other—can end up renewing his engagement to smart, beautiful, stylish Bonnie Hernandez.

I still don't know if remarrying him would have been the right move, but it would have been nice if he'd given me enough time to figure it out.

"Conflict of interest?" I said. "If you don't mind my asking—"

"Detective Hernandez is engaged to be married to a person of interest in this case. What time did you arrive at Dewatre this morning?"

"Wait, what?" I shook my head to clear it. It didn't work. I could have sworn he'd said… "She's engaged to Dom Faso. He's not a person of interest."

"Excuse me, ma'am, but that's not for you to decide. Now, if you would—"

"Trust me." I leaned forward, clutching SB until he yelped. "Dom is my ex-husband. There's nothing at all interesting about him. I mean… I mean, you know, related to Swing's death. He couldn't be less involved."

Detective Cullen balanced the little notebook on his knee. He met my gaze. "What makes you so sure?"

The prudent corner of my brain, the corner I have a habit of ignoring at inopportune moments, whispered, *Careful.* I'd talked myself into trouble before, with Detective Hernandez. It would be nice to think I'd learned from that blunder.

"It's just… he's a good guy. I mean really, Dom wouldn't hurt a fly. He's a *vegetarian!*" I didn't add that he happened to be a vanishingly rare breed: a vegetarian who hunted. He donated the meat to soup kitchens, but still.

Cullen stared at me. "Faso's a vegetarian?"

"Yes! I'm telling you, you're on the wrong—"

"So maybe he's involved with this SEAR outfit," he said. "If he likes animals so much."

"What? No!" I reared back. "He'd never have anything to do with those creeps. The things they do… It's no secret that Dom despises SEAR and its tactics. He and that Romulus Tooley guy, their spokesman, the two of them even got into it publicly last fall when Dom opened some new branches of Janey's Place in Jersey and Connecticut."

"Janey's Place. That's the health-food chain Faso owns." Cullen was scribbling. "Named after you?"

Yep, this guy was a crack detective, all right. "Dom started it back when we were dating," I said. "Listen, those SEAR people, they're who you should be looking at. They even signed their work!"

"Say, you might be on to something there." His expression had morphed from impassive to condescending. It was not an improvement. "Wish I'd thought of that."

"Okay, I get it. Anyone could have written those initials at the scene to implicate SEAR and throw you off the scent. But you must know how that organization operates. Heck, it's not even an *organization*, not really. There's no structure, it's just a bunch of independent cells all over the world. Some of the cells are just one person."

"You seem to know an awful lot about them," he said.

"Oh, please." I rolled my eyes. "As if they aren't on the news all the time for the horrible stuff they do. Or the stuff that's blamed on them anyway. Or that they didn't do but take credit for. They use saving endangered species as an excuse to destroy property, blow stuff up, all of that. Everyone knows about those bastards."

The "signing their work" thing reminded me of other

aspects of the crime scene that pointed to SEAR. I said, "Detective Hernandez asked me not to tell anyone about what they did to Swing after they killed him." At Cullen's questioning look, I added, "The platter? The parsley? Making it look like the chef was being served up for dinner?" The same way he'd supposedly served up endangered animals. That was the unavoidable message.

"Oh yeah, that." He actually chuckled, making me want to belt him.

"Anyway, Bonnie wanted those details withheld from the public," I said. "You know, to aid the investigation? Because it's something only the killer would know?"

He tossed a hand. "Yeah, might as well keep mum about that." Even though it made no difference because he'd already decided who did it. "So this tussle between Faso and Romulus Tooley. Tell me about it."

"Tooley blasted Dom for making a ton of money in the health-food biz and not devoting the profits to saving animals," I said. "It was all over social media for a few days. Got picked up by some of the news outlets. You didn't catch it?"

"I'm not a Facebook kind of guy," he said.

Nor was he, I suspected, a *New York Times* or a CNN or even an online news kind of guy.

"So Faso hangs on to his money." Cullen shrugged. "Nothing wrong with that. You don't get rich by giving it away. That's not how America was built."

I didn't like this police detective with his smirky arrogance and dismissive attitude. I especially didn't like that he was looking for me to help him go after a man I... well, a man I still had feelings for. Just don't ask me to look too closely at those feelings. It didn't even matter anymore now that Dom was back with Bonnie.

"The thing is, he *doesn't* hang on to all of it," I said. "He donates a sizable portion of his profits to various charities."

"So then, what's Tooley's beef with him?"

"Some of the organizations Dom supports *are* involved in conservation and saving endangered wildlife," I said, "but a lot of his money goes to humanitarian causes, especially world hunger."

"So it's not just animals."

I didn't bother reminding Cullen that starving human children are animals too. "No," I said, "and that's what has the SEAR people so worked up. In their twisted thinking, only nonhuman animals count."

"So the two of them got into it on Facebook and what-all," Cullen said.

"Tooley and his minions took advantage of every opportunity to fan the flames and get more media attention for SEAR. They threatened Dom's suppliers, spread false rumors about adulterated food at Janey's Place. They picketed some of the locations, intimidating customers. Dom had no choice but to respond, as calmly and reasonably as he could."

"How'd that work out for him?" Smirky McSmirkster asked. "The calm and reasonable approach."

"Okay, not so well," I admitted, "but the important thing is that Dom kept his cool and never lowered himself to their level. Eventually Tooley and the other SEAR crackpots got bored and moved on to their next public-shaming victim. But the whole thing caused a lot of aggravation and ate into Dom's profits."

"Something like that's bound to make a guy mad." Cullen leaned back in his chair. "Me, I'd be itching to get even."

"Me too," I said. "I guess Dom's a better person than

either of us, because he put it behind him and got on with his life."

That earned me an icy stare. I stared right back and we sat like that for a good two or three seconds until the sound of my back door opening caused me to blurt, "What the heck?"

My alarmed tone put Cullen on the alert. "Anyone else have keys to this house?"

"No. Oh. Hmm…" Strictly speaking, not everyone required a key to get into my house. A certain someone tended to come and go as he pleased, state-of-the-art locks and security system be damned. Before I could verbally backtrack, the detective was on his feet and moving fast, reaching into his jacket as he followed the sound through the family room, breakfast room, and kitchen to the laundry room, where the back door was located.

"Don't shoot!" I yelled, racing after him. Sexy Beast brought up the rear, barking with militant zeal.

I managed to scoot past Cullen and precede into the laundry room, where I found the interloper raising the lid of the washing machine and reaching for a bottle of detergent.

"Hey, Jane," Martin said. "Hey, Paulie."

Paulie?

Detective Paul Cullen looked like he'd just washed down a mouthful of stinging nettles with a swig of battery acid. "What are you doing here, McAuliffe?"

"A load of darks to start." Martin turned on the machine and poured in detergent. "Then I figured I'd move on to the lights, and last but not least, the gentle cycle for my dainties." He gave SB a little scritchie love before dumping the contents of his laundry bag onto the sorting table.

I glanced from Martin to Cullen, and jerked when I spied

the gun in his hand. "Put that thing away!" I barked—probably not the best way to address an armed, pissed-off cop, but the words were out of my mouth before I could stop them.

His dubious glance took in the two of us. "'Scuse me, ma'am, but who's this dirtbag to you?"

"He's a… a friend. He's allowed to be here." I sent Martin a look that said, *We both know that's not true and you owe me big-time for covering your hot little butt.*

Cullen scowled. "You said no one else had a key to this place."

"I, um, left the back door open for him."

From the look Cullen gave Martin, I suspected he saw that statement for the bald-faced lie it was. If these two had a history, as it appeared, then Cullen knew all about my visitor's impressive talents. And the adorable set of lock picks he never left home without.

Martin McAuliffe was six feet tall, with pale blue eyes and sandy hair buzzed ultra-short. I wasn't lying about the hot butt, though I must admit I've never seen it in the flesh, so to speak. I've seen it encased in snug jeans many times, in wet swim trunks once, and on a couple of memorable occasions, in well-fitting black priest's pants. No, he's never taken holy orders, but he finds it convenient every so often to impersonate a man of the cloth for less-than-legitimate purposes.

And for the record, I never invited him to do his laundry at my house. The least he could do was bring his own detergent.

"I heard you found Swing," Martin said to me as he tossed one last item, a black tee-shirt, into the washer and closed the top. Nodding toward Cullen, he added, "Must be true if our friend Paulie decided to pay a visit. What kind of beer you got?" He led the way into the kitchen, where he started rooting through the fridge.

Cullen puffed himself up. "Get lost, McAuliffe. I'm conducting official police business here."

"Jane wants me to stay." Martin gave me a meaningful look, intended to remind me of another occasion when his presence during a police interrogation, or questioning, or whatever the heck it was, had proven fortunate. "Don't you?"

I suspected that if Cullen considered me a "person of interest" in his murder investigation, I'd know about it by now. Still I replied, "Why, yes I do, Padre. Make yourself at home." Not that he'd ever needed an invitation.

Cullen said, "'Padre'? Do I even wanna know?"

If he expected an answer, he was to be disappointed. But I don't mind telling *you*. The priest getup? Martin happened to be wearing it when I first met him, hence the nickname. He hadn't cared for it at first, so I made sure to keep using it, and now I think he kind of digs it.

Martin plucked a bottle of good Belgian beer out of the fridge, along with a half-full takeout container of pad thai left over from last night's dinner. Cullen eyed the bottle as if there were a picture of a naked lady on the label. *Sorry, Paulie.* Even if he weren't on duty, I wouldn't offer him one. I mean, come on, the guy was trying to lock up Dom.

"So how far did you two get?" Martin set the food and bottle on the big granite island that separated the kitchen from the breakfast room. Being better acquainted with my house than I was, he shuffled items in the junk drawer until he came up with a pair of paper-wrapped chopsticks, one of the many sets I'd squirreled away from various food deliveries. He turned to Cullen. "Did you tell her about Dom punching out Swing?"

"*What?*" I cried. "That's crazy. He would never."

"If you're gonna stay here, McAuliffe," Cullen said, "keep your trap shut. I told you, this is official police—"

"Yeah, I had a feeling you hadn't heard about that," Martin told me as he deftly lifted a wad of rice noodles and shrimp with the chopsticks. "Both Dom and Swing tried to hush it up."

And yet somehow Martin knew about it. I wasn't surprised. "Dom doesn't punch people out," I insisted. "He's never been that kind of person. And *Swing?* The two of them are friendly." *Were* friendly, I mentally corrected myself. I looked at Cullen to pronounce yea or nay on Martin's ridiculous statement. He only glared at the other man.

I remembered then. Swing's black eye. I'd sat paralyzed on the floor of the restaurant kitchen after calling 911, holding a squirming SB to my chest and trying to make sense of the scene before me. It was during those interminable few minutes that I noticed details other than the knife protruding from Swing's chest. The flesh around one eye was swollen and purple. He had a small cut on his cheek and a puffy lip.

My overtaxed brain had conflated those injuries with the stabbing. I'd assumed they'd happened at the same time. Now that I thought about it, I realized a shiner like that takes time to blossom.

I couldn't believe I was asking Cullen the question. "Did Dom beat up Swing?"

He nodded. "We have a witness. Faso's daughter was there."

"Karina?" This story was only getting more bizarre. "Kari lives with her mom. Where did this happen? *When* did it happen?"

"Saturday morning," Martin said. "At Dewatre." The same place he died two days later.

"Shut up, McAuliffe," Cullen demanded, "or get out. You're interfering—"

"Excuse me, Detective," I said, "but this is my home and I have a right to include anyone I want in our conversation." Martin offered an approving wink.

Obviously Cullen had a mental script in place dictating which details he would divulge to me and in what sequence, the better to maximize the information he could extract from me in turn—information he intended to use against his one and apparently only person of interest. I had zero desire to facilitate that process. The guy didn't strike me as either a creative thinker or a hard worker. And wouldn't it be a feather in his cap if he was able to "solve" the crime within the first twenty-four hours?

Cullen tried a different tack. "Let's you and me go finish our talk in the living room—"

"No." I lifted Martin's beer bottle and took a fortifying gulp. Good stuff. Brewed by monks, supposedly, and too fine to swig from the bottle. Which was far from my biggest concern at the moment. I took another deep pull and faced the detective head-on.

"First you try to make it seem like Dom has it in for SEAR," I said, "for that guy Tooley, and never once do you mention that he fought with Swing two days before he died. When exactly were you planning to lay that little nugget on me?"

"Oh, I get it." Martin offered a couple of noodles to Sexy Beast, who grabbed them and ran to the sink rug, his preferred snacking spot. To Cullen he said, "You figure Dom killed

Swing, then tried to blame it on the SEAR people for coming after him last year. Two birds, one knife."

"Wait," I said. "Why?"

"Why what?" an exasperated Cullen asked.

"Why did Dom beat up Swing? And why would he let his daughter witness something like that? It doesn't make sense."

"Karina was already there," Martin said.

"At Dewatre? On a Saturday morning when it's closed? Why would…?" I let that hang there as the possibilities—one unsavory possibility in particular—scrolled through my cranium. "No." I shook my head. "No, she's a kid!"

"Karina Faso is sixteen," Cullen said. "A felony in the state of New York."

"She didn't," I said. "She wouldn't. Not Kari. She's a good kid."

Cullen snorted at that, which made me want to punch him.

"No one said she's not a good kid." Martin dangled another rice noodle in front of SB, who did his customary snatch and run.

"Careful with that stuff," I said. "No more for him."

I thought of Karina Faso. Dom's first child. The first child of my beloved ex-husband, who'd sworn up and down as a twenty-year-old newlywed that he never, ever wanted to be a father. It's what had broken up our marriage eight months after the *I do's*. If we'd had that critical conversation before getting hitched, I never would have gone through with it, as much as I loved him.

I'd always wanted children. The need to be a mother was in my bones. Yet here I was, six months away from the big four-oh and fearing it was too late. All because I'd spent the past seventeen and a half years carrying a torch for Dom, while he racked up two more ex–Mrs. Fasos and added three little Fasos to the world. Funny how things work out, huh?

Dom isn't one to stay single long. Within days of our divorce, he'd met Dr. Svetlana Khorkov, a Russian-born endocrinologist eleven years his senior, and married her four months later. Apparently Svetlana had seen no need to consult her bridegroom before going off the Pill. Kari was born nine months after the wedding. Ivan made his appearance eleven months after that. Five years later, following a second amicable divorce, Wife Number Three, a renowned poet named Meryl Hanover, presented him with his third child, Jonathan.

I recalled the day Karina was born. Dom was the happiest, proudest papa you ever saw, once Svetlana had taken the decision away from him. Silly me for wanting to give him a say. He was thoroughly and hopelessly besotted with little Karina. I thought he'd never stop grinning. I can still feel the bittersweet ache of watching him cuddle his newborn daughter, watching them coo to each other, watching her wrap her tiny fist around his finger. Soaking in the heartwarming image while knowing it wasn't our child in his arms and never would be.

Even after his subsequent divorces from Svetlana and Meryl, he remained an involved, loving dad. He's always gotten along with his exes, who both live in Crystal Harbor. It didn't hurt that he worked hard to keep the break-ups civil and is exceptionally generous with child support.

I said, "Kari has too much sense to get involved with someone like Swing."

"Kids that age aren't known for their common sense," Martin said.

"'Someone like Swing'?" Cullen said. "What does that mean?"

"Oh, you know," I said. "Just that he's older, older than her dad even, and he has a reputation for being with a lot of women."

"Some girls would find that a turn-on," Martin said. "He's older, powerful, rich. A famous chef. He's on TV all the time. You telling me Kari would be immune to that?"

"Well, what about Swing, then?" I said. "He has women falling all over him. Why would he mess with a sixteen-year-old and risk being charged with statutory rape?"

"If a girl's persistent," Cullen said, "that can be hard for a guy to resist. Also, some of these girls lie about their age. I've seen fourteen-year-olds, they put on the makeup and the push-up bras and all that, you'd never know they aren't of age. They set the trap and some poor bozo falls right into it, then *he's* the one has his life ruined."

"Okay, can we focus on Kari?" I said. "Kari isn't the type to 'set a trap.'"

Cullen's smirk said, *If you say so.*

"She's an honors student," I persisted. "President of the art club. She volunteers at the local animal shelter, for heaven's sake." I saw Cullen perk up at this. "And no, there's no SEAR connection there, so don't even start."

Martin glanced at Cullen as he wrangled the last of the noodles. "So Dom thought Swing and his daughter were involved?"

"You don't get to ask questions," the detective sneered.

I said, "So Dom thought Swing and his daughter were involved?"

Cullen gave a disgusted sigh. "What do you think? He

finds the two of them alone, meeting secretly, he decides to teach the guy a lesson. That part, I got no problem with. I mean, I have a daughter myself."

"It's quite a leap from punching the guy out to sticking a knife in his chest," I said. "I mean, two days later? You'd think Dom would have cooled off by then."

"Or not, if it looked like Swing was up to his old tricks," Cullen said.

I tried to think like a detective. "I assume you found Dom's fingerprints at the scene since he was there two days before. What about on the knife? Any prints there?"

"I'm not prepared to divulge—"

"Yeah, yeah, police business," I said. "Have you contacted Swing's family at least? He told me his folks have been gone for years, but there's a brother." Swing had mentioned him a couple of times. They were close, despite the geographical separation.

Martin spoke up. "His brother Victor is on a flight right now from Paris."

"How do you know that?" Cullen barked. "Who's feeding you information?"

Martin just smiled and drained his beer bottle. I had little doubt the padre had friendly contacts in the police department. He might have a checkered background—I'd probably never learn the particulars and wasn't entirely sure I wanted to—but there was no doubting the man was a charmer.

"I have things to do, Detective," I said. "Are we done here?"

"We never even got started." He set his notebook on the kitchen island and clicked his pen. "What time did you arrive at Dewatre this morning?"

3

The Chutzpah!

"I LOVED HIM!" Karina Faso screamed. Her pretty face was damp with tears and scarlet with rage and grief. She faced off with her father in the living room of his ultramodern waterfront mansion. White walls and a bleached-wood floor provided the perfect backdrop to elegant black and gray furnishings.

It was almost nine p.m. and fully dark outside. During daylight hours I would have been able to stand there and gaze through the floor-to-ceiling windows past the lush back lawn of the five-acre property, complete with pool, tennis court, and guest house, to the bay and Long Island Sound beyond.

Dom reached for his daughter. She jerked away. At five ten, she was only four inches shorter than her dad. When she wore heels, as she did now, they stood practically eye to eye. In addition to impressive height, she'd also inherited his brown eyes, but she had her mother to thank for her hair color, a light golden brown, several shades darker than my own strawberry blond. She wore it long and straight, and appeared oblivious to the strands clinging to her tear-streaked face.

"I loved him and you couldn't deal with that," she said, "so you killed him!"

"Kari, honey, you know that's absurd." He maintained an air of paternal calm in the face of his child's anguish, though the effort clearly cost him. "When you're less upset, you'll see—"

"I'll never be less upset!" Her eyes looked wild, like a trapped animal's. "Don't you get it? You destroyed my life. It wasn't enough just to beat him up, was it? I hope they put you away for the rest of your life. I hope you rot in jail. *I'll never forgive you!*" She turned and sprinted past me into the foyer and up the curved staircase. After a few moments we heard a door slam upstairs.

Dom sat heavily on the arm of the nearest sofa. I'd never seen him look so helpless. After Detective Cullen had finally left, I'd gone straight to Dom's, needing to get his version of events and see how he was coping with the person-of-interest nonsense. I'd found myself in the midst of a wrenching family drama.

He ran long fingers through his curly, dark hair. "I don't know what to do for her, Janey. Neither does Lana," he said, using his ex-wife Svetlana's nickname. "Kari's accusations, they're insane. How do I get through to her?"

I'd never been a mother, but I'd been a teenage girl. "No one's going to get through to her right now, Dom. She's hurting and instinctively she's directing the pain outward. It's not a conscious thing. She doesn't really hate you."

"I don't know." He shook his head. "We've had arguments, it comes with the territory when you're raising a teenager, but it's never been like this."

She's never been in love with a murder victim. I didn't say it. I didn't have to. And as for the being-in-love thing, we were talking about an adolescent girl in the throes of her first big crush. Did she even know what it meant to be in love?

Then again, at her age I was already deeply in love with her father. By that point we were inseparable. Nothing and no one could tear us apart. Or so I'd assumed in my youthful optimism.

"It's too bad Bonnie was taken off the case," I said.

He gave me a guarded look. We hadn't spoken much in the six weeks since he and Detective Bonnie Hernandez had become re-engaged—shortly after he'd promised me plenty of time to decide whether to remarry him. This was not the time to lay into him about that.

"She took herself off it," he said. "Conflict of interest."

"Yeah, that's what Cullen said." I took a seat on the far end of the sofa he'd perched on. The sofa was gray, the pillows I pushed out of the way black and cream. My ex-husband's decorator had combined refined fabrics, rich textures, and a dramatic color palette to craft a space entirely devoid of warmth or hominess. The result was so at odds with Dom's outgoing personality that I couldn't help but find it a bit sad.

The black-and-white theme carried over into the foyer and giant kitchen. At least his den had been done in warm colors, and there were splashes of red in the second-floor bridge flanked by railings. Altogether, the twelve-thousand-square-foot house felt more like a museum, complete with curved walls and loads of framed art photos illuminated by spot lighting.

"I was surprised to learn that you and Swing actually fought," I said. "As in serious punches thrown."

"It was kind of one-sided, I'm ashamed to say." Dom crossed his arms. "He shoved me when I got in his face, and I used that as an excuse to deck him. I can't remember ever being that angry."

"It's your daughter," I said. "You're allowed."

He sighed. "Well, it's done. I can't take it back. And the worst part is, it only made things worse. With Kari. She witnessed the whole stupid thing and it made her more—" air quotes here "—'in love' with Swing."

"No, the worst part is, it made you a suspect in Swing's murder," I said. "I get the feeling Cullen's not inclined to look any further."

"I'm innocent," he said. "The facts will show that."

Okay, you might be thinking right about now that my ex is dangerously naïve. Anyone who follows the news knows that innocent people are convicted every day of crimes they didn't commit. It wasn't naïveté on Dom's part so much as a perpetually positive outlook. The glass is always half-full in Dominic Faso-land.

"I get why you hushed up the fight," I said, "but why did Swing keep quiet about it? Any idea?"

"One, I beat the tar out of him, so you have the macho thing going on. He wouldn't want to advertise that fact. But also, well…" He looked at me. "I'm wondering if it might have been for Kari's sake. To keep people from talking about her."

"That sounds almost gallant."

"Either that or he didn't want his name publicly linked with an underage girl."

"So how did he explain the black eye?" I asked.

"I gave him a black eye?"

"A real shiner. Maybe he blamed it on one of the SEAR protestors. They're always out there picketing the studio when he goes into Manhattan to tape a TV segment. I mean, when he *went* in. You know what I mean."

"Seems a lot's getting blamed on them lately," Dom said.

"You don't think SEAR had anything to do with his murder?"

"Those vermin might not have the tightest grip on reality, but even they wouldn't be clueless enough to leave a calling card." His expression softened as if he were seeing me for the first time that evening. "Janey. God, that must have been horrible for you. Finding him like that."

Dom sat next to me. He put his arm around my shoulders and pulled me to him. I wish I could claim to be immune to the comfort he offered, to the warmth and familiar masculine scent of him. I leaned into the embrace and let myself bask in it, knowing it would end soon enough.

"It *was* horrible." I would only have admitted it to Dom. I squeezed my eyes against the image that seemed etched into my memory banks. Could it have been only that morning that I'd walked into Dewatre and discovered Swing lying dead? I hauled in a shaky breath. "I hope I never see anything like that again."

Dom pressed his lips to my hair, his breath warming my scalp. "I wish it had been me instead. Who found him. I wish I could have spared you that."

After a moment I looked at him. "Did Cullen ask where you were this morning? When Swing was murdered?"

"Of course."

When he didn't elaborate, I said, "You were at work, right?" At the Janey's Place corporate headquarters there in Crystal Harbor, where his staff could vouch for his presence during the critical window of time.

"No."

I waited. Nothing. I shifted to face him squarely. "What do you mean, 'no'? Cullen never said, but I assume Swing died not long before I got there, which was around ten-thirty."

He nodded as his gaze slid from mine. "The medical examiner estimates he was killed between nine-thirty and ten."

"So today's Monday," I said. "Aren't you at work by nine?"

"Usually, but today there were unforeseen circumstances."

My skin prickled. "What kind of unforeseen circumstances?"

He sighed in defeat. "I didn't spend the night here, first of all."

Bonnie hadn't moved back into Dom's house after they'd renewed their engagement—her decision, I assumed, but whether that held any significance, I couldn't say. Obviously it didn't keep them from sharing a bed on a regular basis.

It shouldn't still get to me, after his two subsequent marriages and his on-again-off-again engagement to Bonnie. He's allowed to spend the night at his fiancée's place, for heaven's sake. But it did still get to me, after all these years.

Hey, I'm in touch with my feelings. Shouldn't that count for something? Oh, what do you know?

The fact that Dom was well aware that stuff like this still got to me was a great big glob of mortification icing on the humiliation cake.

None of which kept me from gamely pretending I didn't give a darn. "Okay, so you were at Bonnie's all night. So?"

"So she left the house before me this morning and then Frederick slipped out the gate and I spent three hours looking for him."

Frederick was Bonnie's magnificent standard poodle, the perfectly behaved, hardworking, blue-ribbon-winning poodle against which all other poodles are to be judged.

Sexy Beast and I hate Frederick.

"Three hours?" I said. "As in the critical three hours?"

Dom flopped back against the sofa, head lolling, eyes shut. "Stupid mutt chased a rabbit into the woods." So much for the "perfectly behaved" part.

"Did anyone see you looking for him?"

He rocked his head in the negative. "It was the woods, Janey. Not exactly teeming with people on a Monday morning."

"Well, did you call anyone? You had to call work, right? So they'd know you were delayed."

"I told them I was working from home this morning," he said. "If I mentioned Frederick, I knew it would get back to Bonnie and she'd pitch a fit."

"So there's no one who can vouch for your whereabouts during the hours in question."

He tipped his head toward me, his expression baleful.

"Too *Law and Order*?" I asked.

"I'm getting enough of that from Cullen. Did you know he showed up here this afternoon with a search warrant?"

"Really? What was he looking for?"

"Shoes," he said. "He took all my sneakers, everything with that kind of sole."

"Ah. The bloody shoe prints."

"You saw them?" he asked.

"Briefly. I was trying hard not to look at… all of that."

He squeezed my hand.

I nodded toward the ceiling, and by extension, Karina. "Is she staying here tonight?" She and her brother Ivan lived with their mother, but visitation was flexible.

He nodded. "Lana's been dealing with her all day. I think she's reached her limit."

I sympathized with Lana, but I didn't think that Karina staying at her dad's place, while she was trying so hard to convince herself he murdered the man she was trying so hard to convince herself she loved, was the best thing for her current state of mind. And Dom had his own person-of-interest headaches. He was not equipped to give his daughter the attention she needed right now.

I sighed.

"What?" he asked.

"I might come to regret this," I said, "but I think Kari should stay with me tonight. Neutral territory." I'd always gotten along well with the girl. "I'll get her to school in the morning."

He was about to dismiss the idea, I could see, but then he stilled and thought about it. He looked at me. "You're okay with that?"

"More to the point, will Kari be okay with it? After all, she can't torture you as easily from my place." I rose.

Dom remained seated. He tossed his hand as if to say, *She's all yours.*

"MOM WANTS ME to go on the Pill." Kari hovered a hand over the griddle, testing the heat.

"And you don't want to?" I asked.

She answered with a shrug, her gaze on the griddle as she swirled butter onto it. The butter melted and foamed on contact, teasing me with its intoxicating perfume.

"So…" I wasn't sure I knew how to do this. "What are you using for protection now?"

Another shrug. Part of me prayed the girl wasn't already pregnant, while another part of me took in subtle clues in her expression and body language as she lifted the bowl of batter and started pouring. Those clues didn't match up with what I was hearing.

We were in my kitchen making a midnight snack. Yeah, I knew she had school in the morning, but if she skipped first-period gym, it wouldn't kill her. I could write the late note. After all, I was her stepmother. Kind of. Well, in a reverse-chronological sort of way, if that counted. And if she was still very upset, I could ask Dom about letting her stay home, although I suspected that sticking with her routine was probably the best thing for her.

We'd already gotten through the sobbing, the accusations, why she hate hate hates her parents and her stupid brother, and the professions of forever-and-ever love for a man who would now remain perfect in her eyes until the end of time. The time had come to decompress with food. Following his initial excitement over seeing Kari, Sexy Beast had curled up in his bucket bed in a corner of the kitchen to alternately gnaw his chew toy and doze.

Kari poured precise, uniform pancakes, each of which landed with a satisfying sizzle. "You're pretty good at this," I said, and meant it.

"I want to be a chef."

"Oh yeah?" It would be so easy to say exactly the wrong thing at that moment. "I bet you'd make a great one."

"Swing was teaching me." She set aside the bowl and lifted a spatula out of the utensil caddy.

What else was he teaching you? "That's… nice," I said.

She looked at me. "It's why I went to Dewatre every Saturday morning. He was giving me lessons."

"Really? I mean, wow. Cooking lessons from a chef of his caliber. That's something. Did your folks know?"

Kari directed her gaze back to the griddle. She shook her head. "It was going to be a surprise. I was going to make Thanksgiving dinner. Including vegetarian stuff for dad."

"So where did your mom and dad think you were going every Saturday morning?" I asked.

"The library. Teen book club." After a few moments she looked at me and said, "I want to know how it was. When you found him."

I took a deep breath. "No, you don't."

She set down the spatula. "I'm not a little kid, Jane. The truth isn't going to scar me for life or anything. I keep imagining all these horrible things and they're probably worse than how it really was." She waited.

"Well, it was pretty bad."

"Was he lying on the floor?" she asked.

"Yes."

"And what?"

"And… the knife was still in him." I cleared my throat. "In his, um, chest."

She nodded thoughtfully. In a quiet voice she said, "There must have been blood."

I nodded again.

"Okay." She sucked in a deep breath and let it out, her gaze unfocused. "So his bloody corpse was lying on the floor with a knife sticking out of it."

Even if I hadn't been instructed to keep quiet about the

platter and the parsley, I wouldn't have mentioned them to Kari. Doing so would have served no purpose except to cause her more pain.

She said, "Did he look… scared or, you know…"

"No." I shook my head vigorously. "His eyes were open, but there was no expression in them. He looked, well, peaceful. I think it was over in an instant, Kari. I didn't see anything to make me think he suffered or… or that it was prolonged or anything."

This was not strictly true. I happen to know that facial muscles, like all muscles, relax in death. If Swing felt terror at the end, we wouldn't know it from his expression. And as for it all being over quickly… anyone who'd witnessed that murder scene and its blood pattern would tell you differently. You didn't need to be a forensic investigator to discern Swing's struggle to live. But there was no way I was going to share that with Kari. I hoped she now had enough information to come to grips with how Swing died and to find some peace.

"Thank you for telling me." She hugged me, and our height difference made *me* feel like the kid. Her voice was watery as she added, "I really needed to know."

I didn't think more tears at this point would do either of us any good. I patted her back and handed her the spatula. "Don't these things need to be turned?"

She shook her head. "Not until the bubbles pop and the holes stay open."

"So I've been making pancakes wrong my whole life," I said. "Tell me. How did you meet Swing?"

"My dad had this big pool party a couple of months ago. It was catered, but I made some hors d'oeuvres and Swing thought they were great. I mean he really liked them. He wasn't just being polite."

"I believe you."

"So we, you know, started talking and he ended up offering to teach me some stuff."

I opened a cabinet and pulled down a couple of plates. The smell of the pancakes had my stomach grumbling. Suddenly I realized that between Cullen's visit and the drama with Dom and Karina—and oh yeah, Martin scarfing down my leftovers—I'd missed dinner. No wonder I was famished.

"So what happened to Tucker?" I asked. This was answered with another shrug. "I thought you two were still going out."

"We are. Kind of. He's like a little boy." Kari started flipping the pockmarked pancakes. "Now that I know what it's like to be with a grown man, I'm not interested in guys my age."

There it was again, the feeling that this girl was having a little too much fun freaking out the adults in her life. "So. Kari." I leaned against the counter and got a good view of her face. "Why don't you want your mom to know you're still a virgin?"

I watched in satisfaction as the pancake she was flipping fell half onto its neighbor. *Yes!* I was right.

Kari scraped the pancakes apart. "You don't know anything about—"

"Don't." I held up my palm. "Save it for your parents."

She maintained her mulish expression for a few seconds, then deflated with a gusty sigh. "I hate them."

"I believe we've covered that ground."

"My mom always assumes the worst," she said. "I can't talk to her. She's *old*. She's *fifty!*" She made a can-you-believe-it face, as if Lana were turning to dust before her eyes. "She's not like you. I can talk to you. Why did you and my dad get divorced? I'd wish I were your kid."

My eyes abruptly stung and I had to turn away. I busied myself getting out utensils and syrup. Just hearing this sweet, confused girl say she wished she were mine brought out all the maternal yearning and disappointment I'd spent decades struggling to suppress. When I felt in control of my voice, I said, "She must be worried about you to suggest you start using birth control."

"They both worry, her and Dad." Kari turned off the stove and deposited pancakes on our plates. "Nothing I do or don't do makes any difference, so why bother?"

We carried our food to the round breakfast-room table. "So did Swing feel the same way about you that you felt about him?"

After a moment she said, "Sure."

I waited.

"It's just, you know, he didn't feel free to express it," she continued. "Because of my age and stuff."

"Is that what he said?" I lifted a forkful of syrup-drenched pancake to my mouth and failed to repress a rapturous groan.

SB had taken up position next to my chair as soon as I sat. Yeah, I know you're not supposed to let them beg at the table, but his original owner, Irene McAuliffe, never got that memo, and by the time he was mine, it was established routine. Plus, well, I hate to disappoint him. I cut a bit of pancake, which he sniffed, then delicately plucked from my fingers.

"We didn't really talk about it," Kari said. "I mean, we really did spend all our time cooking. He only had, like, an hour before he had to get Dewatre ready for the Saturday lunch crowd, so we were too busy to, you know, talk about it.

But I could tell he cared," she hurriedly added.

"Did Swing know that your parents thought you were at the library when you two were together?" I asked.

She shrugged. "It didn't come up."

I wanted to shake her. Instead I waited again.

Finally she said, "Okay, I get why my dad went nuts when he found us together. You know, alone at the restaurant when it was closed and everything. When he thought I was at the library. But he didn't give us a chance to explain. He just, like, *assumed!*"

Considering Swing's reputation as a Lothario, it wasn't an unwarranted assumption. Yes, the chef had been my friend and I'd liked him, but I couldn't say for certain how he'd respond to a pretty teenager in the throes of a major crush. Apparently his pal Dom thought he was capable of taking advantage of the situation.

"Why did your dad show up at Dewatre that morning, anyway?" I asked.

"To return a cookbook Swing lent him. A thousand and one ways to make quinoa or some slop like that."

Dom's children did not share his love for all things vegetarian. I looked down at SB, staring lovingly at my plate and licking his lips. I said, "All gone" in a singsongy tone he knew meant business. He retired to his bed, with a longsuffering sigh.

"He can see it's not all gone," Kari pointed out, reasonably. I still had plenty of pancake on my plate. "Why did he believe you?"

"To him, 'all gone' only means he's not getting any more right now. I'll put some in his bowl when I'm finished."

She grinned. Even with eyes that were red and swollen

from crying, she was a beautiful girl. It was good to see her loosen up after the fraught day she'd had. "You're a good dog mommy. I want a dog—a border collie. They're the smartest. Mom won't let me have one because they shed. I told her I'd dust and vacuum up the hairs every day." She shook her head at the injustice of it.

Yeah, I thought, and she'd walk the dog in the rain and clean up its poop and take it to the vet. Lana was just a teensy bit busy, between her medical practice and raising two teenagers. I didn't blame her one bit for not throwing a high-energy, hard-thinking herding dog into the mix.

I was mentally debating how to persuade this girl to communicate with her parents when my phone rang.

Kari smiled at my ring tone: the 1950s Latin rock classic "Tequila." Favorite drink, favorite song. What can I tell you? I'm simple.

I got up and retrieved my phone from the kitchen island. I didn't recognize the number displayed on it. I sighed.

"Are you going to answer that?" Kari asked.

"The press has been hounding me for statements all day," I said. "I stopped answering the phone."

"Would they bother you this late? I mean, you could be in bed."

"They have a story to write. They don't care." Suddenly I was angry. Kari wasn't the only one who'd had a long, emotionally wrenching day. I stabbed the green "answer" icon and brought the phone to my ear. *"What!"* I barked.

After a moment an accented male voice said, "Is this Jane Delaney?"

"Seriously?" I demanded, looking at the stove clock. "At a quarter past midnight? You people are unbelievable. Do you have any idea what kind of day I've had? Well, of course you do, otherwise you wouldn't be harassing me at midnight, would you? I found a murdered body this morning. My *friend's* body. I had to look at his bloody corpse lying on the floor with a knife sticking out of it!" Kari offered a thumbs-up, clearly unfazed at hearing me parrot her own stark words. I added, "So I can safely say my day has been a little rougher than yours, buddy. *Do not call this number again!*" I broke the connection.

"That feel good?" Kari forked up the last of her pancakes.

"Felt great. Wish I'd been doing it all day instead of letting them go to voice mail." I started cutting the last bite of pancake into itty bitty pieces for Sexy Beast, who abandoned his bucket bed and stood by my side, licking his lips. The smart little brat was fully aware what my dainty cutting motions meant.

"Tequila" started playing again. I looked at the screen. "The *chutzpah*! It's the same guy."

"Let me!" Kari wagged her hand toward the phone. *"Pleeease?"*

Yeah, that's what I needed getting back to Dom and Lana—that I let their daughter cuss out a reporter. It could be someone from *Ramrod News* on the other end. I wouldn't put it past those jackals to record the call and play it on air.

"Sorry, kiddo." I answered the phone. "Listen, you—"

"This is Victor Dewatre."

"What?"

"No, *Dewatre*. Pierre Dewatre was my brother."

I clapped a hand over my mouth, eyes bulging. Swing's brother! I'd just said all that bloody-corpse stuff to Swing's brother!

"What?" Kari looked alarmed. "Jane, what's wrong?"

"Ms. Delaney?" The accent was definitely French. "Are you there?"

I pried my hand off my face. To Kari I mouthed, *It's Swing's brother.* She clapped a hand over her own mouth.

"I… yes, I'm here," I said. "I'm so sorry, Mr. Dewatre. I… the press has been calling all day and I just assumed…"

"I understand." He sounded tired. "My apologies for phoning at this hour. My flight just landed. I'm still on the plane. I wanted to touch base and see if you might be able to make time for me today." His command of the language was perfect.

I frowned. "You want to meet with *me?*"

"I was told you discovered my brother's body, and I suppose you just confirmed it," he said.

I groaned. "That was… I shouldn't have…"

"I'm hoping you might be more forthcoming about certain details than the police detective was on the phone," he said.

Yet one more person who desired a description of Swing's murder scene, in living color. I'd have thought my little bloody-corpse tirade would have sufficed. But I said, "I'll help in any way I can."

He said, "Will you be available during your lunch break? Say, one o'clock?"

"Of course." I could carve some time out of my current assignment, selling the dead doc's antique medical instruments. "Where are you staying?"

"I booked a room at one of the chain hotels near the airport," he said. "All I need is your address. The rental car will have GPS."

This poor man had just lost his brother in the most gruesome way imaginable. He'd been traveling for hours, and

Paris was, what, six hours ahead of New York? He was dealing with grief, exhaustion, and a messed-up body clock. The last thing he needed was some crappy airport hotel and a miserable drive in an unfamiliar car on unfamiliar roads.

Swing had spoken highly of Victor, and I had a good feeling about him just from our brief conversation. Plus I felt I owed him for the, you know, bloody-corpse business.

"I won't hear of you staying at a hotel," I said. "I have more bedrooms here than I know what to do with. I'm picking you up."

"That's very generous of you, Ms. Delaney, but—"

"It's Jane," I said.

"Please call me Victor. Thank you for the offer, Jane, but I couldn't possibly impose."

"Oh please, like you're not about to collapse." When all else fails, turn into the Pushy American. "If there's anyone else traveling with you, they're welcome to stay too." I was thinking no wife or girlfriend would let him make this trip alone.

"It's just me, but you needn't—"

"Which airport?"

He hesitated only a second. "JFK. Excuse me." He turned aside briefly to ask someone a question in French, then told me, "Terminal One."

"This time of night it should only take me about a half hour. Call me again when you clear customs, Victor. I can always wait in the cell phone lot. Oh, and I'll be driving a red Mazda."

"I will be the one asleep standing up."

4

In Which Jane Gets Propositioned

IT'S A GOOD thing I recognized Victor. Which is to say, I recognized Swing. Victor was a younger version of his brother except for his hair color, which was light brown with no hint of gray. He wore it longish, swept back off his face and brushing the open collar of his pale blue dress shirt. The shirt was untucked, the sleeves rolled up. If he'd started out with a necktie, it was history. His gray suit jacket was slung over his shoulder on this warm night in early September.

I say it's a good thing I recognized him because he was indeed nearly asleep on his feet, his bleary gaze staring into middle distance. I pulled up to the curb at the terminal's pickup area, popped the trunk, and rolled down the passenger window.

"Victor!" I called.

He came to attention then, bending to focus on me. He flashed a quick, tired smile—Swing's smile, Swing's silver-gray eyes—before tossing his leather duffel into the trunk and sliding into the passenger seat.

He reached over to shake my hand. "You're a lifesaver, Jane."

"My pleasure. Really." It was no lie. I'd thought Swing was

hot stuff, but his younger brother took that hotness to a new level. Even with strands of hair flopping over his temple and serious beard stubble.

Oh, who am I kidding? *Especially* with the hair flopping and the stubble.

As I drove toward the airport exit, I asked, "Were you able to sleep on the plane?"

"No, I never do. And especially not tonight, with everything." He gave a bleak little shake of his head.

"Of course," I said, just to have something to say.

"It isn't real yet." He yawned. "I've been going, going since the detective called. I had just gotten home from work. I threw a few things into a bag and drove straight to Roissy." At my quizzical look, he clarified. "Charles de Gaulle Airport."

If the circumstances were different, I would have made small talk. Instead I let the silence stretch out. It was a comfortable silence. Victor must have thought so, too, because a couple of minutes later I glanced over and saw he was asleep. I did the arithmetic. It was about seven a.m. in Paris.

Naturally, Kari had wanted to accompany me to pick him up. I'd firmly vetoed that idea and made her go to bed before I left the house, assuring her I'd be back within an hour and a half, tops.

Thankfully, she was sound asleep when we got home. I was glad to see Sexy Beast lying curled on her bed. I offered to make Victor something to eat, but he was only interested in laying his head on a pillow.

I managed to snag four hours of less-than-satisfactory shuteye before my alarm told me it was time to get Kari up for school. The girl's curiosity bubbled over as she passed the bedroom Swing's brother occupied. "Just let me take one little peek," she whispered. *"Pleeease!"*

"Don't even think about it."

To my relief, her mood had improved from the night before. Apparently, midnight pancakes and girl talk with her dad's first ex had been just the ticket. She made noises about skipping school, but I sensed she'd be better off going, and when I pointed out that I had a busy day planned and she'd have to spend the day with one of her parents, she relented.

"I wish I lived here," she announced while pouring her third bowl of Fruity Pebbles. "My mom never lets me have this stuff."

Please don't tell her, I silently begged. Lana and I got along well—heck, all of Dom's exes got along, even if we weren't what you'd call besties—but I wouldn't want to strain the relationship by letting her know I was the Bad Ex feeding her kid sugary breakfast foods. At least she was eating it with milk, so it was, you know, kind of okay.

The Bad Ex gave Kari a late note and drove her to school in time for second-period physics. When I returned home, it was clear Victor was still asleep—nothing but silence from the second floor—so I decided to get a head start on the medical-device project. Step one would be photographing the antiques at my client's home, but I'd gotten a good look at the collection and had a fair idea of what I was dealing with. Meanwhile it wouldn't hurt to scour the Internet for resources to help me identify and price the items.

Over the past few weeks I'd begun using the cozy maid's room down the hall from the kitchen as a sort of office. And yeah, Irene had turned one of the three guest rooms upstairs into a combined library and home office, with sleek, expensive furnishings, state-of-the-art equipment, and yet more modern art masterpieces, including a spectacular Georgia O'Keeffe. Yet somehow I never felt comfortable in there. It was Irene's space. Whenever I tried to work in that room, I always felt her peering over my shoulder, telling me what I was doing wrong. Having known Irene for more than two decades, I could very well believe she'd choose to haunt her former property specifically to micromanage it, and me, from beyond the grave. Don't misunderstand me. I'd loved her, she was like a surrogate grandma, but I'd be lying if I claimed she'd been the easiest person to get along with.

So it was the maid's room I found myself in that morning, curled up in the overstuffed chair with my laptop and my dog. The world of antique medical devices proved more strangely absorbing than one might imagine—I now knew more about cupping lamps and trepanning drills than was probably healthy—and by the time I detected activity upstairs, more than two hours had passed. A few minutes later, I heard muffled footfalls on the carpeted steps.

Sexy Beast sprang off the chair and raced out of the room, intent, no doubt, on separating the dastardly intruder from his jugular. In short order the barking morphed into submissive whimpers as my houseguest cooed to him in French. So much for my fiercely protective watchdog. Victor switched to English to offer SB a treat, as if the language made a difference. He must have correctly deduced that the phony-baloney pepperoni in the glass canister on the counter wasn't intended for human consumption.

He made *nom nom* sounds, teasing SB by exclaiming how delicious the doggie treat was. From my chair in the maid's room I pictured him pretending to eat it. Sexy Beast gave the sharp, imperative bark that meant, *Stop messing around, I know that stupid trick, just give me the darn thing already!* Apparently Victor complied, because SB lapsed into satisfied silence.

Yesterday had been horrendous for the man, and the next few days, as he dealt with the police investigation, the funeral, and settling his brother's affairs, would be trying, to put it mildly, but at least my dopey little dog had managed to give him a few moments of pleasure just by being his dopey little self. The thought brought a dopey little smile to my face.

I heard cabinets opening and closing and knew my guest was looking for a mug. I'd left a half carafe of coffee for him. I closed my laptop and padded down the hall. As I entered the kitchen, I asked, "How did you sleep?"

Victor jumped in surprise, splashing coffee from the carafe onto his bare toes. They weren't all that was bare. My houseguest wore a pair of snug black boxer briefs and nothing else.

"Oh," I said.

"Ow," he said, balancing on one foot as he grabbed a paper towel to blot scalding coffee off his foot. His hair was rumpled and his stubble was even more pronounced.

With great reluctance and through sheer force of will, I averted my gaze. I'm telling you, this was a genuine mind-over-matter moment. My eyeballs had to be dragged kicking and screaming from the sight of the gorgeous, sleep-tousled, nearly naked Frenchman hopping around my kitchen.

And really, it was so wrong of me to even register his hotness quotient, considering what the poor guy was going through. Not to mention that he had to be, what, seven or eight years younger than I was.

Wait, I forget. That's supposed to make him less appealing why?

We started talking simultaneously. I motioned to him to

proceed.

"Apologies," he said. "I assumed you'd be at work."

"I work from home," I told the refrigerator. "So, uh, yeah." Then I said, "Sorry, I should have warned you," because it was the right thing to say, although between you and me I was not in fact at all sorry. Yeah, big surprise.

"I'll go grab a shower." He headed toward the foyer.

"Great. I'll start breakfast," I said. "French toast sound good? Wait. What do they call that in France? Do they have it in France?"

"Pain perdu." Victor turned and regarded me seriously, apparently unembarrassed by his state of undress. Which made sense because, let's be honest, the man had nothing at all to be embarrassed about. "I appreciate the offer, Jane, but there's something I need to do first."

"What's that?"

"I need to see my brother."

I stood speechless for a moment, then managed, "You, um… There's no need to officially identify him if that's what you're thinking. They already, um… That's been done. If you can wait a day or two until they release him to a funeral home—"

He shook his head, looking so bleak something in my chest squeezed. Quietly he said, "I need to see him."

I took a deep breath to steady myself. "Of course. Of course you do, Victor. If it were me…" I swallowed hard. "I'll make a couple of calls. I'll find out where we need to go."

WHERE WE NEEDED to go, as it turned out, was the Forensic Sciences Building in Hauppauge, a big, modern structure about twenty miles east of Crystal Harbor that housed the medical examiner's office. Despite what I do for a living, I'd never before had occasion to visit the place. I'd phoned an old college pal, Sheryl Singer, who worked as a forensic investigator at the crime lab there, where specialists investigate stuff like DNA, drugs, firearms, and microscopic trace evidence. Sheryl was waiting for us by the time we arrived about an hour later. She was a zaftig woman of thirty with long blond hair.

Victor cleaned up nice, which was no surprise. He'd presented himself clean-shaven and fresh-scrubbed, wearing khakis and a long-sleeved navy sport shirt made of some soft, drapey material that was probably part silk. Or maybe part linen. Or maybe silk *and* linen.

No, I didn't run my hands over it to check! Jeez, why would you even think that? Okay, I know why you would think it, but give me some credit.

Naturally, he'd insisted my presence wasn't needed, he knew I was a busy person and I'd already gone above and beyond and yadda yadda. Get this, he thought I was going to let him take a taxi to the car-rental place. Yeah, that might happen. I discovered there really was a Pushy American deep down inside and that she liked to come out and play.

Sheryl led us into the viewing room, located immediately off the building's large first-floor lobby. Someone had taken pains to make the space look homey and welcoming. There were sofas and chairs in a soothing shade of green, a few simple decorations, and an adjacent bathroom.

And a big interior window. We couldn't see what was

beyond the window because of the concealing screen behind it. My mouth felt dry and I took slow, calming breaths, grateful Victor hadn't let me make us a big breakfast of French toast and bacon. Why was I nervous? I'd already seen the worst of it. I knew Swing had been autopsied the day before but felt sure they'd make him as presentable as possible.

I glanced at Victor, at his stolid expression. I placed my hand lightly on his arm.

"Are you ready?" Sheryl asked.

He nodded. She pushed a button next to the window. The screen slowly rose to reveal a small room and a sheet-draped gurney. Swing's face was exposed. After the briefest glance, I looked away.

Victor drew in a long breath and slowly let it out. He stood there unmoving for a minute or two. Sheryl didn't rush him.

At last he said, "They beat him."

"What?" Automatically I looked at Swing again and saw what he'd noticed: the livid bruises on the pale, slack face.

Victor cleared his throat. "Whoever killed him. They…" He gestured limply toward his brother's body. "They beat him. Do you see?"

"Um, no," I said. "That happened before. Two days before. I can explain. Later, okay?"

Never was I happier to drive away from a place. Victor, sitting in the passenger seat, emitted a deep sigh. He placed his hand on my shoulder. "Thank you, Jane. I know I said I could do it alone, but I'm very glad you were with me."

My throat tightened. "I was glad to do it, Victor."

He smiled crookedly, the first genuine smile I'd seen on him. "Liar."

"Okay, truth? That particular adventure was not exactly high on my bucket list. You know what that means? 'Bucket list'?"

"Sure. I lived here for three years. Earned my graduate degree at Columbia."

"Really? What kind of degree?"

"M.Arch. Master of Architecture."

"So that's why you're fluent in English." I didn't add, *Yet you never lost the swoon-worthy accent.* "You're an architect, then? In Paris?"

He nodded. "The firm I work for handles a lot of international projects, especially for U.S. companies. We have branches in San Francisco, D.C., even right here in New York, down in SoHo."

"Why did you get your degree here instead of France?" I asked.

"To be near Pierre. He was all the family I had."

"He told me your parents died a long time ago. In a car accident, I think?"

"That's right," he said. "I was twelve. Pierre was ten years older. I was a handful, let me tell you. I got into every kind of trouble you can imagine. The world had dealt me this terrible tragedy and the only way I knew to deal with it was to lash out at everyone and everything. Even at my brother, who loved me."

I thought of Kari and the shrieking, sobbing vitriol directed at her father, the ugly, unjust accusation of murder, which she had to know deep in her heart couldn't possibly be true.

"Did you do your undergrad in New York, too?" I asked.

"No, I went to school in Nice. That's where I met my wife."

Ah. A wife. He didn't wear a ring. Maybe they did things differently in France.

"Pierre had already received his training by then, he'd apprenticed with important chefs," Victor said. "When I went away to college, he left for New York. He felt he had a better chance of breaking out here, becoming a culinary star."

"And he was right," I said. "I understand he was close to getting his own show on the Food Network."

"They offered it to him."

I failed to restrain a gasp. I could think of nothing to say except, "When?"

"A few days before he died. His agent was negotiating the details. Chloe Sleeper—I haven't met her yet. They were supposed to finalize the deal and start production very soon." Victor lapsed into silence, staring out the windshield as we merged onto the parkway. Finally he said, "There's one thing about New York I miss more than anything."

"Pizza rats on the subway tracks? Drunk tourists puking in Times Square?"

"Real New York diners. I'm certain you make delicious *French toast*." He said this last with an over-the-top American accent that made me laugh out loud and pray my speech didn't sound like that to him. "But what do you say we find a diner? I haven't had a black-and-white cookie in years."

"You have to wash it down with an egg cream. It's the law. Don't worry, I know just the place."

Twenty minutes later we slid onto padded vinyl benches while our surly waiter cleared away the detritus of the previous meal, set down paper placemats and coffee mugs, and slapped a couple of five-pound menus on the table. Our booth had a view of the parking lot. A toddler at the next booth was screaming and throwing toast. An elderly couple at a nearby table argued loudly about whether eggs were good or bad for you this week.

It was perfect.

Victor turned to the breakfast page of the menu, glanced briefly at it, and set it aside.

"That was fast," I said.

"Western omelet. Sausage. Home fries. White toast. Orange juice. Lots of black coffee."

"The man knows what he wants. I still have my heart set on French toast, plus they make it with challah here." I slapped the menu shut. "Done deal." Pancakes at midnight, French toast at noon. I'd have to count calories for a week to make up for this carb-fest.

Victor waited until our food had been set in front of us before saying, "The bruises."

I sighed as I poured syrup. "My ex-husband did that to him. Dom. Dominic Faso."

He forked up a mouthful of Western omelet, patiently awaiting details.

"Okay," I said, "so the thing I want you to know is that Dom is a nice guy. Really. This was an aberration."

Mouth full, he gestured for me to continue. Sunlight slanted through the window, illuminating his silver-gray eyes. It took me a moment to get my brain back on track.

"Um, what happened is that, well, Dom thought Swing—I mean Pierre—"

"It's all right, I know everyone called him Swing," he said. "It's funny. He liked it."

"Okay, well, Dom thought Swing was, um... involved with his daughter."

"*His* daughter," Victor said. "Not yours?"

"No, our divorce was ages ago," I said. "We never had kids. I still don't." Why did I feel a need to tell him that? "Kari is his second wife's daughter."

"So…" I could almost hear him doing the math, applying his big architect's brain to the task of guesstimating the girl's age.

"She's sixteen," I said.

"Then no." Victor put down his fork. "Not a sixteen-year-old. Not Pierre. No way."

"I didn't think so either. I talked with Kari. Don't worry, she says nothing happened, and her dad will figure it out if he hasn't already."

"What does it matter now? Pierre's dead. It's not as if he could be arrested for statutory rape." He sat back against the blue vinyl, regarding me steadily. "How badly did your Dom hate Pierre?"

My Dom? Did something in my tone give away my lingering feelings for my ex? I glanced around and lowered my voice. "If you're asking whether Dom could have murdered your brother, the answer is no. He doesn't have it in him."

"He thought Pierre was sleeping with his underage daughter," he said. "He was enraged enough to beat him up. Why are you so sure he'd stop there?"

"Because I know this man." I told Victor about Kari's cooking lessons, the lessons Swing hadn't known she'd kept secret from her parents until Dom stumbled upon the two of them at Dewatre and went ballistic. "Dom was caught off guard. He regretted it later. The thing is, the detective in charge of the investigation is thinking along the same lines as you. I have to tell you, he thinks Dom did it."

Victor stared out the window. He scrubbed a hand over his jaw.

"This detective, Paul Cullen," I said, "he's not even looking at anybody else. He's lazy and out for a quick solve."

"Are there no other suspects?" he asked.

"Well, I'm sure you know about that animal-rights organization," I said. "The Society for Endangered—"

"Yes, of course. Is there any evidence they were involved?"

I hesitated, recalling all too vividly how the killer had staged Swing's corpse: the platter, the parsley, the acronym SEAR spelled out in balsamic syrup. The police had instructed me to keep those details to myself, and for that I was grateful. I had no desire to share them with the victim's brother. Instead of answering, I said, "Cullen refuses to consider that SEAR could have anything to do with Swing's death."

He sat awhile, thinking, then picked up his fork. "I'll speak with your Dom. I'll see if I agree with Cullen."

I didn't like the sound of that. What would Victor do if he failed to get a warm and fuzzy feeling from Dom? If he came to the conclusion that sure, this guy could have offed his brother? "Please stop calling him *my* Dom," I said. "He's not... we're divorced. I told you."

"It was friendly, I assume." He took a swig of orange juice. "What's the word you Americans always use? Amicable. It sounds like it was an amicable divorce."

"Yes, it was amicable. We've remained friends."

"My divorce, it was not so amicable."

"Oh," I said. "You're divorced?"

He nodded. "After Columbia I returned to Paris to marry Emmie. It turns out we get along better when there's an ocean between us."

"Children?" I asked.

"No. It lasted precisely three years. The last two years and eleven months we struggled to make it work." He shrugged. No one can shrug like a Frenchman. "What do you do, Jane?"

"Hmm? Oh, you mean for a living?"

"You said you work from home. And what a home, yes? In such a well-to-do neighborhood. I hope you don't think me rude, but I'm curious what kind of home-based business affords such a lifestyle."

I almost told him that my newly elevated lifestyle was unrelated to what I do for a living, but that wasn't true. My first after-school job had been pet-sitting for Irene McAuliffe all those years ago when I was still in high school. Which led eventually to my Death Diva business, which Irene helped to foster with frequent assignments and recommendations. Which led to the two of us becoming close enough for her to trust me to care for her beloved Sexy Beast after her death.

By the time I'd laid it all out to Victor—the history of my bizarre business and how I'd come to be the guardian not only of Sexy Beast but of the grand mini mansion he'd inherited— we'd finished breakfast and were lingering over third cups of coffee.

He signaled for the check. "I have a proposition for you, Jane."

And yes, I managed not to giggle, but it was a close thing. "What would that be?"

"Pierre needs a proper funeral," he said, "and a proper, what do you call it, a gathering. After the funeral. 'Party' doesn't sound right."

"A reception."

"Yes. A reception. He had many friends, and some of those

friends were prominent people. I wouldn't know where to begin."

"Don't worry, I'm an old hand at this," I said. "I'm happy to help."

"Then I'll hire you to do this for me," he said. When I started to object, he raised a palm. "I won't take advantage of your expertise, Jane. Don't insult me by asking me to do so."

"Oh brother," I muttered. This guy was good.

"This will entail a great deal of work," he continued, "and you'll no doubt need to hire assistants. I assure you that as my brother's sole heir, I can afford your professional services. Pierre would have wanted this done right."

He was correct about that. The Swing I'd known was a perfectionist.

"So do we have a deal?" he asked.

"That depends," I said. "Are you going to stop threatening to rent a car and move to a hotel?"

He pretended to struggle with the question. "Oh, I suppose so. If I must."

"Then I guess we have a deal."

5

Stinking Badges

"SO THEN SWING SAYS..." The man holding the microphone slathered on a ridiculous French accent that sounded nothing like his deceased friend. "'Why? Doesn't it *taste* like orangutan?'"

Laughter and applause rippled across the ballroom. About a hundred fifty people sat at round tables and congregated near the bar and buffet tables. Everyone present was a vetted friend of the late Pierre Dewatre's. This was an invitation-only funeral reception.

I wore the fade-into-the-background outfit I reserved for funeral homes and other assignments that require a more respectable appearance: gray skirt suit, white blouse, and black pumps, my layered reddish-blond hair pulled back into a ladylike French twist.

For flair I'd paired my usual fake pearls with an inconspicuous surveillance headset, which coordinated nicely with the small two-way radio attached to my waistband. The transparent earpiece and behind-the-ear coil were connected to a tiny microphone clipped to my lapel. This rig allowed me to remain in constant contact with my designated head of security and his two assistants.

I pressed the button on the mic and murmured, "Hey, guys, how's it looking out there?" Members of the Society for Endangered Animal Rights had picketed the interment at Whispering Willows Cemetery and then reconvened on the sidewalk at the entrance to the Crystal Harbor Country Club, where the reception was being held. Thankfully they hadn't disturbed the funeral mass at Holy Resurrection, but only because the law forced them to keep a distance of three hundred feet. A couple of cops were out there keeping an eye on things, for what that was worth.

Martin's voice filled my ear. "They're keeping to the sidewalk. So far."

Yeah, that's right, I'd put the padre in charge of keeping out the crazies. "The fox guarding the henhouse" was how Detective Cullen had put it when he'd found out. What did he think Martin was going to do, pickpocket his way through the mourners? And okay, it was entirely possible Cullen knew Martin better than I did, or at least was privy to some of the more intriguing aspects of his background, but the padre and I had been in a couple of tight spots together, and I liked to think I was a pretty good judge of character. Also I'd seen him in action and knew he was capable of subduing someone if necessary, even a strong, emotionally excited someone.

Tina's voice replaced Martin's in my earpiece. "I don't like it," she said. "That *Ramrod News* lady is still out there, stirring things up. She's stopping everyone coming and going, getting the SEAR idiots all whipped up. And her cameraman's getting it all on tape."

"Great," I said. Tina was Tina Cullen, an off-duty NYPD cop and—in case the last name sounds familiar—Paul Cullen's daughter. When he'd found out Martin had hired his darling baby girl to work security today, he'd turned all kinds of interesting colors. I was afraid the poor guy would stroke out right there in Holy Resurrection. It was a good thing we were in a church and Cullen couldn't get too vocal.

By the time they were packing Swing's box into the hearse, and the mourners' cars were queuing up for the drive to the boneyard, Cullen had managed to get himself under control. Plus Tina was having none of it. She was as tall as her dad and as wide, only on her it was all muscle. Any poor sap who let the pink streaks in her spiky platinum hair fool them into thinking she was a pushover was in for a rude education, and that included her old man. Cullen continued to grumble and shoot Martin venomous looks, but that was as far as he took it.

The padre's other assistant was Ben Ralston, a local private investigator and mutual friend of ours. He also happened to be living with Martin's mother, Stevie.

It was more than two hours into the affair and the speechifying finally appeared to be winding down, thank goodness. Victor had been the first to take the mic. He'd spoken movingly of his brother, of Swing's role as Victor's surrogate parent, of his love of food and hospitality, of the hard work and determination that had helped him rise to prominence in the culinary world. He didn't gloss over Swing's personality quirks or the fact that he could be difficult to live and work with, but his wry observations were made with love and elicited warm smiles all around.

After Victor had taken his seat, various pals and associates of Swing's took their turns with the mic. Many of them were celebrities of one sort or another and not shy about public speaking. I'd never worked a funeral reception with so many mourners hogging the limelight, particularly those of the female persuasion who'd shared Swing's bed at one time or another. The more liquor they imbibed, the more rambling and off-topic the speeches became. On a couple of occasions I'd had to gently wrest the cordless mic from a speaker, ostensibly to give the next person a turn but in reality to keep too much private knowledge from becoming drunkenly public.

I stood ready to snatch the mic once this guy was done and then spirit it away for good. Across the room I spied Maia Armstrong, a local caterer and buddy of mine, giving instructions to an assistant. In addition to Maia's own delicious food, the buffet tables held some of the deceased's signature dishes contributed by his assistant chefs. Prominent among them was, yes, the outrageously sexy Dixie Brisket. I couldn't look at it without my mouth watering like a faucet. I was there to supervise, I reminded myself, not to stuff my face.

Detective Cullen had no such qualms. I assumed he was also working that day, on the alert for guilty behavior by funeral-goers. Isn't that what detectives always do on TV? But he appeared to take more interest in the Bluepoint oysters and lobster mac and cheese.

And why not? After all, the guilty party—which is to say his one and only suspect—was absent from the proceedings. Although Dom and Swing had been friends until that final, fateful blow-up, Dom had decided his presence at the funeral would constitute both a distraction and fodder for the seamier news outlets.

Kari, however, was there. She'd told me Dom hadn't wanted her to attend but that her mom had thought she needed "closure." I'd promised Lana I'd keep a close eye on the girl and make sure it wasn't all too much for her. So far she was holding up. Perhaps Lana's maternal instincts had been on the money. Stranger things had happened.

Unfortunately, the guy with the mic did not appear to be running out of steam. He was a wealthy Japanese-American fellow in his mid-thirties named Joe Oshiro who'd inherited a chain of popular sushi restaurants. Joe kept riffing on the theme of Swing's supposed penchant for serving up endangered species. Apparently he thought the idea had enormous comic potential. But then, if his anecdotes were accurate, so did Swing.

Joe sipped from the martini in his other hand. "So Swing invites them into the kitchen at Dewatre," he said, "the whole *Sixty Minutes* crew with their cameras and everything. And very seriously he tells Lesley Stahl he wants to address the rumors that have been circulating about him. The public has a right to know, he says."

I scanned the ballroom, happy to see that Sophie Halperin, Crystal Harbor's mayor and a close friend of mine, had made it. She and Sten Jakobsen, a local attorney who'd done legal work for Swing, were chatting as they piled their plates at the buffet. Through my earpiece I heard Ben say, "I caught one of the busboys taking video on his phone. Turns out he's a production assistant for *Ramrod News*."

Tina cursed. Martin said, "You need any help?"

"Nah," Ben said. "I deleted the video and put the fear of God into him. He won't be back."

I pressed the speaker button and said, sotto voce, "Guys, we need to be doubly on the alert if they're pulling stunts like that." I'd liked Swing and was glad to be able to help his brother, but I was ready for this whole stressful day to be over.

Joe finished his martini and wound up for the pitch. "So Swing opens up the big steel freezer and shows them what he has inside. It's crammed top to bottom with packages wrapped in white butcher paper. They're labeled 'Mountain Gorilla,' 'Snow Leopard,' 'Spotted Owl'…"

His audience roared with laughter. "Needless to say, that segment never made it onto the show." Joe's grin lost some of its luster. "Swing enjoyed tweaking anyone gullible enough to believe the rumors, but those of us who knew him knew that he never could have done what they accused him of. He loved animals. The World Wildlife Fund was his favorite charity. Right, Victor?"

From his seat across the room, Victor nodded. He looked especially handsome today in a brand-new dark navy suit he'd managed to have rush-tailored in time for the funeral. He'd paired it with a snowy white shirt and subdued striped tie.

I knew that the members of SEAR wouldn't be at all impressed that Swing supported the World Wildlife Fund. They saw it and similar organizations that actually accomplished something as mainstream sellouts.

Joe finished by inviting Swing's friends to make contributions in his memory to the World Wildlife Fund and finally relinquished the mic. I pretended not to see the two or three raised hands as I slipped the mic to Maia's assistant with a command to make it disappear.

I made my way through the room to Victor, who sat chatting with a thirtyish redheaded woman I knew to be Swing's agent, Chloe Sleeper. I recognized her from that *Ramrod News* episode when she faced off against Romulus Tooley, the SEAR spokesman, as well as from her picture on Swing's phone. She'd tried to call him the day he died.

The two of them stood. Victor introduced us and we shook hands. The television didn't do justice to Chloe, who was a petite beauty with large green eyes and enviable cheekbones.

"How long were you Swing's agent?" I asked.

"Just under a year," she said. "Did you know him?"

I nodded. "For the past three years since he opened Dewatre." Was it my imagination or did her expression alter, just slightly? Probably wondering if I'd been one of his myriad bed partners. It occurred to me that Victor might be wondering the same thing. For some reason, that bothered me more than any speculation on the part of Swing's agent.

"I saw you on *Ramrod News*," I told Chloe. "For what it's worth, you came off much more favorably than that blowhard Tooley."

At the mention of his name, she looked like she wanted to spit. "That's not hard to do. The man's a parasite. He's just after publicity."

"That's what worries me." I jerked my head in the general direction of the sidewalk picketers. "I can't see Tooley and his pals quietly leaving today without putting on some sort of show."

Victor spoke up. "Especially with those TV cameras on them."

A reluctant smile tugged at Chloe's mouth. "Swing would have enjoyed this. He'd have been out there goading them."

I glanced at Victor. He wasn't smiling, and I sensed he was thinking the same thing I was. Swing's goading of these unstable fanatics might very well have gotten him killed. Sure, writing "SEAR" at the crime scene would be counterintuitive if the murderer really was connected with the organization. Why draw the police right to you? On the other hand, I didn't see Cullen giving them the slightest glance. If Tooley or one of the other SEAR nut jobs put that knife in Swing's chest, then leaving their calling card might have been intended as a kind of reverse diversion, as in *Why on earth would I murder someone and take credit for it? I* must *be innocent.* Either that or the killer was so off the deep end that pride in his accomplishment overcame any concern about getting caught.

Bottom line: SEAR and its spokesman were in no way off the hook as far as I was concerned.

In my earpiece I heard Martin check in with Ben and Tina: their locations, what they were observing. All quiet on the country-club front if you didn't count the more or less peaceful demonstration going on the requisite three hundred-plus feet from where we stood.

Victor glanced around the ballroom. To Chloe he said, "You must know Lee. Leonora Romano."

"Of course."

"I haven't seen her today. I know things were strained between her and Pierre, but I can't believe she wouldn't show up."

"She's here. She was at the church and cemetery, too." Chloe wore a knowing smile. "You just didn't recognize her. She's had a little work done."

He looked dubious. "Unless she's inhabiting a totally new body…"

She shrugged. "That's kind of what we're talking about." She quickly scanned the room and pointed to a small cluster of people at the bar. "There she is."

He peered at the group, shaking his head in bewilderment.

"In the bright red suit," she said.

After a stunned moment, he said, "No." The head-shake turned vigorous. "Impossible."

The object of their discussion was a mature, stylish woman with carefully coiffed blond hair and a good figure. The crimson suit looked like it had been sewn on her, with a nipped-in peplum jacket and short, body-hugging skirt. Sky-high, pointy-toed heels completed her sedate funerary attire. She stood conversing with a dapper, portly man I knew to be a bigwig at the Food Network. She noticed Victor gaping at her and sent him a little wave, raising her finger in a "one minute" signal.

Victor turned to Chloe. "The last time I saw Lee, she weighed at least three hundred pounds and lived in sweats and overalls. Her hair was a frizzy gray mess. And that is someone else's face."

Chloe lowered her voice. "Scarlett Johansson's if we're being specific. That's who she was going for."

"Where are those thick eyeglasses she always wore?" he asked. "Contacts, finally?"

She shook her head. "Vision-correction surgery. Weight-loss surgery. And she hired a wardrobe stylist."

He shook his head sadly. "Why? To turn herself into some kind of plastic doll when she's such a gifted chef? She's the best."

"Better than—" Chloe faltered "—than almost anyone."

"Better than Pierre." He gave her a knowing smile. "You can say it."

"There's no point in getting into all that now. They moved apart, but they never stopped respecting each other." Chloe seemed to recall my presence. "Lee and Swing had a history."

"So I gather." I watched Lee detach herself from the network exec and begin to make her way toward us. "How long were they together?"

"Eight years," she said. "Hummingbird in Manhattan—that was their restaurant. Oh." She noted my reaction. "You thought they were a couple?"

"Well…" I shrugged.

"Understandable," Victor said, "considering Pierre's reputation. Lee was one of the few females of his acquaintance he did not… was not involved with," he ended politely.

I wagged my hand. "Add me to the short list." My face heated. Why had I felt a need to say that? It might be because I didn't want this accomplished, discerning, and yes, sexy man to view me as just another of his brother's many conquests.

Chloe lowered her voice further still. "Plus she's seven or eight years older than Swing. He liked them younger."

Okay, by my calculation I was seven or eight years older than Victor. I wondered whether he shared his brother's preference for younger women. Then I hated myself for wondering.

Lee swept up in a cloud of high-end perfume. The distinctive floral scent had some fancy French name I can't recall. What I do recall is standing in Nordstrom's fragrance department a couple of weeks earlier staring longingly at the obscenely expensive bottle after letting the saleslady spritz my wrist. Judging from the overpowering miasma that announced her arrival, Lee must have spritzed it on from head to toe.

"Victor." She embraced him, managing not to spill a drop of the white wine in her full glass. "Isn't it just awful? Poor Pierre. Awful business, just awful." She looked into his eyes. "How are you holding up, dear?"

"I'm all right," he said. "I'm glad you decided to come, Lee."

"Oh, don't be ridiculous." She gave an airy wave. "How

could I stay away? I choose to remember the good times. The rest of it, it's all water under the bridge."

Victor and Chloe responded with polite little nods that, to my eye, lacked conviction.

Victor made introductions. "Jane, this is Leonora Romano, Pierre's former business partner." To her he said, "My new friend Jane Delaney. Jane is a wonder. All of this is her doing."

We shook hands, said our nice-to-meet-yous, and agreed to call each other Lee and Jane. Chloe had said Lee was trying for the Scarlett Johansson look, and I guess I could see it in the fat lips and sultry eyes. A stranger to cosmetic procedures, I could only guess at how many separate procedures and how much cold hard cash had been involved in her transformation.

I suspected Victor was wondering the same thing when he said, "You look amazing, Lee. I didn't recognize you. Ask Chloe."

She laughed. "Well, that's the point, isn't it?" She struck a pose. "The new me. I consider it an investment, and so far it's paying off in spades."

"In what way?" he asked.

Chloe appeared uncomfortable. "Perhaps now isn't the best time to get into this."

"Why pussyfoot around?" Lee said. "It'll be public knowledge soon enough."

"*Maybe,*" Chloe cautioned her. "It's not a done deal yet."

Lee waved away the other woman's caution. "Did you see who I was chatting up over there? Dennis Rothbart! We're close to signing on the dotted line."

Working a high-powered business deal at a funeral. Oh, and? Bragging about it in front of the deceased's brother. Classy.

"It's not done until it's done," Chloe said. "I don't want you to be crushed if it falls through."

Victor wore a frown. "How are you involved in this, Chloe?"

She tried to look him in the eye, and almost succeeded. "I'm representing Lee now."

His features hardened fractionally, though his overall expression remained neutral. "That was fast."

Lee did not appear to share Chloe's embarrassment at how swiftly she'd snatched up her estranged former partner's agent. She sipped her wine. "This is a cutthroat business, Victor. I'm sure you're aware of that."

"Which business are you referring to?" he asked. "Not the restaurant business."

"Oh, please don't be willfully naïve, dear. It's unbecoming in a man as handsome as you. We all know to what cutthroat business I refer. Well, perhaps Jane doesn't."

"Oh, I'm pretty sure I do," I said.

Victor pitched his voice dangerously low. "We just buried my brother today and already you've moved in to snap up the television show they offered him. You don't procrastinate, I'll say that for you."

Her chin rose. "We both know that if I hadn't 'moved in' with alacrity, someone else would have beaten me to it. Someone younger, fresher, sexier." Hot color suffused her face under the skillfully applied makeup. "It's no longer about who has more talent, who works harder. Do you think Julia Child could have become a TV sensation in the twenty-first century? Why do you think I went through all this?" She indicated herself, her whole self, from her sleek, highlighted hair to the pointed toes of her designer four-inch pumps. Now wine did slosh out of her glass, but she didn't seem to notice.

"Your miraculous—" he groped for the word "—metamorphosis might work for a while, but if that's what you're pinning your hopes on, your efforts are doomed to fail. How long do you think it will take before someone 'younger, fresher, sexier' comes along and displaces you?"

"Let them try." She got in his face, quivering with vehemence. "By then the world will have seen who I am and what I can do." She stabbed a manicured finger at her own chest. "They'll see that *I'm* the best and they'll *have* to pay attention! I just needed to get a foot in the door, and that was never going to happen for a fat, ugly fifty-year-old, no matter how exceptional a chef I was."

"Guys, please…" Chloe spread her hands. "Let's not—"

"How long has this been in the works?" Victor gestured to indicate Lee's new look. "You must have been planning this for some time."

"Since Hummingbird closed three years ago if you must know," she said. "I spent the time writing a cookbook—it's just been published—and getting the surgeries. My eyelids just finished healing. The timing for this show was—" She clamped her mouth shut. Apparently even this bigmouth had her limits.

"Fortunate?" Victor took a deep, calming breath. He stepped back and shifted his gaze to Chloe, who looked like she wanted to teleport off the planet.

She pushed a strand of chin-length, coppery hair behind her ear. "It's business, Victor. It doesn't… it doesn't mean I don't miss Swing terribly—"

"Excuse me, I need to breathe some fresh air." He strode swiftly to the exit.

Chloe tried to soothe her new client. "Don't worry, Lee,

he'll come around. This was just the wrong day to—"

"The hell with him." Lee drained her glass in one swallow. Her bee-stung mouth—by all appearances stung by the whole damn swarm—stretched wide to show off blindingly white, implausibly straight and even teeth. "One of the best things about losing half your body weight is you get drunk faster. Can I bring either of you something from the bar?"

At that moment Tina's voice erupted in my earpiece. "All hands out front!" she barked. "We have a fight."

I didn't hesitate. I ran as fast as my pencil skirt and modest heels would allow through the ballroom and foyer and out the front doors of the redbrick English Tudor-style clubhouse, startling Victor where he paced and smoked—he *smoked?*—on the brick walkway fronting the building.

I heard the ruckus before I saw it. I pressed the button on my lapel mic as I ran under the long green awning and across the enormous front lawn toward the street. "What's going on?" I breathlessly demanded. "Where are the cops?"

I received no response, which meant all three members of my security crew were up to their eyeballs in whatever was going on down at the entrance to the country club.

Victor sprinted past me toward the hubbub and I muttered a winded oath. This was not exactly what I'd had in mind when I'd promised him a memorable, dignified send-off for his brother. Sure, I'd aced the memorable part. Dignified, not so much.

By the time I reached the street, the brawl was already breaking up. Traffic, however, was still snarled in all directions, with drivers slowing to rubberneck and shout opinions regarding the moral character of those who chose to picket funerals, along with helpful suggestions of the anatomically impossible variety.

Officer Geri Marvin, a young female cop with more attitude than sense, stood guard over a gaggle of demonstrators sitting on the curb, almost all of them young women in their twenties. Their picket signs lay on the grass behind them, sporting such messages as *Murderers Deserve Murder* and *Swing Had It Coming* and *Score: Swing, Zero – Animals, One.* That last one was decorated with a picture of a panda swinging a bloody knife at a man in a chef's toque. I was tempted to challenge that measly zero. I mean, if Swing had indeed butchered all those critters as they claimed, shouldn't the sign give him credit for, I don't know, a few hundred kills?

Sergeant Howie Werker, a tall, dark-skinned cop in his early forties, actively encouraged the rest of the picketers to shut the heck up and sit their bottoms down on the curb. Only, he didn't say "heck." Or "bottoms."

I liked Howie. He was smart, sensible, and even-tempered—positive attributes in any law-enforcement officer. Recently he'd informed me, over pints at Murray's Pub, a popular local watering hole, that he'd taken the detective's exam and aced it. The thing is, he wanted to remain in the Crystal Harbor PD, which has only two detective positions, both currently filled. I couldn't see either Bonnie Hernandez or Paul Cullen resigning anytime soon. Nevertheless, I wished him luck and toasted his success on the exam.

Howie's crowd-control efforts were being aided by Martin, who wore the same impeccably tailored charcoal-gray suit I'd seen him in at his daughter Lexie's wedding the previous spring. With his impenetrable aviator sunglasses and the surveillance headset, he could have been mistaken for a member of the Secret Service. When he said, *"Sit!"* the SEAR chicks plopped their cute little fannies on the curb without a peep and stared at him wide-eyed as if awaiting the next order.

When I'd initially seen the picketers earlier that day at the cemetery, the first thing that had popped into my head was Charles Manson and the adoring young followers who would have done anything for him—and did. Here was Romulus Tooley, an older man with presence, a strong leader who was blindly committed to his cause. The SEAR members trailing him with picket signs, yelling chants, were for the most part young, female, and probably quite impressionable. I suspected they were seeking direction, a higher purpose. I wouldn't go so far as to speculate about daddy issues, but who knew? That could be part of the mix for some of them.

Considering the gooey-eyed way most of them looked at Tooley, I couldn't help but wonder whether he took advantage of their devotion, in the sexual sense. And if so, was that the only similarity between Manson and Tooley? The young people who'd killed on Manson's orders had written on the walls in blood. Swing's killer had chosen balsamic syrup.

The girls sitting on the curb looked sweet and innocent, but chances were that some of them had been involved in the notorious activities SEAR was known for, including vandalism, harassment, burglary, and arson. Their criminal acts had yet to be connected with a death, but it was only a matter of time. Their targets included fur farms, research labs, whaling ships— and okay, I can't help but sympathize with some of their goals. They aren't wrong about wanting to protect endangered species and require humane treatment of animals. I want that too. Heck, so did Swing. But please. Arson?

Platinum-haired Miranda Daniels from *Ramrod News* was busy shoving her microphone in people's faces while her cameraman captured the action for that evening's show. The local Long Island news station had its people there as well. As I watched, a white NBC News van pulled up. The other networks couldn't be far behind.

Romulus Tooley wasn't about to cool his heels with the others, not while the cameras were rolling. Beefy Tina Cullen restrained him with apparent ease as he and a tall teenage boy engaged in a screaming match. Tooley accused the teen of playing into the hands of the animal-slaughtering establishment. For his part, the boy called Tooley a shameless, publicity-hogging terrorist while Ben Ralston, the third member of Martin's security team, held him back. Ben, a middle-aged Black man, was four or five inches shorter than the youth but sturdily built.

This, then, was what had started the melee: this irate young man deciding to mix it up with the SEAR spokesman.

"Tucker!" It was Kari, dashing into the throng before I could stop her. Some of the funeral-goers had wandered down from the clubhouse, drinks in hand, as if this were a spectator sport. Most of them also held up cell phones, taking photos and video. Victor was not one of them. He stood to the side, scowling at the spectacle.

Kari got between Tooley and her boyfriend. So this young hothead was Tucker Nearing. I'd heard about him but had never seen him in the flesh until then. Tucker was a good-looking six-footer with short black hair and light brown eyes. He had powerful shoulders and arms above a slim waist, and I recalled Kari mentioning he was the star of the swim team.

"Tucker, what are you doing?" Kari demanded. "Why are you here?"

"Somebody has to stand up to these people, Kari. They're vultures, picketing a funeral. *Vultures!*" he hollered at Tooley, prompting an angry outburst from the seated SEAR members, which Martin immediately quelled simply by crossing his arms and frowning at them from behind the dark shades.

"What they're doing is legal, Tucker," she said. "Disgusting but legal. You're not making it any better by stirring things up."

Her disapproval took some of the starch out of him. He looked like a chastised puppy. "I did this for you," he said softly. The TV cameras honed in on the couple, and without a word exchanged between them, Martin and his team forcibly redirected them away from the teenagers.

Miranda Daniels was clearly unaccustomed to being thwarted. "We have a right to be here!" she told Martin. "You can't order us around, you're just rent-a-cops. If you're real police, then show me your badges."

He whipped off his shades and shoved his grinning mug right in front of the *Ramrod News* camera lens. With a jaunty wink and an over-the-top Mexican accent, he said, "Badges? We don't need no stinking badges!"

I rolled my eyes at the beaten-to-death movie line, popularized by *Blazing Saddles* but having originated with *The Treasure of the Sierra Madre*. Miranda, apparently not a film buff, looked at him as if he'd lost his mind.

Victor and I took advantage of the diversion to herd Kari and Tucker through the gates of the country club, well away from the action.

"That's the brother!" Miranda yelled to her cameraman, signaling him to follow her. This prompted Tooley and his minions to scream lovely things at Victor, such as "Your brother was a murderer!" and "Swing got what he deserved!" The cops and my security team did their best to control them.

Where the heck was Detective Cullen?

Miranda and her cameraman attempted to follow us, only to have Tina block their way like a human bulldozer with pink-streaked hair. "This is private property." She placed her big hand over the camera lens. "You can't enter."

"You don't have the authority to keep us out," Miranda said. "Where's the owner?"

"The club's owned by all the members," Tina said. "If you can get every last one of them to provide written permission, I'll step aside. Until then..." She advanced, forcing the newswoman and cameraman to back up to the sidewalk. "You go no further."

I hadn't a clue who owned the club, and I doubted Tina knew either. Judging by Miranda's uncertain scowl, she was unwilling to risk being charged with trespassing, especially with this belligerent broad and the crazy guy with the shades guarding the gates. But that didn't keep her from trying to get some juicy footage of Swing's brother. That he was easy on the eyes no doubt intensified her determination to get him on camera.

"Victor!" Miranda hollered. "Victor, come here and talk to us! Talk to the American public!" He ignored her. "Victor, this is your chance to send a message to your brother's killer!"

He responded with the kind of disdainful glance only the French can pull off, before steering our little group behind one of the broad stone gateposts, concealing us from the cameras.

Tucker scrubbed a hand through his short black hair. "I wasn't trying to make things worse, Kari, I swear. It's just..." Had any teenager in the history of teenagers ever looked this hopelessly lovesick?

I thought of how Kari had compared her boyfriend with

Swing, that night at my place while we made pancakes. She'd said Tucker was like a little boy. He was not, in fact, like a little boy, he was like precisely what he was: a besotted adolescent trying hard to hold on to his girlfriend and making boneheaded mistakes in the process—like trying to impress her by picking a fight with the guy he figured she must hate more than anyone in the world at that moment.

He looked searchingly into her eyes. "I know you and Swing had a thing going. I forgive you."

I intercepted Victor's questioning glance as we turned our backs on the young couple and took a few steps away to give them privacy—or the illusion of it, considering we could still hear every word exchanged between them. I'd assured Victor that his brother hadn't seduced a sixteen-year-old. Had I been lying?

"No, Tucker," Kari said, "it wasn't like—"

"It doesn't matter what you did with him," he said. "That's over. All I care about is that you and I are together now."

"Tucker, for God's sake, we didn't do anything!" she insisted.

"You don't have to lie to me," he said. "I told you, I forgive you. I love you, Kari. I'd do anything for you. *Anything!*"

"Okay, play time's over!" It was Detective Cullen, ambling across the lawn at last, picking at his teeth and brushing crumbs off his jacket once he spied the TV cameras. "Who's ready for a statement?"

6

Il Est un Bouffon

VICTOR AND I were about to exit my parked car and brave the torrential downpour the next evening when his cell rang. He glanced at the number on the screen and shrugged. He didn't recognize it. After he and the caller exchanged greetings, he said, "I'm not at Jane's right now. We just got to the pub. Murray's Pub? You know it?" He listened for a moment, then said, "You're welcome to join us. We'll save you a seat."

"Who was that?" I asked after he ended the call.

"Chloe. She says she has something for me."

"Sounds mysterious." I flipped up the hood of my rain jacket and reached for the door handle.

"Wait." He had the huge, black golf umbrella I'd found in the coat closet after Irene had died and left me the house. It had a curved wooden handle and enough fabric to make a six-man tent. A man's umbrella. "I'll come around."

Be still, my heart. Obediently I waited while Victor circled the car in what had turned into a biblical deluge and opened my door. He held the enormous canopy over us while we made the half-block dash to the pub.

Here, too, he held the door. I could get used to this. I welcomed the pub's cheery ambience, the aromas of fresh beer and spicy fries, the bluegrass music played at a volume that allowed patrons to converse without shouting, the warm golden light from original antique wall sconces that had started life as gas fixtures long before anyone in the whole dang place had been born. I hung my dripping jacket on the row of hooks by the door.

Victor glanced around approvingly as he deposited the umbrella in the stand by the door. It gave the little automatic umbrellas that were already there inferiority complexes. *It's chilly outside*, they whined. *Shrinkage. You know.*

Despite it being a Friday evening, the pub was less than a third full. Anyone who had a micron of sense had taken one look out the window and hauled out the Scrabble board. The rest of us found ourselves at Murray's.

I could feel Victor begin to relax as we slid onto barstools, and was glad I'd insisted on dragging him out of the house that night. The funeral had been yesterday. He'd spent all day today on the phone taking care of a variety of personal and business matters.

I'd gone out for a few hours in the middle of the day to start inventorying and photographing all those antique medical devices at my client's home. When I'd returned with groceries, Victor was where I'd left him, sitting at the breakfast table, filling a legal pad with notes. His phone was on speaker and the conversation was in French.

Unlike my houseguest, I spoke no language other than the one of my birth, despite having gotten decent grades in Spanish for six years. For what it's worth, I do remember all the important vacation words, the most critical being *baño* and *cerveza*. Drink enough Mexican *cerveza* and you'd darn well better know how to say, *Dónde está el baño?*

I did catch a few words as Victor wrapped up his conversation with someone named Michel. *Bien* and *merci* and *oui* were easy enough to pick out. Then Michel asked something and Victor said, "Crystal Harbor." Michel responded with the French version of *Say what?* Victor smiled at me as he slowly repeated the name of the town, followed by the translation: *"Cristal Port."* Then he added, "Long Island." Ah. A place Michel had heard of. He proceeded to share his encyclopedic knowledge about Long Island—I heard "Billy Joel" and "Gatsby" and "Amityville *Horreur*"—while Victor made yappy hand gestures for my benefit.

After saying *adieu* to Michel, he'd helped me throw together a spaghetti dinner. He might not be the world-class chef his brother had been, but he knew his way around a meatball, endearing himself even further to Sexy Beast. Once we'd eaten, I'd been determined to get us out of the house. Victor had spent the entire day working and no doubt intended to spend his evening the same way. While it might be true that work was preferable to wallowing in grief, there was a third option that beat them both out.

Martin was behind the bar when we took our seats, flirting with a trio of pretty young women while he worked the blender for their girlie drinks. Hiring the padre had been a canny move on the part of Maxine Baumgartner, the pub's owner. The place now attracted far more female customers, whose presence in turn attracted even more male customers.

When I'd met Martin, he'd been bartending in Southampton, an hour's drive from his mother's home in working-class Rocky Bay. Yeah, that's right, he'd lived with his mom back then—temporarily, he'd insisted, and dang if he hadn't been telling the truth. When he'd started working at

Murray's two months ago, Maxine had rented him the apartment upstairs, which reduced his commute to a lazy stroll down a flight of stairs.

He glanced over and spotted us as he poured the last slushy, neon-colored concoction for the young ladies. He joined us, shook Victor's hand, and quietly mentioned that Dom was there.

"Oh," I said, and "Jeez." I looked at Victor, who was well aware that Dom was the primary suspect—heck, the *only* suspect—in his brother's murder. I slid off the barstool. "Um, maybe we should find another place to unwind."

"Where is he?" Victor asked.

Martin nodded toward a booth in the far corner. Only then did I recognize the back of Dom's head. Bonnie noticed us first, gazing past her fiancé with a sober expression.

"There's a great wine bar the next town over," I told Victor. "We'll come here some other—"

But he was already making his way toward Dom. The background music seemed to get louder as conversation ground to a halt throughout the pub. Everyone there knew who Victor was. The family resemblance left little doubt, not to mention a few funeral shots of him that had made it onto the news last night. And they also knew the investigation had targeted my ex. Most of them politely feigned disinterest, while a few gawked outright. All three of Martin's cuties were furiously thumbing their phones, no doubt tweeting this latest sighting of #SwingsSexyBro.

Reluctantly I followed Victor. Dom had risen at his approach, his expression outwardly neutral to anyone who didn't know him as well as I did. The Dom I saw was wary and watchful and prepared for things to turn ugly. His fiancée kept her seat as she watched Victor close the distance between them. Casually she unbuttoned her slate-colored jacket, and with a start, I realized why. Cops carry guns, even when off duty if they choose to. Bonnie struck me as the type who would choose to.

Victor stopped in front of Dom and extended his hand. He didn't smile. "We haven't met. I'm Victor Dewatre."

After a moment Dom stiffly shook it. "Dominic Faso. This is my fiancée, Detective Bonnie Hernandez." Yeah, he said *Detective*. Can you blame him?

"I would have preferred for Jane to introduce us," Victor said, shaking her hand, "but this is making her nervous."

An abrasive female voice rang out. "When did this place turn into a damn church?" It was Maxine, bellowing from behind the bar. The pub's owner was in her late fifties, with a blond ponytail and a grating smoker's voice. "Does the sign outside say Saint Murray's? No? Well then, stop praying for something exciting to happen over there—" Max jerked her head toward our little group "—or I'll have to shut the place down and join a convent."

She stared hard at her patrons, eliciting a few self-conscious titters, followed by a gradual resumption of conversation. I caught her eye and mouthed a thank-you.

"Would you, uh, like to join us?" Dom asked, while Bonnie gave him the Death Stare.

"For a moment only," Victor said. "It's not my intention to intrude." He sat next to Bonnie, forcing her to scoot over to make room. Dom did the same for me. He was halfway through a beer, while his fiancée sipped red wine. Nothing but crumbs and an errant tentacle remained of what had once been a pile of crispy fried calamari.

Well. Wasn't this cozy. What was Victor trying to prove?

As if I weren't sufficiently uptight, Bonnie's left hand rested lightly on the tabletop, with that four-karat diamond frantically waving at me and *nyah-nyah*ing and generally making a nuisance of itself. Oh yeah, *so* mature.

Victor addressed Bonnie, pitching his voice low enough to discourage eavesdroppers. "Detective, I understand you had to remove yourself from my brother's case due to the—" he gestured toward Dom "—conflict."

"That's right." Bonnie was in her early thirties, with short, stylishly cut dark hair and a mild lingering accent from her native Dominican Republic.

"This Detective Cullen," he said, "I have little faith in him. I know you're not free to comment, but from what I can tell, he is a buffoon."

Bonnie and Dom exchanged a look. It was clear they shared his assessment.

"Is it me," I asked her, "or is it weird that Cullen has chosen to zero in on the fiancé of a fellow detective? I mean, I can see Dom being, you know, a person of interest and all, but Cullen has obviously made up his mind. Is he even looking seriously at anyone else?"

"Like Mr. Dewatre said, I'm not free to comment on any aspect of the investigation."

I leaned forward, my voice low and steady and deadly serious. "Do you get that we're all on the same side here, Bonnie?"

Her eyes cut to the Frenchman sitting next to her. "Are we?"

"Since Victor wants to find out who killed his brother," I said, "and since you and I both know Dom didn't do it, then yes, I'd say we're all on the same side." Even if Victor didn't know it yet. In time he would.

I could almost hear the internal debate being waged behind Bonnie's green eyes. Finally, with a look of mild disgust, she said, "What I *can* tell you is that Cullen's always had a problem with me, because I've always had a problem with him. I've made no secret of the fact that the guy has no business wearing a gold shield."

"There's a good-old-boy thing going on here," Dom said. "He's pals with Chief Larsen. The department's stuck with him."

"I hate to think that my brother's killer might remain free due to police incompetence," Victor said. "I'll do whatever is required to keep that from happening."

"Mr. Dewatre—" Bonnie said.

"Call me Victor," he said. "Please."

"Victor, I sympathize with your frustration, but I must warn you not to take the law into—"

"Yes, yes," he said impatiently, "I know you must say this, but tell me. What would you do? If it were your brother. What would you do?"

She took a deep breath and sagged a little as she released it. "I'd try to see what I could find out. *Legally*," she added. "Without stepping on the detective's toes. And keeping him in the loop."

Dom addressed Victor. "It sounds to me like you're not convinced Cullen's on the right track."

"If you're asking whether I think you're guilty," Victor said, looking straight at him, "my honest answer is, I don't know. As for Cullen, I think if he somehow stumbled onto the right track, he would likely stumble right off it."

No one spoke for several moments while I envisioned a particularly hazardous minefield stretching between us, just waiting for someone to jump in and blow this civilized conversation to bits. No one, for example, brought up why Cullen had homed in on Dom as a suspect. Answer: because he'd beaten the snot out of Victor's brother, the murder victim. And why had Dom done that? Because he'd thought Swing was sexing up his teenage daughter. For all I knew, he believed it still. These were issues none of us appeared eager to explore at this juncture.

"Well, here's something to get you started," Dom told him. "The killer wears size thirteen shoes."

"But isn't that—" I cut myself off.

"My size?" he said. "Yes, unfortunately. Cullen made off with all my sneakers for testing. They're the right size, but none of them match. Wrong treads or whatever. Of course, he's claiming I threw away the shoes I wore that day." To Victor he explained, "Whoever committed the murder apparently left footprints."

"It's true," Victor said. "I saw."

I looked at him sharply. "What do you mean you saw? When could you have seen?"

"Cullen finally released the crime scene," he said. "He brought the restaurant keys over this afternoon when you were out. It was a good walk. I needed the exercise." Dewatre was about two miles from my house.

"Oh, Victor, that must have been..." I shook my head. "Why didn't you wait for me? I would have gone with you."

"You've been through enough," he said. "You found him."

"Why didn't you tell me about this earlier?"

"I knew you would be upset. I wasn't going to mention it,

but now we're talking about the shoes and…" He shrugged.

"You stubborn… *Frenchman!*" I accused.

He rewarded that with a little smile, quickly squelched. He gave a sad shake of his head. "Pierre loved that kitchen. Now… now I feel like bulldozing the place."

It had been four days. I thought about the blood. I thought about the meat and other cooking ingredients that had been left out on the counter, certain the cops would not have bothered disposing of it. Four warm days with the place all closed up.

"I'll bring someone in to clean it up," I said.

He frowned. "Who would do a job like that?"

"There are professionals who do this for a living, believe it or not. Crime scenes, suicides… you know. They come in with hazmat suits and special equipment. There's a very good company. I know the owner. I'll call him tomorrow."

Lie. I'd call Denny Pinheiro from the privacy of my bedroom as soon as I got home. In his business, prospective customers were assured of getting someone on the phone twenty-four seven. Plus I was a valued client, thanks to my unusual line of work, so I had Denny's personal cell on speed dial. I had little doubt he'd meet me at Dewatre the next morning. Victor, however, did not need to know that. I planned to quietly swipe the keys Cullen had just given him and run out in the a.m. to do "a little shopping."

Yeah, I'm a big fat liar, so sue me. Swing's brother had already viewed the grisly aftermath of his murder. He didn't need to experience it again.

An awkward silence ensued, which Bonnie finally broke with, "I wonder what size shoes Romulus Tooley wears."

"I'll ask Ben to find out," Victor said.

"Ben Ralston?" I asked. "The private investigator?"

Victor nodded. "I phoned him today. You mentioned that he's done work for you. He's competent, yes?"

"He's very competent. What exactly did you ask him to do?"

"To find out where Tooley was on Monday morning when Pierre was stabbed to death."

"I wonder if Cullen even did that much," I said.

"Well, we can eliminate fifty percent of the population," Bonnie said. "The killer was almost certainly male. I don't know any woman who could wear a men's size thirteen."

"How long until you have to go back home?" Dom asked Victor. "I mean, I assume your employer offered a few days' bereavement leave, but I'm just wondering how you'll manage to look into your brother's murder from… is it Paris?"

Victor nodded. "My architectural firm is located on the Champs-Élysées, but we do a lot of work for U.S. companies, so we have several branches over here as well. One of them is in Manhattan, down in SoHo. I told my boss I wanted to work out of the SoHo office for, well, I'm not sure how long, with flexible hours, and he has graciously agreed."

"That's quite a concession," Bonnie said. "They must be eager to keep you happy."

Victor shrugged. "I'm good at what I do. Also I've brought the firm a couple of valuable clients. It's not just the investigation keeping me here. I need to sell Pierre's house and the restaurant, settle his affairs."

I said, "Well, you know you're welcome to stay at my place for the duration. The truth is, I enjoy the company." I felt Dom stiffen slightly.

"You've been exceedingly generous, Jane," Victor said,

"and I thank you for it, but I couldn't continue to impose—"

"We have a deal," I reminded him. "No hotels, remember? You're hurting my feelings, Victor. I feel a big, juicy cry coming on."

He shook his head, grinning. "You are impossible."

"So you've been staying at Janey's all week?" Dom sounded casual. Too casual. Bonnie thought so, too, judging by the flat stare she gave him.

"That's right," Victor said. "Jane is my guardian angel. I don't know what I would have done without her these past few days."

"Yeah, she's… That's great," Dom said, "that you have someplace local to stay and all. What about Swing's house? I'd have thought you'd want to stay there."

"At first the police wouldn't let me near it. And now…" Victor hesitated. "I know I need to go there and begin sorting through his things. To be honest, I'm not looking forward to it."

"Well, listen," Dom said, "if you get tired of the scenery over at Jane's, you can always bunk at my place. Plenty of room—"

"Dom," Bonnie interrupted, "that's probably not a good idea, considering."

He looked blank for a moment. *Considering…? Oh!* Considering the fact he was still the police department's sole suspect in the murder of Victor's brother.

And okay, yeah, I'll admit it. I dig the fact that I can still inspire jealousy in my ex after all these years. Hey, I'll take what I can get.

Something in Victor's smile told me the subtext wasn't lost on him either. "It's no problem. I appreciate the offer.

Congratulations to the two of you, by the way."

Dom looked at me, confused.

I said, "I think he means you and Bonnie."

"Your engagement," Victor said.

"Oh!" Dom said. "Yes, of course. Thanks."

Victor asked when they were planning to tie the knot. Dom responded with a dismissive "No rush," which naturally made a big hit with his fiancée. If I were Dom, I'd be thinking hard about the fact that his significant other carried a loaded weapon.

As we made our way back to our barstools, Victor whispered, "You and Dom have been divorced for many years, yes?"

"Yes, but…" My sigh was the kind normally associated with the word *eloquent*.

"You two are not done with each other," he pronounced.

"What makes you say that?"

He shrugged. "I'm French. I know these things."

I made a rude noise and smacked his arm, and he snickered.

We resumed our seats. A cognac snifter awaited me. I knew what the golden liquid was even before I lifted the glass and sniffed. I smiled. My favorite añejo tequila.

From behind the bar, Martin winked. "I know what you like." He turned to my companion. "What'll you have, Victor?"

"Guinness. A proper pub drink."

"The man has good taste." He grabbed a glass and started working one of the beer taps.

Was it my imagination or had the padre's words been directed at Victor? *I know what she likes.* Or had that business with Dom messed with my head and was I reading coded messages in the most innocent of statements?

Of course, it was possible I wasn't imagining a darn thing and that I should have started playing house with a French hottie years ago. It certainly had a way of making the men in my life sit up and take notice.

Martin returned with Victor's ale and we clinked glasses.

"Cheers."

"*Santé.*"

I took a sip. "I'm impressed by the way you handled yourself over there, Victor. You displayed admirable aplomb. How do you say that in French?"

"*Aplomb.* But really, what's the sense in passing judgment at this point when we have so few facts? Dom might be a very bad man, that is possible. Or he might be a good man caught in a very bad situation."

"Well, you know what I think," I said.

"You believe Dom is innocent. Setting aside your history with him, let me say I believe you to be a good judge of character. I can tell this already. Perhaps it's because of your work, the different types of people you interact with."

"Most of whom no longer have a pulse."

"You know what I mean," he said. "Your clients are the ones who are left behind, those who are devastated, and bitter, and remorseful. You see people at their worst."

"I see people at their best too. I see people summon strength and goodness when no one, including themselves, thought they had it in them. Anyway, thank you for the compliment." I studied my snifter, took another sip. "You know, if Dom were guilty, he probably wouldn't have shared the fact that he and the killer wear the same size shoe."

"And if Bonnie thought her fiancé might be guilty," Victor said, "she would not have encouraged me to see what I could dig up on my own."

"Don't kid yourself," I said. "If Detective Hernandez suspected her fiancé was a murderer, he would not get a pass, believe you me. Conflict of interest or no, she'd get to the bottom of it. She might not be my favorite person, but she's a dedicated cop."

Victor looked past me, hand raised in a wave. I followed his gaze to the entrance, where Chloe Sleeper stood folding her little umbrella and scanning the room. She spied us and smiled. Two guys at a nearby table tracked her progress as she joined us. Not surprising really. She was young and attractive, even rain-damp and wearing jeans and a pink fleece jacket.

Victor rose and they pecked cheeks. When he continued on to her other cheek, the old Gallic two-step, she responded with a surprised "Oh!" and a self-conscious giggle.

She looked around. "There are some tables free. That might be more comfortable." And more private, which I realized was her primary concern when she pointed to the most out-of-the-way booth, away from curious ears. Before moving from the bar, she asked Martin for one of the IPAs the pub offered on draft, then did a classic double-take.

"Aren't you…?" she asked. "Weren't you at the funeral yesterday? Working security?"

He grinned. "I'm a man of many talents. Ask Jane."

Okay, that was *not* my imagination, right? I mean, this guy was as subtle as Pepé Le Pew. I doubt the padre was referring to his *talent* for lock-picking, which I'd seen him do. Or his *talent* for winning a poker tournament, which I'd seen him do. Or his *talent* for talking dirty to a corpse, which I'd also seen him do.

Oh, don't start! It was a paid assignment. Sheesh.

Once we'd settled into the booth, Victor and me on one side, Chloe on the other, she dispensed with the *Some rain huh?* chitchat, instead reaching into her jacket pocket and producing a small plastic bag. Inside was a folded tissue. She withdrew the tissue and unfolded it, revealing a ring.

It was clearly an antique, judging by the fussy Art Deco setting, which appeared to be platinum. The rectangular diamond, perhaps half the size of Bonnie's showy boulder, was flanked by smaller diamonds and two good-sized sapphires.

Victor breathed something in French and lifted the ring, turning it to view all sides. "This is my great-grandmother's engagement ring."

Chloe nodded, with a sad smile.

"When our parents died," he said, "Pierre and I divided everything of value, including *Maman*'s jewelry. He got this."

Chloe's eyes were moist. "He gave it to me two months ago. July Fourth. We went to this huge fireworks display out east. Swing threw together this whole gourmet picnic, complete with candles, champagne, even a white tablecloth. And then during the big crescendo he brought out this ring and—" Her voice cracked. "It was… magical."

"You two were going to be married," Victor said.

She nodded again, too overcome to speak.

"I had no idea," he said. "I didn't even know he had someone special."

"No one knew," she said. "About some things, Swing was very private. He planned to surprise you the next time you visited."

"This is typical Pierre." He wore a gentle half smile.

"Plus there was his public image, the playboy chef," Chloe

said. "He was trying to get that Food Network show, and he figured he had a better chance if he kept the bad-boy persona going awhile longer."

I nodded politely, but even Chloe had to know that the playboy reputation hadn't been undeserved. Just yesterday she'd sat in the ballroom of the Crystal Harbor Country Club and listened as more than one tipsy female grabbed the mic and shared far too many details of recent intimate encounters with the dead chef. Sure, maybe they were trying to outdo one another, but I didn't believe it was all lies and exaggerations.

And then there were the rumors that had swirled around Swing the whole time I'd known him, as recently as the day before his death. That last one had involved a well-known female food writer who'd been on the judging panel of his latest competitive TV cooking bout. Even discounting the rumor mill, we'd all seen pictures of Swing on those entertainment-news programs cozying up to this or that dewy starlet.

Is that still a word? *Starlet?* I can't help picturing Jean Harlow.

Okay, if nothing else, I know for a fact that just last week he tried to seduce my friend Maia Armstrong, the caterer. Yes, the same Maia who'd provided the vittles for his funeral reception a few days later. Maia is levelheaded, ego-free, and honest. If she says Swing tried to get into her pants, then you can take that, as the saying goes, to the bank.

Did Chloe really believe her fiancé was putting on an act for the sake of his playboy image? Could she be that much in denial?

"Thank you, Chloe." Victor reached across the table and squeezed her hand. They were both misty-eyed. "You didn't have to return the ring. That was… It means a lot to me."

"It's a family heirloom," she said. "It doesn't belong to me anymore, not really. Not without Swing—" She broke off, her hand covering her mouth as she struggled for control.

I was reminded of another family heirloom I'd encountered last spring, a gaudy, gem-encrusted brooch in the shape of a mermaid which Irene McAuliffe had hired me to liberate from the corpse of her former best friend during said bestie's wake. Don't judge me, it was complicated! That theft hadn't gone quite as planned, but in the end that heirloom, too, had ended up where it belonged.

Chloe cleared her throat and collected herself. "I'd appreciate it if you kept this to yourselves, about me and Swing. At this point it would just be… well, that kind of attention would make me uncomfortable. You're the only ones who know besides Detective Cullen."

"I understand," I said. "It's nobody else's business."

Victor nodded in agreement.

Considering how private Chloe and Swing had kept their engagement, I assumed she'd never had the opportunity to show off that beautiful ring in public, never had the pleasure of accepting congratulatory hugs and well-wishes. The thought made me sad.

I was mentally groping for a conversational topic that didn't involve dead fiancés and their fake (yeah, right) bad-boy reputations when I remembered something I'd been meaning to ask Victor about. "So. I didn't know you're a smoker."

"Me? No," he said.

"Don't tell me no. I saw you smoking outside the country club yesterday."

"Ah, that. I quit years ago, but when I'm upset, sometimes

I…" He searched for the word. "I relapse. I bummed a smoke from one of the busboys."

"Well, I guess you're allowed. That business with Lee Romano was certainly upsetting." I regretted the words the instant I said them, recalling that Lee was now Chloe's client.

"I'm so sorry about all that," Chloe said. "I didn't think Lee would, I don't know, gloat like that."

Victor said, "You have no control over what other people do."

"No, but…" She groaned. "I didn't want you to find out that way. That I'm her agent and all."

"You're entitled to represent whoever—"

"Yeah, I know." Chloe raised a palm to stop his polite disclaimer. "But it still felt crappy to hear her go on like that at the worst possible time." She trailed a finger through the condensation on her beer glass. "I keep telling myself Swing wouldn't have wanted me to sit around and let my business languish after he was gone."

I didn't glance at Victor, but I suspected his thoughts mirrored mine. There are plenty of ways to keep your business from languishing that don't involve signing your dead fiancé's estranged partner as a client before he's even in the ground.

She added, "I know for a fact he would have wanted me to take care of myself."

Since she seemed to need approval, Victor and I made the appropriate noises.

I asked, "How did Lee and Swing end up as partners in that Manhattan restaurant? Hummingbird."

"Oh, this is going back, what, fifteen years?" Chloe turned to Victor.

"Eleven," he said. "Pierre spent his first few years in New

York working in various kitchens, learning the ropes and making connections. He wanted his own restaurant, but he didn't have the capital."

"He did have the talent, though," she said.

"Talent wasn't the only thing Lee was looking for in a partner," he said, "or even the most important thing."

"What?" I said. "You already told me they weren't a couple."

Chloe said, "That doesn't mean she didn't appreciate his killer looks and lively personality. To say nothing of the sexy accent, that whole French thing."

I looked at Victor for his take on that last part.

"What can I tell you?" he deadpanned. "It's a burden."

"Okay, I think I'm getting it," I said. "Having a partner like Swing would bring attention to Hummingbird, enhance its visibility."

"Lee had been a renowned chef for many years at that point," he said. "She owned a successful midtown Manhattan restaurant. But she had bigger plans for it."

"So she brought Swing on board to help those plans along," I said.

"She made him a partner," he said, "under very favorable terms. Favorable to him, that is, although I don't know the details."

"So he got his restaurant," I said. "And in return, Hummingbird reaped the benefit of all that raw sex appeal and *joie de vivre*. Sounds like everyone came out ahead."

"Lee would disagree," Chloe said. "To hear her tell it, Swing spent the next eight years absorbing everything she had to teach him, about both cooking and the industry, while he established himself as a major player. Then... and this is her version of events, not mine."

"Understood," I said.

Victor finished for her. "Then he left Hummingbird and opened Dewatre."

"She puts it differently," Chloe said. "He 'abandoned' Hummingbird. 'Gutted' it. Destroyed everything she'd spent her entire career working for."

"Well, that's just Lee being bitter." My gaze bounced between the two of them. "Right?"

Victor looked uncomfortable. "She had to buy out Pierre when he left. By then he possessed substantial equity in the business. Hummingbird closed its doors a few months later."

"Lee was off the scope after that," Chloe said. "Now we know why."

She'd been busy remaking herself for the small screen.

"Let's face it," she continued, "she wasn't wrong when she said it's no longer about talent. Nowadays you have to be telegenic, glamorous even, to make it on TV."

"Well, all those nips and tucks apparently paid off," I said, recalling Lee's boasts the day before. "She's close to getting her own show."

"Maybe." Now it was Chloe's turn to look uncomfortable. "Negotiations have kind of... hit a rough patch."

"Well, even if that one falls through," I said, "there are other opportunities, right? I mean, the Food Network's important, but they're not the only game in town."

"Lee's pinned all her hopes on that one show," she said.

"Pierre's show." Victor's expression was stony. "The one they offered him right before he died."

Chloe nodded miserably. "She has blinders on. I've been trying to get her interested in starting at the bottom, like Swing did. Working the local media, doing talk-show gigs, gradually building a fan base."

"Let me guess," he said. "Lee Romano isn't interested in working her way up. It's her own show or nothing."

"That's kind of where we're at," she said. "She feels the world owes her."

"Well, that show they offered Swing," I said, "it wasn't even up for grabs until... while he was still alive. So how can she be so fixated on it?"

"She wasn't ready for *any* media appearances until very recently," Chloe said. "I mean, you know, with the surgeries and all. Like she said yesterday, the timing for this show is perfect. Sorry," she murmured to Victor.

He took a long swig of his Guinness. "So why is the network balking?"

"Well, you know, it's very competitive..." Chloe started.

"It's because she's difficult, yes?" he said. "They don't want to work with her."

She looked like she wanted to deny it, but what would be the point? Victor had known his brother's former business partner for years. Finally she said, "I tried to set her up with a professional image consultant, one who specializes in communications skills and dealing with the media. She refused to even consider it. But I don't have to tell you, her personality can come across as, well, abrasive. Even more so on the small screen."

"So she makes this huge investment in her body," I said, "transforms herself top to bottom, but when it comes to her attitude problem, what, she's in denial?"

"'What attitude problem?'" Chloe said, mimicking Lee. "As far as she's concerned, it's the rest of the world that has the problem."

7

Smoking Jacket

"HAVE YOU THOUGHT about what colleges you want to apply to?" My question was directed at Tucker Nearing, sitting next to Kari in the backseat of Dom's dark-blue BMW. I was in the front passenger seat, looking at the couple over my shoulder as Dom drove. Mine was the typical chatter of an adult trying to make conversation with a teenager she didn't know all that well. "I mean, I know you're still a junior, but I assume you've given it some thought."

"My folks want me to go to NYU. They want me close to home," Tucker said. He held hands with Kari, and from the way she gazed at him, you'd never know she was supposedly grieving for the love of her life, a celebrity chef more than twenty-five years her senior.

Dom had just picked me up at my house. He and I had somewhere to be—somewhere I really, really had no desire to set foot, but it had to be done—and we were giving the kids a lift to the train station on the way. They were headed to Manhattan to stroll the High Line, the mile-and-a-half-long elevated park built on long-disused railroad tracks, before dinner and a concert.

"But where do *you* want to go to school?" I asked him.

"Johns Hopkins."

"Baltimore," I said. "Not so far away. Why Hopkins?"

"I want to go into medicine. Orthopedic surgery probably."

"Wow. That's pretty focused for someone your age. Why that specialty?"

He shrugged. "I broke my leg a couple of years ago. That's when I started getting interested. It fascinates me, our skeletal structure, the way we're put together."

"Tucker's a whiz at science." Kari squeezed his hand. "Math, bio, all that stuff. He'll totally get into any school he wants."

He offered an embarrassed smile. "Maybe. Depends on the SATs. I'll need some coaching for the writing portion."

"I didn't know any of this about you," I admitted. "I guess I just associate you with the swim team."

"Hey, if someone wants to pay me to swim for a living, no problem," he said with a grin.

This was the longest conversation I'd had with Tucker Nearing. I found myself liking him. "You know, Tucker, your interests kind of tie in with an assignment I'm working on."

Kari looked dubious. "One of your Death Diva things? Really?"

"Hey, it's not all gore and goop." Today's unpleasant task notwithstanding. "This dead surgeon's kids are having me catalog and sell his collection of antique medical instruments."

Tucker was immediately animated. "Cool! You think I could take a look?"

"I don't think they'd mind." I grinned. "And from what I know of Dr. Walters, I'm pretty sure he would have approved."

Dom flashed me a surreptitious smile. He approved of

Tucker, I knew. And he had to be relieved that his daughter appeared to be directing her romantic energy to a more suitable, age-appropriate, not to mention living boyfriend. Also, the fact she'd accepted this ride from the father she'd accused of coldblooded murder a mere five days earlier had to be a positive indicator of family harmony.

"So where are you guys off to?" Kari asked.

Dom glanced at me. He offered a minute shrug, not lost on his daughter.

"What?" Eagerly she leaned forward. She shook my shoulder. "Tell me!"

Her dad seemed to be okay with it, so… "Well, the restaurant needs to be cleaned," I said.

She stared for a heartbeat, then fell back against the seat, her face drained of color.

She wasn't the only one. Tucker appeared just as shaken. "You mean you…" He cleared his throat. "You're going to clean up all that blood and everything?"

"No!" I assured him. "No, no, we're hiring someone. Professionals. They do this sort of thing all the time." I offered a weak smile.

Kari's voice was tiny. "Well, I asked."

Tucker directed his blank gaze out the window. She grabbed his hand again, clutching it with both of hers. He seemed not to notice.

After we dropped the kids off, we drove through the town in silence. It was a typical Saturday morning in Crystal Harbor, with heavy vehicular traffic and plenty of locals and day tourists patronizing the quaint stores and eateries.

As expected, Denny Pinheiro had agreed to meet me at Dewatre that morning to inspect the scene, with Victor none the wiser. Dom, however, was not so easily evaded. Last night at Murray's, he'd heard me mention the impending cleanup and, thanks to his long association with yours truly and my creepy vocation, was familiar with how swiftly these things get done. No sooner was I off the phone with Denny than he'd phoned. He was going with me. It was nonnegotiable. What time should he pick me up?

When Dom makes up his mind about something, arguing is pointless. And the truth is, I didn't want to go alone. Ushering Denny into an environment in need of his distinctive services wasn't something I'd ever get used to, but in this instance it was worse because I knew the victim. He'd been a friend. So yes, I was grateful for Dom's solid presence. I told him so again, for about the dozenth time.

He patted my jeans-clad thigh. "This nasty business will be over before you know it, Janey. Then what do you say we go get a bite to eat?"

We thought about that for about half a second before shaking our heads in unison and muttering, "Maybe not" and "Some other time."

"Don't park on the street," I said. "Go around back and park in the alley behind Dewatre. We'll let ourselves in through the service entrance. No need to attract attention." I'd already told Denny to meet me back there.

He showed up eight minutes early, pulling up behind the reeking dumpster in a gleaming, tomato-red VW Beetle. I made the introductions. Denny, lean and wiry with thinning chestnut hair and a neat goatee, stands about five seven on a good day and looks like a shrimp next to my ex. But what he lacks in physical presence, he makes up for with a thundering baritone voice that positively oozes authority. He carried a clipboard.

Dom grabbed the keyring out of my hand before I could stop him. "You stay out here, Janey. I can show Denny—"

"No," I said. "I appreciate it, Dom, but that's not—"

"Don't be stubborn," he said. "You don't have to prove any—"

"I'm not trying to *prove* anything. This is my responsib—"

"You two are just adorable," Denny boomed, "but I have other stops this morning, so if one of you could please unlock this door?"

With a disgruntled sigh, Dom did so. The instant the heavy door swung open, the smell hit us. It wasn't the worst odor I'd experienced in my two-decade stint as Death Diva—use your imagination—but it was no spring meadow either. Denny didn't hesitate but strode right into the restaurant's kitchen. I hauled in a nice, deep lungful of Dumpster-scented air, held it, and followed him inside. Dom brought up the rear, making a funny little sound deep in his throat that reminded me of Sexy Beast entering the vet's office.

And there it all was. The dried blood, which we carefully avoided. The flies. The shoe prints, featuring a distinctive pattern of chevrons and concentric circles. The letters S, E, A, and R squirted on the floor tiles. The abandoned cooking ingredients. Noticeably absent was the serving platter, collected as evidence, no doubt. I catalogued all these things in the nanosecond it took to make a sweeping visual survey of the room.

There was one thing I needed to do before the place was cleaned up and any lingering evidence obliterated. It had occurred to me in the middle of the night as I lay awake trying to determine my next move. I hauled out my cell phone and snapped a bunch of pictures of the bloody shoe prints. I had to retake several that were out of focus due to a slight tremor in my fingers and the fact I was still holding my breath.

I exhaled on a hurried "I'll meet you up front" as I sprinted through the kitchen and shoved through the double doors. The dining room was a sea of bare tables supporting upturned chairs, by all appearances untouched since before Swing's death if you didn't count the dark fingerprint powder that now begrimed various surfaces.

I made my way to the very front of the building, gulping air and aiming for a corner spot away from the big picture window. I had no desire to be spied by curious pedestrians strolling past. The odor from the kitchen lingered in my nostrils.

The shoe prints. Yep, they were big. Size thirteen, according to Dom. His own size. Romulus Tooley's size, too? I hoped Ben would be able to provide an answer to that one, along with Tooley's whereabouts the morning Swing was killed.

Okay, I could shove away the thought no longer, much as I'd tried.

Tucker. Kari's sweet, besotted scholar athlete. Passionate about swimming. Passionate about a future in the healing sciences. Passionate about his girlfriend. I recalled his heartfelt declaration after he'd faced off with Tooley the day of the funeral.

I love you, Kari. I'd do anything for you. Anything!

Tucker, who seemed to know a little too much about things he couldn't, shouldn't, know about.

You're going to clean up all that blood and everything?

Well, the blood was a given, right? I mean, everyone knew how Swing had died. A stabbing equals blood. But then

Tucker had gone and said *everything*. What kind of *everything* would the average walking-around person assume to be present at that kind of crime scene? I happened to know what everything meant in this case because I'd been there. I'd seen the cooking ingredients, the platter, the word scrawled on the floor. *Everything.*

Was I overreacting? Probably. *Blood and everything.* So what? Didn't teens in particular throw around words like *everything* without even knowing what the heck they meant by it?

At that moment I dearly wished I'd thought to look at Tucker's feet when we'd dropped off the kids at the train station. His feet could be puny little size sevens for all I knew, and then I could stop obsessing about the *everything*.

Dom entered the dining room in under a minute. Only his male pride had kept him in the Kitchen of Horrors for that long, I was certain.

"The guy's thorough, I'll give him that," he said, as he joined me in my secluded little corner. "He's checking out the storage areas, office, everywhere."

"The cops and crime-scene techs were probably all over the building," I said. "Traces of blood could be anywhere—it's a biohazard. Denny's guys use Luminol or something to test for it. By the time they're done decontaminating this place, no one will be able to tell anything happened here. It'll be like new."

Dom looked dubious. "If you say so. Why would anyone go into his line of work?"

I shrugged. "Why would anyone go into *my* line of work? Denny used to be an EMT, so he has the stomach for it. Years ago he did a suicide clean-up as a favor for a pal and ended up starting a business."

After a moment Dom said, "Victor doesn't know you're here, does he?"

"He's been through enough."

He nodded in a noncommittal way. "So. You like this guy?"

"He seems nice enough."

He grunted. "He really seems to have made himself at home."

"That's what houseguests do."

"And he's working in the city?" he asked. "Commuting?"

"For now."

"Interesting." There was that dopey nod again.

"Interesting how?" I had no intention of making this easier for him. After all those years watching my ex cycle through multiple fiancées and wives—and me, let's face it, not giving him all that much to feel jealous about in return—I was having fun watching him squirm.

Oh please, there's nothing mean about it. After what that man put me through? Okay, maybe not intentionally. I mean, you could say he was just, you know, "living his life" or whatever after our divorce. But still.

"Be careful, Janey. That's all I'm saying."

"'Be careful'? What does that mean?"

"It means I don't want you hurt," he said. "That's all."

My jaw hinged open to respond, but my good sense locked it in place while the withering comebacks scrolled harmlessly through my brainpan.

"What?" he asked. "What does that look mean? Come on, let's have it."

I took a calming breath. "Yeah. I do."

"You do what?"

"Like him," I said, and watched with satisfaction as that simple statement hit home. "I've really enjoyed getting to know Victor. I'm looking forward to getting to know him better."

"You met the guy less than a week ago, Janey."

"That's where the 'getting to know him better' part comes in."

Dom gave an exasperated sigh. "Fine. I just don't want you to get—"

"Do not say it again," I warned. I was staring at the only man who'd ever really hurt me. The fact that he hadn't meant to was immaterial.

"Well, does he feel the same way?" he asked.

I was saved from trying to formulate an answer by the sudden squeal of car brakes from beyond the big front window. Dom and I edged close enough to peek outside without being seen. A nondescript beige sedan had stopped in the middle of the street right in front of Dewatre. The driver remained behind the wheel as two individuals jumped out of the car.

I say *individuals* because their gender wasn't immediately apparent. This was due to the full-head masks they wore. The driver was a panda. The one carrying a brick was a rhino. And the one holding the flame of a cigarette lighter to the rag sticking out of a bottle was a lion. As my brain began to register the strangeness of this—Halloween? No, not for another few weeks—the rhino hurled the brick through the window.

I screamed as glass sprayed in all directions. The alarm system kicked in with an earsplitting wail. Dom yanked me out of the line of fire as the lion hauled back to toss what I belatedly identified as a Molotov cocktail.

He successfully chucked the makeshift firebomb into the

restaurant, but not before the flaming wick and dripping gasoline had ignited his mask and the back of his jacket. His shrieks were audible over the alarm as he fell to the street, yanking off the mask and rolling to extinguish the flames.

The bottle shattered on a table a few feet from us. The fireball was instantaneous, a column of flame engulfing the table and its upturned chairs as puddles of burning gasoline littered the floor around it. The dining room contained no shortage of fuel—the whole place would go up in no time. The fierce heat and acrid smell compounded my terror as Dom seized my hand and started running. We gave the conflagration a wide berth as we raced for the front door.

Outside, a crowd was beginning to form. As usual, most held up their cell phones. Hey, why be merely a passive observer or—now, here's a crazy thought—offer assistance when you can document the moment for Facebook and YouTube?

The thrower of the Molotov cocktail lay curled on the street, not due to any injuries he'd sustained from having inadvertently set himself on fire—singed hair and black streaks on his windbreaker appeared to be the worst of it—but because Cheyenne O'Rourke was gleefully kicking him with her stratospheric, money-patterned platform sneakers, in between licks of a soft-serve chocolate ice-cream cone with rainbow sprinkles. The crowd urged her on with cheers and shouted encouragement.

I happened to know that Cheyenne, a sullen local teenager who worked for Dom at Janey's Place, wasn't above a bit of hooliganism herself, but it would appear she had little use for arsonists. Either that or she simply enjoyed kicking a man while he was down. Meanwhile the arsonist's buddies laid rubber, abandoning the poor schmuck to the vindictive bystanders, their vehicle's swiftly retreating license plate obscured with a liberal coating of mud.

Oh, did I mention? The poor abandoned schmuck was Romulus Tooley.

"All right, Cheyenne, I think he got the message." Dom managed to separate his employee and the SEAR spokesman, but not before she got in one final, well-aimed kick that had Tooley squealing in agony, and every male in the vicinity wincing.

"That crazy SOB," Dom muttered.

Tracking his gaze to the restaurant, I realized he was not referring to Tooley. Denny Pinheiro had wheeled a full janitor's bucket into the dining room, where the fire was rapidly spreading.

Silly me, I'd assumed Denny had escaped out the back when the excitement started. Turned out the former EMT had been preparing to battle the blaze single-handedly. Once a first responder, always a first responder. Black smoke billowed through the broken window. Sirens warbled in the distance.

"Denny! Get the hell out of there!" Dom sprinted back into the restaurant, leaving Tooley to the less-than-tender mercies of the onlookers. The sniveling SEAR spokesman offered little resistance as a couple of burly construction workers dragged him onto the sidewalk opposite Dewatre.

"I did it for the animals," Tooley bleated.

"Don't even." Cheyenne lobbed the sloppy remains of her cone, nailing him in the kisser.

I peered into the restaurant, squinting through the smoke to see what Dom and Denny were up to. *"What are you doing?"* I screeched, trying to be heard over the brain-skewering alarm. *"Get out!"*

The flames abruptly abated. I saw the two men drop the big janitor's bucket. They'd flung the contents onto the fire, extinguishing much but not all of it. I kept hollering for them to get out—the fire trucks were rounding the corner, for crying out loud!—but instead the men grabbed a stack of folded white tablecloths off the bar and used them to snuff out the remaining flames.

Twenty minutes later, the firefighters had finished tromping through the place, ostensibly to ensure the danger was past but really, I suspect, to get a good eyeful of the notorious murder scene in the kitchen. Juicy grist for the Crystal Harbor gossip mill. They pretended to chastise Denny and Dom for risking their hides putting out the blaze, but no one was fooled. The guys had received congratulations and backslaps from the cheering throng. Even Cheyenne was being hailed as a hero for "subduing" the dangerous ecoterrorist, who was currently on his way to the police station, with a detour to Harbor Memorial Hospital to check out any injuries.

The cops had pushed the looky-loos a half block from Dewatre, which had now become the site of two, count 'em two, major crime scenes in less than a week. Dom and I stood chatting with the milling bystanders, watching the cops string yellow crime-scene tape yet again, when I heard my name being called.

I turned to see Victor bulling his way through the crowd. "Are you all right?" he said when he reached me. "The alarm company called. I left you a voice mail."

"I guess I didn't hear my phone," I said. "Things were kind of loud." The alarm had finally been silenced, thank heaven.

His worried gaze should have made him less handsome. Ask me if it did. Go ahead, ask.

"You smell like smoke," he said. "Were you in there when it happened?"

I nodded. He pulled me into a bone-crushing hug. "Jane, *mon Dieu*, you could have been killed." He pulled back for a second to ask if I was hurt. When I shook my head no, he hugged me even tighter. And yeah, it felt as good as you're imagining.

I was aware of Dom's silent presence next to us. I said, "I'm all right, really, Victor."

He released me but kept hold of my hands. "You met the cleaning person here," he accused. "You thought to spare me, yes?" Correctly interpreting my expression, he said, "Foolish woman. I'm not so fragile as you think."

"Um, Dom helped to put out the fire." Gently I extricated myself from Victor's hold. "Along with Denny—that's the cleaning guy. He's around here somewhere." When last I'd seen Denny, he'd been schmoozing with some of his firefighter buddies.

Belatedly Victor took in Dom's rumpled appearance, the soot clinging to every square inch of him. "Another case of temporary insanity." But he said it with kindness. He extended his hand. "Thank you, Dom."

Dom appeared momentarily perplexed—why was Victor thanking him? I watched comprehension slam home with the realization that my houseguest now owned Dewatre, being his brother's sole beneficiary. He mumbled something appropriate and moved away through the crowd as Victor slid a protective arm around me.

8

This Is a Serious Matter and Everyone in This Reum Is Under Suspicion

I WAS IN my kitchen examining the front page of the *Harbor Herald*, the town's weekly newspaper, when I heard the doorbell ring, to the accompaniment of Sexy Beast's territorial hysteria. This was followed moments later by the sound of the front door opening and the indistinct murmur of male voices. It was Wednesday evening, sevenish. I'd just picked up Victor at the train station. He'd spent the day working at his firm's Manhattan office.

For sure this had to be a worse commute than what he was used to in Paris: an early-morning car ride to the local Long Island Railroad station, followed by an hour-and-a-half train ride, followed by a trek through crowded Penn Station to catch a packed subway to Spring Street in SoHo, followed by a final walk to his office building. Close to two and a half tedious hours, and that's if things ran smoothly and on time. Throw a canceled train and/or funky weather into the mix and hilarity would ensue. And then at the end of the day, Victor got to do the whole thing in reverse.

I was kind of surprised he'd decided to remain at my place rather than move into the city, closer to his job. He must have friends in town from his grad-school days who'd be happy to put him up. On the other hand, Crystal Harbor was the best location for looking into his brother's death and settling his affairs. And I hadn't been lying when I'd told him I was glad for the company. The big house would seem like a tomb when he finally moved back to Paris.

And then there was that other thing. The thing that had been simmering between us during the four days since Romulus Tooley had tried to turn Dewatre into a pile of smoking rubble. Oh, you know the kind of thing I mean. No? Try sticking a capital *T* on it.

Yeah, that's right. A Thing.

We didn't talk about it. And we didn't do anything about it. It was just there. Like when we squeezed by each other in the upstairs hallway. Okay, yeah, it was a wide hallway, but somehow it was never quite wide enough. Or when my fingers brushed his as we both reached for the last cookie on the plate. Or when his fingers brushed something else as he lifted Sexy Beast out of my arms. The narrow-eyed look SB gave him was eloquent. *Real subtle, my friend. You owe me a Vienna sausage for that one.*

So anyway, I was curious about who Victor had just let into the house, but as I mentioned, I was also distracted by the front page of the *Harbor Herald*. The feature story applauded Crystal Harbor High's swim team for its victory over a neighboring school during a recent meet. The article was accompanied by a photo showing several boys poised to dive off the edge of a pool.

Tucker Nearing stood smack in the center, his sleek, broad-shouldered body balanced on a pair of long feet. I stared at those feet. Maybe they were twelves. Or fourteens. Yeah, they were pretty big, they could easily be fourteens. No way were they thirteens, though. I was almost certain.

I tossed aside the paper and followed the sounds of conversation to the living room, where I found Detective Paul Cullen sitting on the same pretty, linen-upholstered armchair he'd occupied more than a week ago. Had it been only nine days since Swing's murder? Since his brother had taken up residence in one of my guest rooms? It felt like the distant past.

The detective had produced his little notebook. The hairs on my nape leapt up and shrieked dire warnings. Clearly those hairs knew something I didn't.

"Detective Cullen wants to get me up to speed on the investigation," Victor said.

"Uh-huh." I took a seat next to him on the sofa. Sexy Beast had curled up on Victor's other side, but as soon as I joined them, he bestirred himself, stretched, got a good shake on, and daintily tiptoed across our laps to smoosh himself close to my side, his chin propped on my thigh. SB liked Victor well enough, but let's face it, he was no alpha female.

"You don't need to be here," Cullen told me.

"I live here."

He opened his yap to explain to my dense self that he meant I didn't need to be present there in the living room while he spoke with Victor, but something about my expression stopped him. Maybe it was the stony, don't-mess-with-me stare I fixed him with. Yeah, I'm thinking that was it.

Our little stare-down wasn't lost on Victor. "I've had a long day, Detective," he said. "If we could get on with it?"

"We still don't know who killed your brother," Cullen said, "but we're following every lead."

That was it. That was his report. I looked at Victor. Victor looked at me. Sexy Beast looked from one of us to the other and then gave Cullen a single imperative bark. *Quit kiddin' around,* this bark said. *Tell us something we don't already know.*

"What about Romulus Tooley?" I asked.

"What about him?"

"Isn't he one of the leads you're following? I mean, since he tried to burn down Dewatre?"

"That was a political statement," Cullen said.

"Political?" I sneered. "It felt pretty darn personal to me considering I was inside at the time. Along with two other people."

"Yeah, and he'll have to answer for it, him and his pals, but he was just trying to bring attention to his cause." The two other thugs had been apprehended a few blocks from the restaurant. "He isn't a person of interest in the murder of Pierre Dewatre, is what I mean." He flipped open his notebook.

"So you're still fixated on Dom?" I demanded. "What do you know that takes Tooley out of the running?"

"Trust me." There was that condescending smile I'd come to loathe. "The guy didn't do it, all right?"

"You don't think it's even remotely possible," I said, "that Tooley might have been trying to destroy evidence by burning down the restaurant? Evidence of his guilt?"

"Five days after the murder?" Cullen said. "Five days after my boys went over that place top to bottom? You think the guy's that slow-witted? Or lazy?"

"So that's it?" Victor said. I could tell he was getting

steamed. "That's what you came all the way over here to tell me? That you've made no progress at all?"

"I didn't say that. As a matter of fact, new information has come to light." Cullen clicked his pen. "If you'll bear with me, I have a few questions for you, Mr. Dewatre. This shouldn't take long."

Those hairs on my nape? They were now slapping their foreheads and whining, *Don't blame us. We tried to warn you.*

I sat forward. "What kind of questions?"

Cullen didn't answer. He looked at Victor. "What was your relationship with your brother like?"

Victor said, "Why are you asking this?"

"Jeez," Cullen griped, "this isn't gonna work if all of us are doing the asking and no one's doing any answering."

"I think it's a reasonable request," Victor said. "What does my relationship with Pierre have to do with his murder? I was in Paris when he was killed."

"Now, don't go getting all worked up. No one's accusing you of anything. I'm just following up on new information."

I said, "New information, huh? I assume it involves Victor?" I turned to Swing's brother. "Just so you know, you don't have to—"

"I know," he said, "I don't have to say anything. I've watched plenty of American cop shows." He turned to Cullen and patiently waited for him to fill in the blanks.

An angry flush mottled the detective's face, but he managed to keep his cool. After a few moments he said, "It seems you and your brother didn't get along so good."

"We got along very well." Victor's voice was tight.

"Not according to his former partner," Cullen said. "She says he was afraid of you."

"What?" I cried. "That's ridic—"

Cullen held up a palm. "Miss Delaney, did you ever see the two of them together? Victor and Pierre?"

"No, of course not, I didn't meet Victor until after the... after Swing died. But—"

"Then I'm gonna have to ask you to let me do my job. That okay with you?"

I flopped back against the sofa with a frustrated sigh. I crossed my arms and did my best not to glare at Cullen.

"It's all right, Jane, I don't mind answering the detective's questions. Anything that moves this investigation along." Victor refrained from inserting the phrase "so-called" before "investigation." Out loud anyway. Turning back to Cullen, he said, "So you spoke with Leonora Romano. What other lies did she tell you?"

Cullen puffed himself up. "You calling Ms. Romano a liar?"

I'm telling you, nothing gets past this crack detective.

"If she told you Pierre was afraid of me," Victor said, "then yes, I'm calling her a liar."

"The lady worked with your brother every day for years," Cullen said. "She knew him real good. Maybe better than you."

Obviously Cullen was trying to get a rise out of Victor, trying to get him to slip up and blurt something self-incriminating. Sitting next to Victor, I sensed the tension in his body even as he leaned back and slowed his breathing. Good. He had no intention of falling for it.

"What specifically did Lee say?" he asked.

"Swing told her that if anything ever happened to him, it would be *you* that did it." Cullen gesticulated with his pen.

"He said you threatened to kill him."

"Preposterous."

"Really?" The detective wore a nasty, cream-lapping smile. "Ms. Romano witnessed the whole thing. The fight you two had in the kitchen there at that restaurant she used to own. She says some of her employees saw it too." He flipped through previous notes. "Hummingbird, that's the name of the place."

Victor became very still. I looked at him, at his frigid features, and shivered. Yeah, I knew I wasn't going to like this next part, whatever it was.

"Brothers have disagreements," Victor said. "This happens in all families."

"Yeah? A guy sleeping with his brother's wife?" Cullen said. "Is that the kind of disagreement that happens in all families?"

Whoa, what?

Angry spots of color marred Victor's handsome face. "Emmie was not my wife at the time. We were divorced."

"Just barely." More page flipping as Cullen located the pertinent note. "Ten months. Ink was still wet on the divorce papers."

I recalled Victor telling me he and Emmie had struggled from the beginning to make their marriage work. They hadn't been suited, according to him.

"Hey, I don't blame you for losing it like you did." Cullen spread his hands. "I got an ex, too, and I got a brother. If Ralphie pulled something like that, I'd want to take him apart limb from limb."

"It was a long time ago," Victor said. "Seven years."

"Six." Cullen tapped his notebook. "It was six years ago that your wife flew to New York on vacation. Seems that while she was over here, taking in the sights, her and your brother got it on."

"My *ex*-wife. She told me about it herself. Pierre invited her to his place for dinner. They had too much to drink and…" Victor tossed his hand to indicate the rest. "She felt awkward about it and didn't want me to have to find out from him."

Cullen chuckled. "Yeah, I bet she felt awkward. What did she expect, that you'd pat her on the head and say—" he adopted an insultingly over-the-top French accent "—'Think nothing of it, *ma chère*, we are *French*, after all!'"

Sexy Beast's head jerked up, making me wonder what was going on in that wee brain of his: *Nous sommes français?*

"Me and your wife had a cozy little chat today," Cullen continued. "Nice lady. Speaks English almost as good as you. She says when you found out, you were spittin' nails. You know that expression? It means—"

"You're inflating the incident out of proportion," Victor said. "It was a long time ago, as I said, and we all got over it."

"Maybe *they* got over it. *You* were mad enough to hop a flight to New York and storm into Hummingbird and threaten your brother with a knife." Cullen added, "One of his own cooking knives."

My stomach executed a slow roll.

"This part is not true," Victor said. "I was angry, yes, more with Pierre than with Emmie. I flew to New York, yes. I confronted him, yes. But there was no knife."

"That's not how Ms. Romano remembers it," Cullen said.

"As you say, there were others present," Victor pointed out. "I defy you to find anyone else who claims I picked up a knife."

"Being in a highly emotional state and all," the detective said, "it's possible you forgot about the knife."

"There was no knife."

Cullen held up a placating hand. "Okay, we'll get back to the knife. You don't deny you threatened to kill him, though."

Victor hesitated. "This is what people say when they're angry. It meant nothing."

"So, what, you and your brother have this big blow-up, then you go home and forget all about it? Like whew, glad I got that out of my system, I feel all better now."

"It took time, but eventually we got past it."

"You trying to tell me you haven't been carrying around a grudge for six years?" Cullen said. "I mean, come on, your wife and your brother? What kind of man wouldn't want to get even?"

When Victor failed to rise to the bait, Cullen scratched his jaw in perplexity. "I don't know, I guess guys are different where you come from. I guess we're not as *sophisticated* over here."

Real smooth, Detective. Through a heroic effort of will I avoided rolling my eyes. Okay, maybe I rolled them a little.

"The fact remains," Victor said, "I was in Paris when my brother was murdered."

"You ever hear of hit men? You must have those in France, too, right? You hire a guy to do the deed?"

"I know what a hit man is," Victor said. "I would assume a hired killer would bring his own weapon. A gun in most cases. The man who killed my brother used one of Pierre's own cooking knives. Let me ask you as the expert in such things. Is this not odd behavior for a hit man?"

"Nothing surprises me anymore." Cullen gave an elaborate

shrug to indicate how jaded he'd become after so many years of tracking down dastardly killers. Meanwhile I strongly suspected this was his very first murder case.

The good news? Cullen was no longer concentrating solely on Dom. The bad news? He'd targeted another blatantly innocent person. I mean, Victor couldn't possibly have murdered his brother. This man had spent the past nine days living in my home, breaking bread with me, sleeping right down the hall from me. I'd *know* if he was a coldblooded killer.

A memory swooped in then. Victor's second night at my house, after I'd taken him to view his brother's body. I'd awoken in the middle of the night thirsty—we'd had pizza with anchovies for dinner—and was headed downstairs for some orange soda, my bare feet silent on the carpeted stairs. Halfway down, I glanced into the dining room and spied him sitting there, illuminated only by moonlight.

Had I ever seen anyone look so anguished? So bereft? I felt his soundless sobs as a stabbing pain in my own chest. Quietly I turned and made my way back to my room, unwilling to intrude on his private grief.

Because that's what I'd been witnessing, right? Simple grief for a murdered brother. Not something else. Not something more complicated involving guilt or regret.

"The timing seems off, no?" Victor asked. "This argument I had with Pierre, it took place six years ago. If I was angry enough to murder him, why would I wait all that time?"

"I have an answer for that," Cullen said.

"I thought you might."

"Your brother wasn't so famous back then. Or rich. All that came later, especially the last few years when he had his own restaurant and was on TV all the time."

"So it was greed?" Victor asked. "My motive for killing Pierre?"

"The guy was worth plenty," Cullen said. "He died a wealthy man. I mean, you probably do okay, you're what, an architect? So a professional, but still, a working stiff. Nine to five, am I right?"

When Victor refrained from answering, Cullen charged right ahead. "Plus you had to be jealous—it's only natural. I'm not just talking about the money here. Swing Dewatre was a bona fide celebrity. The mayor of New York bragged about being pals with *him*. And the women?" He wagged his hand. "From what I hear, he had his pick of the models, the actresses... Now, I'm not saying you're a slouch in that department, you're a good-looking guy and all, but come on. We're talking hot and cold running—" he shot me a quick look "—female companionship."

"My brother was engaged to be married," Victor said.

"Huh? Oh. Yeah, I know," Cullen said. "Chloe Sleeper's one of the first people I talked to, on account of she tried to call him around the time he got killed. What's your point?"

"You speak of all the women," Victor said. "I'm just setting the record straight. That was in the past."

Cullen wore a smarmy little smile. "What, because he was getting married?"

"That was not Pierre's way. Yes, he loved women and they loved him. But over the years he has had several serious girlfriends, and I can tell you that he never betrayed any of them. He had too much honor for that."

"Or maybe he was just careful not to get caught," Cullen said. "Or maybe, once he was rich and famous and women were falling all over him, maybe all that 'honor' kinda lost its appeal. I mean, how well did you really know him? You guys lived on different continents."

"He wasn't like that," Victor insisted.

Yeah, well. It was nice that he had so much respect for his dead brother and all, but seriously? Swing had had an active and varied sex life right up until the end, including trying to seduce my buddy Maia Armstrong a few days before he died. That's just fact. As much as I hated to agree with Paul Cullen about anything, I had to give him this one.

Someone needed to clue Victor in, and I wasn't about to volunteer for the job.

There was something else, however, I couldn't keep quiet about. I said, "Detective, you must know that Leonora Romano had it in for Swing ever since they parted ways three years ago."

"I know what you're getting at, but Swing was killed by a man." He held up a palm. "Don't ask how I know."

"I don't have to. I'm the one who found him, remember?"

As I waited for the genius to figure it out, I thought again about Tucker and his long feet. Tucker, who was passionately in love with Kari Faso and convinced that Chef Pierre Dewatre had been taking advantage of her youthful infatuation.

No. I couldn't, wouldn't, mention him to Cullen. Not yet, not on such flimsy evidence.

Cullen grunted. "Okay, so you saw the bloody shoe prints."

"I just heard you tell Victor that he could have hired a hit man to do in his brother," I said. "Why couldn't Lee Romano have done the same thing? Oh, and there's something else— did Chloe mention it? Swing was offered his own TV show shortly before he died, and now it's probably going to Lee.

She's pulling out the stops to make it happen. There's your motive."

"Do the police a favor, Ms. Delaney. Don't try to do our job for us. You'll do more harm than good, trust me."

I'd been wondering why Lee would falsely incriminate Victor in his brother's murder. After all, her beef had been with Swing. What had Victor ever done to her? The answer became obvious, however, if Lee herself was indeed the murderer. In that case her accusation could be chalked up to simple self-preservation, an attempt to throw the cops off the scent.

"Another possibility," Victor said, "is that Lee accompanied her hit man to Dewatre that day. The elaborate way Pierre was arranged—his head on a serving platter—I could picture her doing that to him."

Cullen's smug expression told me he thought he'd cracked the case wide open. "How'd you know about the platter if you weren't there?" he asked Victor, then jerked his thumb toward me. "She's the only civilian that knew, and she was told not to blab."

"She didn't have to. I *was* there." Before the detective could get too excited, Victor added, "You dropped off the keys to Dewatre last Friday. That's when I went."

Cullen wasn't ready to relinquish his juicy bone. He leaned forward. "We took that platter as evidence the day of the murder. It was long gone by the time I handed you those keys. The only way you could've known about it is if you were there when he died."

"I was in Paris when Pierre was killed, remember? This is not in doubt. Which must mean that the hit man I hired told me about the platter. Perhaps I instructed him to do that very thing with it. To help make it look like SEAR was responsible."

Cullen closed his notebook. "Let's take this conversation down to the station." Where Victor's impending confession could be recorded and his adorable French butt tossed into the hoosegow.

I released an exasperated sigh. Without lifting his chin from my leg, Sexy Beast did the same.

Victor shook his head. "Thank you, Detective, but I'm comfortable right here."

So how *did* Victor know about the platter? I'd been told to keep my yap shut, and shut I'd kept it. Because I always do what authority figures tell me to.

I heard that. Yes, I can too hear you think. Deal with it.

Victor didn't keep me in suspense. "When I entered Pierre's kitchen, it was several days after he died. The blood—" his voice hitched, ever so slightly, belying his calm demeanor "—had dried, but one could see where it had pooled around his upper body and the object under his head. The size and oval shape suggested a platter identical to those stacked nearby. It was clear that the blood had dried or at least become… what is the word? *coagulé* by the time the police removed the platter. And Pierre."

Gosh, the word sounded downright sexy in French.

Cullen slumped back. "Huh."

I said, "Let's say Lee Romano did hire a hit man, and let's say she accompanied him to the murder and did all the… arranging like Victor said. His larger shoe prints could have obliterated any she might have left." Especially if she'd worn the kind of dainty high-heeled shoes she'd had on during the funeral reception.

Cullen still had some fight left in him. "Don't you think it's kinda strange, Mr. Dewatre? First chance you get, you run right over there to look at the place where your brother was stabbed to death? Most folks, you couldn't pay 'em to do that."

As a certified Death Diva (hey, I'll get out my crayons and make a certificate one of these days), I knew the detective's comment for the self-serving BS it was. The fact is, everybody's different. Victor had wanted to see where his brother had died. So what? He'd also wanted to view Swing's corpse. Doing these things apparently helped him cope with his loss, and it wasn't for Cullen or anyone else to judge.

Victor let his silence indicate that he did not in fact consider his behavior kinda strange.

"Okay, well, was anyone with you at the restaurant last Friday?" Cullen asked.

"No, I was alone."

"Did anyone see you go in or come out?"

Victor shook his head. "I used the back entrance. I didn't want to speak with anyone."

"So no one can corroborate your presence there that day," Cullen said. "It would look better for you if they could." The message being: With no witnesses to put him at the restaurant on the day he claimed to have slipped in through the back door, Victor's knowledge of the crime scene still appeared mighty suspicious.

"For what it's worth, Detective," I said, "Victor told me about his visit to Dewatre. I learned about it that evening." I refrained from mentioning that he also told Dom and Bonnie. *That's right, Detective, the four of us are conducting our own little investigation into the murder since you're a dangerously inept buffoon.*

Cullen stood. Finally! We walked him to the door as he slid the notebook and pen back into his pocket. "Mr.

Dewatre," he said, "you're gonna need to stick around and not take any trips for the foreseeable future."

"Um, Detective," I said, "Victor is, as you're aware, a citizen of France. He possesses a valid passport and, if I'm not mistaken, the legal right to vamoose at will. Unless you're prepared to arrest him?"

The look Cullen gave me prompted Sexy Beast, tucked against my chest, to deliver a long, low growl of warning.

I stroked him lovingly. *Someone's going to get his own little bowl of Fruity Pebbles tonight, yes he is, such a good boy!*

"How about this, then?" The detective's voice was flat. "If you gotta leave town for any reason, please do me the courtesy of letting me know in advance. That work for you?"

"If I'm able." Victor halted before the huge double doors. "Now I have a request of you."

"Yeah?"

"Are you ever going to return Pierre's cell phone to me? I know it's considered evidence, its contents, that is, but you've had ample time to examine it, no? His laptop too."

"Oh yeah, thanks for reminding me." Cullen reached into his suit jacket and handed over a phone, by all appearances the same one that had rung just before I'd nearly tripped over Swing's body. "I'll have to check on his computer, see where it's at."

Victor opened the doors and we all turned to look as a white Acura pulled up and parked in the circular courtyard behind Cullen's gray Impala.

"Ralston," he sneered, as the private investigator slammed his car door and headed up the steps of the colonnaded porch.

Ben noticed Cullen. His smile was not friendly. "Well, if it isn't Crystal Harbor's answer to Inspector Clouseau." He shook with Victor, kissed my cheek, and scratched Sexy Beast behind the ears. He did not extend his hand to Cullen.

"What's he doing here?" Cullen demanded.

"Ben is a friend," I said. "Friends visit each other."

He skewered Ben with a hard look. "Did she hire you to look into the Dewatre murder?"

"Nope."

He wasn't lying. It was Victor who hired him, not me.

"I better not catch you interfering with my investigation," Cullen said.

"I'm confident that you won't," Ben said.

"The hell's that supposed to mean?"

I knew Ben used to be a cop before taking his pension and opening Ralston Investigations. I also knew he wasn't crazy about Bonnie Hernandez, though he respected her as a detective. Respect had nothing to do with what I was observing here.

I ushered Cullen through the doorway, more or less forcefully. "Thanks for coming by, Detective. Call ahead next time, I'll bake brownies."

As we watched the Impala disappear down the long cobblestone drive, Ben said, "What did that idiot want?"

"He wanted to accuse me of murdering my brother," Victor said.

"Based on what?"

I said, "A bunch of lies Swing's old business partner fed him." We were still standing in the foyer. I invited him to sit and visit awhile. "Stay for dinner."

"Thanks, but Stevie and I have reservations. I just wanted to fill you in on what I found out. Tooley has a solid alibi for the time of the murder. Guy's an accounting temp, can you believe it? He was working in an office in Mineola. Couple of dozen people can vouch for his presence there all day."

I didn't register all of that. I was still trying to get past the idea that Romulus Tooley, the big, bad ecoterrorist, made his living as a bean counter for hire.

"And his shoe size?" Victor asked.

"Ten. He's not your guy."

"Not him personally," I said, "but he could have gotten one of his SEAR hangers-on to do it for him."

Victor said, "It's also possible one of them acted on his own after listening to Tooley's inflammatory rhetoric about Pierre."

"I can write up a report and invoice you," Ben told Victor, "or if you think you might have something else for me, we can wait on that."

"Why don't we wait," Victor said. "I have a feeling I'll be calling on your services again."

I would have liked to call on Ben's services right then and there, but I said nothing. I needed to know what size shoe Tucker Nearing wore and where he was the morning Swing was killed—in school, I hoped. I had no intention of sharing these concerns with anyone else, though, based as they were on nothing more than a vague uh-oh feeling. I'd have to figure it out on my own.

9

I Spat in Your Soup Every Day

"WHERE DID YOU even *find* that getup?" I asked.

Martin stood next to me in front of the door to Apartment 3B in a prewar building called The Americana. "I have my sources." He brushed a speck of lint off the front of his blue uniform and reached up to straighten the brim of his cap, similar to a police cap but with a metal plaque on the front sporting the old-fashioned Western Union logo.

"Well, you look ridiculous," I said. "I hope you didn't spend money on it. If you did, it's coming out of your cut."

"Clearly you have no appreciation for men in uniform. Is this guy even home?" He stabbed the doorbell again.

"It's the son," I said. "Chronically unemployed. Probably still in bed." This was our first visit of the morning on behalf of a client named Claude Meyer, recently deceased, who'd had zero intention of going gentle into that good night.

Across the hall a door opened. We turned to see a thirtyish Latina wearing one of those front-pack baby carriers, currently occupied by a tiny, dark-haired infant, fast asleep. The woman turned back in to her apartment, clucking and cooing and tugging on a leash. A dog reluctantly emerged, specifically a Chinese crested, its small, spotted body devoid of hair if you didn't count the explosion of white fluff on its forelegs and the crown of its head. It wore a neon-green sweater.

Suddenly I wished Sexy Beast were there. Here, at long last, was a dog guaranteed to boost my pet's fragile self-esteem.

The instant the animal spied Martin, it lunged for him, fangs bared, drool spraying as it growled and snapped.

"Seriously?" the padre said.

"Pickles, stop that! Be a good boy." The woman struggled to control the little demon as it strained at the leash. "It's the uniform," she explained. "Pickles doesn't like uniforms." The racket woke the baby, who began to wail.

"See?" I told Martin. "I'm not the only one who thinks you look preposterous. Pickles concurs."

Fury had imbued the little dog with the strength of ten Rottweilers. Unable to drag him away, the woman finally bent down and scooped Pickles into a football hold before hurrying toward the stairs.

Meanwhile a male voice hollered from the other side of the door to 3B. "Are you cops?"

"Nah." Martin grinned at the peephole and doffed his silly cap, tapping the Western Union shield. "Delivery."

"I didn't order anything."

I said, "We're here to deliver a message, Mr. Meyer. We'll only be a minute, I promise."

We waited while Claude's son thought this over. Finally the locks turned and the door swung open. Brandon Meyer was in his midtwenties and soft looking under the plaid pj bottoms and dingy white undershirt. It would appear we had indeed roused him out of a deep sleep at close to eleven in the morning.

He stood scratching his armpit and glaring through puffy

eyes. "Message from who?"

Martin said, "Your father, Claude Meyer."

Suspicion tugged Brandon's eyebrows together. "He's dead."

I spoke up. "That's true, I'm afraid. Please accept our sympathies. We're here because your father arranged for the delivery of personal messages to his loved ones after his death."

Martin produced a pitch pipe and played a note. He cleared his throat and proceeded to sing, to the tune of "I Wish I Was in Dixie": *Someday you'll be in the land of hell, because of my beloved cat Belle, she ran away, ran away, ran away, 'cause you left the door open."*

Seconds passed. Brandon scratched the other armpit. Finally he said, "Stupid cat. So that's why Dad left me squat?"

"I'm afraid I'm not privy to his reasons," I said. Which, of course, was a big fat lie. Hell yeah, it was because of the cat. Claude had been a mean old crank. If the cat hadn't decamped, he'd have found some other excuse to cut his only child out of his will and give it all to an organization that claims gravity is a hoax and that only the iron in our blood keeps us from floating away, thanks to the tunnel-dwelling mole people and their giant electromagnets. But I had no intention of standing there chewing the fat with my client's careless son. The sooner we got to our next stop, the sooner I could put this whole stupid assignment behind me.

Claude had insisted that only a male voice would do for his postmortem singing telegrams. No problem—Martin and I collaborated on the occasional assignment. What I hadn't counted on was the padre showing up in that moronic costume. Why couldn't he be normal? Predictable?

And if he were? a niggling voice asked. If Martin were

normal and predictable and steadfast and responsible, like—

Okay, yes, I'll say it. Like Dom! Are you happy? If Martin were more like Dom, would I still feel…

All right, for the record, I'm not saying I feel anything special for Martin. Lord knows he's never said he feels anything special for me, though he did come close once. I'm kinda almost a hundred percent certain about that. But to get back to my point…

Wait, I forgot my point. You know what? Forget it. I had no business playing what-if when I should be concentrating on getting through Claude's vindictive little song list so I could cash his final check.

Brandon was still scratching himself when we took our leave, and no, he does not possess a third armpit, so use your imagination. We drove to the swanky house in Crystal Harbor that Claude had shared with his third wife, Margaret Mary. The fortyish widow opened the door promptly, looking both hotsy and totsy in a revealing wrap top, sprayed-on white pants, and blingy mules. Big hair and an e-cigarette completed the look.

Martin grinned appreciatively. Margaret Mary grinned back, taking note of the Western Union cap, which she flicked with a lacquered nail. "Well, don't you look cute. I thought telegrams went the way of the dodos."

I jumped right in with, "Mrs. Meyer, we're here to deliver a personal message from your late husband, Claude."

She rolled her eyes and took a drag of her e-cigarette, whose telltale skunky aroma hinted it was not in fact an e-cigarette but one of those vape pens whose use had nothing at all to do with nicotine.

In a bored tone Margaret Mary said, "I should've known I

hadn't heard the last from that old bastard. All right, lemme have it."

The padre went through the same silly pitch-pipe-and throat-clearing routine before singing, to the tune of "Oh my darling, Clementine": *"Oh my darling, oh my darling, oh my darling Margaret Mary, you are gone and lost forever, 'cause you cheated on me with Fred McCuddy."*

Margaret Mary pulled a face. "That doesn't even rhyme."

"I'm not responsible for the lyrics," Martin said.

"No, I know that. Sheesh." She sucked her vape pen, thinking. "I should've done it with someone named Harry. Or Larry. Or, oh, I know! Stanley Perry. Oh wait, I did."

"I'm sure you were provoked," Martin said, then grunted as my elbow connected with his ribs. *Stick to the script, Padre.*

"Was I ever," Margaret Mary said. "You ever meet the dearly departed?"

"No." Martin pointed to me. "But she did."

Before the widow could get up a good head of steam on the subject of her infidelities and their perfectly justifiable provocations, I said, "Our sincere condolences on your loss, Mrs. Meyer."

She gestured with the vape pen as if to say, *Yeah, whatever.* Her gaze was unfocused as she said, "Listen, am I supposed to tip you?"

"It's not required," Martin said, "but I wouldn't turn it d—*oof!*"

There was my pesky elbow again, with a mind of its own.

"There's no need for that," I said. "Mr. Meyer took care of our fee. We'll just be on our—"

"You know," she purred, gesturing inside the house, "I just opened a bottle of good pinot noir. I hate drinking alone, don't you?" Her smile encompassed both me and Martin in a way that told me she was on the prowl for more than a couple of drinking buddies.

Martin was all over that. "I think we could be persuad—*Ow!* Jane, knock it off!"

"Unfortunately, we have another stop to make," I said, dragging Martin back down the porch steps.

"Rain check!" he hollered over his shoulder.

Our last stop was a three-story office building in western Nassau County that housed Aiello Packaging Solutions, where Claude had toiled for twenty-one years in the sales department. The administrative floor was an expanse of generic cubicles ringed by private offices and conference rooms. The receptionist eyed Martin's outfit warily as she buzzed her boss to let him know he had visitors.

By the time Gunther Aiello joined us several minutes later, whispers had spread about the Western Union messenger, and all the employees had either drifted out of their cubicles or were peeking over the partitions to see what was going on. Gunther, the third generation of Aiellos to head the company, was tall, fiftyish, well dressed but flabby around the middle. Genially he introduced himself and asked our business.

I said, "Mr. Aiello, we're here to deliver a personal message from Claude Meyer."

It took a second for that to sink in. "Claude!" He pressed his hands together. Shook his head. "Poor Claude. We were all so shocked. A message, you say?"

I nodded. "To be delivered to you personally after his passing. Perhaps, um… well, I'm sure you'd prefer the privacy of your office." That big, bright corner office from which Gunther had emerged. The one with a door that closed.

"Not at all." Gunther gestured expansively, indicating the dreary sea of cubicles under buzzing fluorescent ceiling lights. "Everyone here knew Claude. I think we all want to hear what he had to say."

Before I could pursue the point, Martin said, "Sure thing!" and produced his pitch pipe. He played his note. He cleared his throat. The lyrics that followed were sung to the tune of "Swing Low, Sweet Chariot": *"You're low, Gunther Aiello, lower than I can say, you passed me up for promotion, so I spat in your soup every day."*

Gunther jerked. A livid flush crawled upward from his starched collar as his employees gasped and snickered. One of them murmured a smug, "Claude, too?" making me wonder how much disgruntled employee spit his boss had consumed over the years.

Gunther yelled himself hoarse kicking us out of the office and ordering his staff back to work. Martin slipped the receptionist a stack of my business cards on the way out.

As we crossed the small parking lot, headed for my red Mazda, I said, "What are you doing tomorrow around four?"

"In the a.m.?" There was that silky smile. "Depends how much you've worn me out by then."

Yeah, he had the sexy innuendo down. The guy was a born flirt. I'd long ago stopped thinking it meant anything. Well, mostly stopped.

"Do you remember Tucker Nearing?" I asked. "Karina Faso's boyfriend. He was the kid that got into it with Tooley—"

"Yeah, sure, what about him?"

I beeped the door locks and we let ourselves in to the car. "There's something I need done," I said. "Something that requires your particular skill set. I don't know who else to ask."

I must have looked pretty grim since he chose not to have fun with my reference to his skill set. He said, "I'm listening."

THE ROSE BOOKSHOP was that rare breed, an independent bookstore that was solidly in the black and in no danger of going the sad way of so many of its brethren. The Rose had occupied the same location on Main Street since 1946. It had grown over the years, spreading into a neighboring space and morphing from your basic bookstore into a sort of community center.

A full third of the store was a children's area, selling kids' books, toys, games, and arts and crafts supplies. In a well-to-do town like Crystal Harbor, folks didn't hesitate to open their wallets if it meant nurturing Junior's budding genius. The store housed a funky café where those who worked locally could grab coffee and a breakfast burrito, or a prosciutto and mozzarella panino at lunchtime. The dining area doubled as a venue for musical performances on Friday evenings and occasional book-signings during evening hours and weekends. With The Rose, as with so much else in life, adaptation had proved to be the key to survival.

It was a book-signing that had brought me there that Thursday evening. I'd seen the notice in the same issue of the *Harbor Herald* where I'd spied Tucker's big feet. In light of Detective Cullen's visit two days earlier, I couldn't pass up this opportunity.

Leonora Romano sat on a hard wooden chair behind a

table piled high with copies of her newly released cookbook, *Leonora's Kitchen.* It was a slick hardback with a hefty price tag and a close-up of Lee's grinning face on the book jacket.

How had Chloe put it? *She feels the world owes her.* Well, first it would be nice if the world realized she existed, and I saw no evidence of that at this pitiful excuse for a book-signing.

Few others occupied the café area at the moment. A guy around eighty sat nursing a cup of herbal tea while perusing the *New York Times.* A harried-looking young mother chatted with a friend while shoving cookies at a fussy toddler in a stroller. They all ignored Lee, who had yet to notice me. This was because her attention was on the twenty-something customer asking her for directions to the ladies' room. Lee answered, wearing a smile that could only be described as strained.

I almost felt sorry for her. Until I recalled that this woman was trying to convince the detective in charge of Swing's murder investigation that his brother had done him in. She was spreading the news of Victor's supposed guilt far and wide. It was all over the Web. The town was buzzing with it. My empathy had its limits.

After the bathroom seeker wandered off in search of relief, I approached Lee, who didn't recognize me at first. We'd met just the once, after all, at Swing's funeral reception. She probably assumed I, too, was a random customer looking for the loo. Or the latest Stephen King novel. Maybe an inquiry about store hours.

I stuck out my hand and reintroduced myself, getting another lungful of that pricey French perfume. The woman must stand under a waterfall of it every morning.

Her smile turned even more brittle. I'm not kidding, I wouldn't have been surprised to see fault lines appear in her plastic face. "Oh yes, Jane. Of course." She pulled the top book off the stack and opened the cover. To keep her from scribbling my name on the flyleaf, thus forcing me to plunk down forty clams at the register, I blurted out the first thing that leapt to my tongue.

"Why did you accuse Victor of murder?"

She froze momentarily, then straightened and rearranged her awesomely realistic features into something resembling dismissive hauteur. "I have no intention of discussing this matter with—"

"You know very well he had nothing to do with it." I braced my arms on the table and leaned over her. I wasn't shouting, but I was making no effort to whisper either. Lee glanced nervously at the handful of customers in the vicinity, who were pretending not to listen.

"What makes you so certain your precious Victor didn't do it?" she snarled.

"Oh, please," I said. "If you really think he's capable of something like that, you don't know him."

"And you do?" she said. "After, what, a week? A week and a half? You don't want to believe it because this sexy young Frenchman is paying all this attention to you. Think about it, Jane. Ted Bundy was young and good-looking too."

I managed not to guffaw at her comparing Victor Dewatre to one of the most notorious serial killers in history. "What's this really about?" I asked. "Why are you going after him like this? Siccing the cops on him, savaging his reputation, after the loss he just suffered. What did he ever do to you?"

Unless I was right and her attempt to frame Victor was a ploy meant to divert attention from her own guilt. In which case I'd just managed to piss off a coldblooded murderer.

"Excuse me?" came a timid female voice from behind me. I glanced over my shoulder at a middle-aged woman toting one of The Rose's pink-and-white shopping bags. It was crammed with expensive-looking books. "I'd like to meet the author and get her to sign—"

"She's busy." I gave the woman my back as Lee leapt to her feet in an attempt to salvage what was probably her first and only sale of the day.

"You have no right," Lee growled, jerking this way and that, trying to make eye contact with the departing customer as I mirrored her movements, thwarting her. I hadn't woken up that day planning to hone my hip-hop dance moves, but hey, you never know what life will bring.

"Answer the question," I said when she finally gave up. "What could Swing's brother possibly have done to make you retaliate in this hateful fashion? And don't give me any nonsense about his big fight with Swing over boffing the ex-wife. We both know that's a smokescreen."

As Lee pondered how to respond, she chewed those big, fake lips of hers, smearing crimson lipstick on her big, fake teeth. Finally she shrugged and, in a near whisper, said, "What the hell, it'd be your word against mine. I'll tell you what that son of a bitch did. He sabotaged my chances with the Food Network."

"What?"

"My show," she snapped. "It was supposed to be Swing's and—"

"I know about the show," I said. "So you didn't get it, huh? I just can't believe you think Victor had anything to do with that."

"Chloe broke the news to me yesterday." Her carefully

applied makeup failed to conceal the patches of hot color that had bloomed in her sculpted cheeks. "They're giving it to this young—" she threw her arms wide, at a momentary loss for words "—*hipster* chef. From *Brooklyn*."

"Morgan McNair?" I said. "Wasn't he a contestant on *Kale Wars*? He has an awesome food blog."

"How could they give it to someone like that?" she demanded. "I deserve it! That show was supposed to be mine!"

"I know it's easier to blame someone else," I said, "but has it occurred to you that—?"

"No!" Her face twisted into something I hardly recognized. "*He* did this. Victor. You were there at that funeral thing. That reception. You saw how angry he was. He practically accused me of trying to profit from his brother's death."

Well, weren't you? I opened my mouth to ask it, then snapped it shut. I didn't need her more worked up than she already was. Customers had begun drifting into the café, lured by our juicy contretemps. I had no desire to be banned from The Rose for life. It wasn't even book browsing or the weekly live music I'd miss the most. Their bacon-cheddar scones were to die for.

"You can't seriously believe Victor somehow wrecked your standing with the network," I said.

"Oh, I don't doubt it," she said. "Who knows what lies he told them about me?"

This woman had nerve complaining about damaging lies. But she wasn't done.

"And I know why he did it," she continued, leaning closer and truly whispering now that we had an audience. "It wasn't just the TV show, the fact that I saw a chance to advance my career and acted on it, like any good businesswoman would.

No, it was the endangered species thing, too."

"Umm…" I said.

"Victor must have found out I'm the one who started the rumor."

After a second of stunned silence, I sputtered, "*You* did that?"

Lee had the bad taste to look pleased with herself. "Three years ago, right after Swing abandoned Hummingbird and forced me to close." Her face fell. "How was I to know the whole thing would backfire and he'd thrive on the notoriety? That bastard could step in a pile of dog crap and it would turn into twenty-four-karat gold."

I left her muttering about the unfairness of it all, about how some people have all the luck and it's her turn now, dammit. As I headed for the exit, I recognized a familiar form from the back. Short, stylish dark hair, elegant clothes, gigundo diamond on the left ring finger.

Bonnie stood in front of a bookshelf labeled *Wedding Planning*, a subsection of the *Self-Help and Relationships* section.

How did that make me feel? you ask. How do you *think* it made me feel?

I would have liked nothing more than to slink out of the store and try to forget about Bonnie and Dom and their impending nuptials—no firm date yet, don't ask me the significance of that—but there was something I'd kept meaning to run past her, alone, and I had no desire to cede home turf advantage by dropping in on her at the PD.

I tapped her shoulder. She turned with a pleasant expression, which morphed into a blend of annoyance and embarrassment when she saw me. The annoyance needed no explanation. As for the other…

I glanced at the book she'd been perusing, which billed itself as the *Supreme Wedding Planner & Organizer*. It was the most girly thing I'd ever seen her do. She slammed it shut and crammed it back on the shelf between *The Bride's Memory Book* and *The Creative Wedding Planning Guide*.

I'm not going to apologize for the little zing of satisfaction I felt at her obvious discomfiture. And face it, if I did, you wouldn't buy it for a second.

"Getting ready for the big day?" I asked. Sweetly.

"What do you want, Jane?"

I blinked at her abrupt tone, a little hurt. At least I hoped it looked that way.

Okay, you know what? You do not get a vote in how I conduct myself with the woman who was gearing up to marry the love of my life. Or… whatever he was at the moment.

Her expression said, *Give me a break.* This seasoned detective wasn't about to be fooled by my little act.

"Listen, Bonnie, there's something I think we should be doing." I glanced around and lowered my voice. "You know, about the investigation?"

"I have nothing to do with the investigation," she said, "and *you* certainly don't—"

"Yeah, yeah, we've been through that. Do you want to see your fiancé go to prison for a crime he didn't commit?"

"I happen to know Detective Cullen is looking at someone else," she said.

"Right. Victor. And only because Nip and Tuck Barbie over there—" I jerked my thumb toward the café where Lee Romano sat before her sad pile of cookbooks "—is trying to frame him. Even that idiot Cullen will figure that out if he hadn't already. Meanwhile there's still only one serious 'person of interest.'" How I was coming to loathe that term.

"So when you say there's something 'we' should be doing," Bonnie said, "what you're really saying is there's something you want me to do."

I got in her face. "Same side, remember? We're supposed to be on the same side here?"

I waited for her to acknowledge that, which she finally did, more or less, by sighing and glancing at her watch. It was all I was going to get.

"Cullen has this little notebook," I said.

She shrugged. "So? He's a detective. We all carry them."

"*So,*" I said, "Cullen works at the PD. You work at the PD. That thing must come out of his pocket at some point. Like when he's reading it over, filling out forms, I don't know…"

Her eyes popped. "You want me to sneak a look at his notebook?"

"Why not? Is there some kind of rule against, you know, two detectives sharing information?"

"It's not 'sharing' if one of the detectives doesn't know he's doing it," she said, "and there's no way he'd willingly show me his notes. You know very well I removed myself from the case due to—"

"Conflict of interest. So? I'm just asking you to check up on him, find out if there are any details we don't know about."

Bonnie pulled herself up. "What you're asking is not only unethical, it would get me in serious trouble if I got caught. I won't do it."

10

He Really Stepped in It

"ONE PAPAYA-GINGER smoothie, large." Cheyenne O'Rourke set a plastic cup in front of me. "One Dracula Special, large." This one was for Victor, who sat across from me at a blond-wood bistro table placed next to the huge picture windows overlooking Crystal Harbor's Main Street. He'd decided to work from home that day and I'd persuaded him to take an afternoon break at Janey's Place, Dom's health-food joint. It was a warm, welcoming space decorated in the store's signature light beige and apple-green, and fragrant with the soups, salads, and blended drinks that drew discerning vegetarians from miles around. Plus regular meat-eating folks like us who enjoy the pleasant ambience and occasional healthier alternative to pizza and orange soda.

Victor eyed his drink dubiously. "I didn't know it would look so…"

"Disgusting," Cheyenne helpfully supplied. Today the girl's well-nourished form had been poured into red-and-white-striped leggings—was the circus in town already?—and ultra-high stiletto ankle boots crisscrossed top to bottom with buckled straps. Her apple-green Janey's Place T-shirt was tied tight at the midriff, exposing a pale roll of bare muffin top.

I didn't bother advising her not to describe the food she served in terms that were so, well, honest. She'd been working for Dom for seven months. By this point he was well aware of her shortcomings, but nice guy that he was, he kept her on despite them. Some people might view his tolerance as weakness, but I thought it was sweet. More than sweet, it was indicative of the kind of man he was. Despite all he'd accomplished, Dom had never let his success go to his head. He never forgot what he owed his family, his town, his friends who'd stood by him, and yes, even me, his ex-wife. He always gave back.

Whoever said a touch of humility couldn't be sexy?

Victor said, "I assumed 'Dracula Special' is just a silly name."

"It looks like blood," Cheyenne said. "That's why they call it—"

"Yes, thank you, Cheyenne," I said. "We get it." The stuff was a blend of carrot, orange, and beet juices. It was chock-full of vitamins and supposedly great for your blood pressure and circulation and all that.

"You want anything else?" she asked.

You mean besides an IV bag and needle? One look at Victor's face was enough to call forth my inner Pushy American. Without consulting him, I shoved his drink back at Cheyenne. "Take this away and bring him one of these." I indicated my papaya-ginger smoothie, thick and pale orange, which I knew from experience was as sweet and yummy as a milk shake and would in no way remind him of his brother's murder scene.

"He doesn't want the Dracula stuff?" she asked.

"It's not his type."

As she tottered away, Victor produced a cell phone, which I recognized as Swing's. "I've been going through Pierre's emails and texts," he said. "Also his calendar."

"Find anything interesting?" I stuck the straw into my drink.

"Not really," he said. "Nothing on his social media either."

"No posts like 'So-and-so wants to do me in, I'd better watch my back'?"

"If only it were that simple." Listlessly he thumbed the screen, his forehead marred by a slight frown.

"What?" I said. He didn't look up. "What's bothering you, Victor?"

"Nothing. It's just… I'm frustrated by the lack of progress. Every day that passes makes it's less likely Pierre's killer will be caught."

I sensed that wasn't the whole story. Instead of harassing him further, I held out my hand for the phone. With a sigh he passed it to me.

As I scrolled through Swing's emails, I began to comprehend the source of Victor's discomfort. He'd told Cullen that whenever Swing had found himself involved in the occasional serious relationship, he'd never cheated. *He had too much honor for that*, according to Victor. And yet the emails I was now reading, sent to and from several women in the days before Swing's death, left little doubt that Cullen was right and that Victor hadn't known his brother as well as he thought he had. Swing had been cheating on his fiancée big time.

He and Chloe had exchanged emails, too, of course, but surprisingly, those all pertained to business. Where were the intimate little messages? The cloying emoticons and XOXOXOs? It seemed odd until I considered that they were engaged and lived in the same town. Why waste effort on lovey-dovey emails to your betrothed when the two of you can get your lovey-dovey on in person anytime you want?

Maybe that was their problem, the whole absence-makes-the-heart-grow-fonder thing. Maybe Swing was the kind of guy who thrived on the chase and got bored once he'd snagged his quarry. He wouldn't be the first.

His emails were brief and to the point, composed for the most part of sentence fragments and abbreviations, with few fancy-schmancy flourishes such as punctuation or capitalization. The communications of a busy man.

I glanced at Victor, who sat staring out the window, lost in thought, even after Cheyenne plunked his smoothie in front of him. I thumbed an icon on the screen, producing Swing's texting history. More of same. Terse, get-to-the-point texts, even when arranging an assignation with this or that nubile young thing. I recognized the name of a well-known model who'd tossed back a few before grabbing the mic during Swing's funeral reception. So. I was right. It hadn't been all lies and exaggerations.

"Victor, I..." What could I say? *I'm sorry you had to find out your revered late brother was fallible?*

He shrugged and held out his hand for the phone. "Did you look at the calendar?" When I shook my head, he pulled up Swing's electronic calendar and angled the phone so we could both see the screen. The entries here were downright cryptic. Plus they were in a combination of English and French that made them next to impossible to decipher—for me at least.

"The calendar agrees with the emails and texts," he said.

"You mean like when he arranged his, um, meetings—"

"His dates. Like here after he texted this Brianna to meet him at the Greenwich Hotel at seven o'clock on August nineteenth." Swing's calendar reminder for seven p.m. that day was *b green*.

"You know," I said, "maybe Swing had every intention of settling down and being a faithful husband once he and Chloe got married. Maybe this was kind of a last hurrah?"

His expression said, *Thanks for trying*. "I know you think I'm being unrealistic about Pierre, about his character, but I *knew* him, Jane. This…" He tossed his hand at the phone. "It just doesn't feel right." He meandered through his brother's calendar, scrolling backward in time through the summer. A gentle smile tugged at his mouth.

"What?" I peered at the entry for July 4: *dom p*. "He saw Dom that day? What does *p* mean?"

His smile grew lopsided. "Naturally you would read it that way. Pierre took Chloe to the fireworks on July Fourth, remember? The white tablecloth, the champagne? Dom Perignon has always been his favorite."

"Ah, I get it. But that's his whole calendar entry for the night he proposes to Chloe? A reminder to bring champagne?"

"This is typical Pierre. It would be tragic if he forgot the most important thing—the Dom Perignon! Without that, it's just a picnic with explosions."

"And, hello? An *engagement ring*," I reminded him.

"Yes, but without the right champagne?" Victor let his Gallic shrug say the rest.

Movement from beyond the big picture windows snagged my attention. Three teenage girls stood on the sidewalk staring in at us, their faces practically pressed to the glass. I say they were staring at *us*, but that's not quite accurate. All their attention was on Victor.

The instant he turned toward them, they erupted in giggles. "Do you know them?" he asked.

"The blond one looks familiar," I said. "I think I've seen her around town."

She appeared to be the bold one, egging on the other two. Within seconds they stood next to our table.

"Mr. Doo-wat?" The girl wore fashionable black-framed glasses, her pale hair cut in a severe bob. She blushed fiercely. "I'm Ariel. This is Phoebe and Mandy," she added, indicating her pals. All three had backpacks slung over their shoulders. Clearly they'd just gotten out of school. Phoebe was a tall Asian girl. Mandy had a blue streak in her long brown hair.

"A pleasure to meet you," Victor said, which triggered another bout of giggles. "This is my friend Jane."

They dutifully murmured "hi," with barely a glance in my direction.

"We just want you to know," Ariel said, "that we think you're totally innocent."

"We *know* you're totally innocent," Mandy said.

Phoebe said, "Like you *couldn't* have done what they say you did."

"How can they even *think* that?" Ariel said.

"Uh…" Victor glanced at me as if seeking guidance.

My eye-shrug said, *You're on your own.*

"Well, I appreciate your confidence," he said. "Thank you."

I asked, "Do you girls go to Crystal Harbor High?"

They nodded in unison. Phoebe said, "Like, everyone at school's talking about Swing and who might've killed him."

"What are they saying?" I asked.

"Well, some kids think Victor did it," Mandy said, "'cause they read it on some stupid site or something."

"It's so *unfair!*" Ariel said. "*Anybody* can tell you're innocent."

Why? Because he was a hottie? Lee Romano's words invaded my thoughts. *Ted Bundy was young and good-looking too.*

Phoebe shoved her phone and a Sharpie at Victor. The phone was enclosed in a pink metallic case. "Would you, like, sign my phone?"

"I'm… not comfortable doing that," he said.

Ariel smacked her friend's shoulder. "I *told* you not to ask him."

"Listen, girls." I stood, prompting Victor to do the same. "We have to get going, but it was nice meeting you."

"Hang in there," Mandy told him.

"We're rooting for you," Ariel said, as if Swing's murder investigation were some sort of sporting event.

After I dropped Victor off at the house, I swung by the high school, where swim practice had just let out. Tucker hopped into the car and I drove us to the home of the late Dr. Walters, whose collection of antique medical instruments I was in the process of cataloging. I'd promised the boy he could take a look at the collection, and the doc's family had no problem with it.

Yeah, don't tell me yet what a swell person I am. I had an ulterior motive for keeping Kari's boyfriend busy for an hour or so, and even though it was something that had to be done, it didn't keep my conscience from tweaking me when the boy thanked me yet again for doing him this cool favor.

He was fascinated by the bizarre old devices. I'd wondered

about the sort of people who collect this stuff, but viewing the artifacts through Tucker's eyes as he fiddled with the wooden stethoscope, the brass-and-glass syringe, the stained chloroform inhaler, I began to see the appeal. He spent a long time examining a military amputation set from the Civil War, speculating aloud on how many limbs this particular bone saw might have severed.

And okay, this whole exercise could be considered kind of creepy in light of our town's recent unsolved murder, but I chose not to dwell on that. And nearly succeeded.

Tucker was lifting the lid on an exquisitely decorated porcelain jar labeled "Leeches" when my cell phone burped, informing me a text had come in. It was Martin: *Where are you?* I texted back: *Doc's house.* His response came almost immediately: *Address.* I supplied it, adding, *You done yet?*

He didn't text back and I forgot about it as Tucker began to tell me everything he knew about the medical use of leeches, both historical and current. Yeah, that's right, the medical establishment has essentially come full circle and once again embraces the application of blood-sucking worms as a viable therapy. Oh, and maggots, too.

No, I did not make that up! Tucker told me all about it, and for the record, I'll take leeches over maggots. Just in case I'm ever, you know, unconscious and you have to make the decision for me.

Tucker, no doubt inspired by the look on my face, was still regaling me with the gruesome particulars of how maggots are used for wound therapy ("Open your laptop, there are some cool videos") when the doorbell rang a few minutes later. *Thank you!* I mentally cried as I jumped up to answer it.

"What are you doing here?" I asked, looking past Martin

to that big Harley of his parked haphazardly in the driveway. "I thought we were going to—" I shut my trap since Tucker was within earshot, in the living room just beyond the front vestibule.

I couldn't recall ever seeing the padre look so grave. We'd planned to meet up at Murray's Pub a few hours later so he could report back on the thing I'd asked him to do. Not a Death Diva assignment, more along the lines of a personal favor.

Relief softened his expression as he looked me over. Relief at what? He ignored my inquisitive expression and gazed past me to Tucker, who was carefully repacking the leech jar in bubble wrap. They exchanged greetings and Martin joined us as we finished perusing the collection. The boy didn't ask what the padre was doing there, for which I was grateful since I didn't know myself.

When we were finally done, it was nearly dinnertime. I asked Martin, "Do you still want to, um, go for a beer later?"

He shrugged, clearly preoccupied. "Maybe."

As I drove Tucker to his family home on the other side of Crystal Harbor, Martin stayed right behind us on his Harley. Tucker didn't appear to notice, but my gaze kept flicking to the rearview mirror. I shivered. I wasn't liking this one little bit.

Martin hung back a half block while I dropped off Tucker, who thanked me yet again before disappearing into his house. My phone burped. I really should find a more polite-sounding text notification. It was the padre, natch, telling me to meet him at the railroad station a couple of miles away.

We pulled up next to the waiting room at the same time. He dismounted and joined me in my car, sliding into the passenger seat recently vacated by Tucker. Afternoon rush hour was in full swing. An eastbound train had just come through. Passengers descended the staircase from the platform level, some headed to the parking lot, some to idling cars and taxis.

Martin turned to me, his expression bleak. "It's him."

I clapped a hand over the gasp that erupted. My heart kicked. "No! No, it can't be Tucker."

"We have to call this in." The cops, he meant. Cullen.

"Wait." I grabbed his hand, which felt hot under my icy fingers. "Just… Just tell me. Tell me what you found."

I'd asked Martin to watch the Nearings' house that afternoon. I knew their housekeeper went home at four o'clock. I knew the boy's parents would both be at work. I knew Tucker had one sibling, an older married sister who lived in Jersey. Once he was certain no one was home, Martin was to quickly and quietly enter the house—and yes, we're talking about that cute little lock-pick set he never leaves home without—and slip up to Tucker's room to check on his shoe size while I kept the boy occupied clear across town with assorted bone saws and leech jars. Quick and simple, no harm done.

All right, yes, technically it was breaking and entering, but you tell me what you would have done under the same circumstances, with Detective Paul Cullen in charge of an investigation that threatened to send your ex-husband, who just happened to be The Nicest Guy in the World, to prison for the rest of his life for a horrible crime that he definitely, no doubt about it, could not have committed.

Martin is the only person I could have asked to perform this particular favor. He knows it and I think he likes it that way, likes being the bad boy with a shadowy past, likes having me depend on him when things get hairy.

He said, "I found the shoes, Jane."

"So he wears size thirteen, so what?" I swallowed hard. "That doesn't make him a killer. It doesn't prove anything."

"No, I mean I found *the* shoes." He waited for that to sink in.

A strange sound escaped my throat, a small animal sound.

Martin squeezed my hand. He sighed. Something told me he didn't want this to be true any more than I did. "The sneakers in Tucker's closet have the exact same soles as the pictures you sent me," he said. I'd emailed him the shoe-print photos I'd taken in the restaurant kitchen.

"There must be hundreds of guys with those exact same sneakers," I said. "Thousands. It doesn't—"

"There's blood," he said. "Dried blood in the treads."

"How can you be sure it's bl—" I cut myself off and raised a hand, forestalling his answer, knowing it would come under the broad category of Things I Would Rather Not Know About Martin.

So. I'd spent the past couple of hours at the doc's house with the person who'd almost certainly plunged that big knife into Swing's chest. Just the two of us, Tucker and me. "Why didn't you call or text me with this as soon as you knew?" I asked.

"I was afraid that if you knew, you wouldn't be able to keep your cool," he said. "You might have given it away, put yourself in danger—more danger than you were already in, that is, just being there alone with him."

I wanted to tell him he was wrong, that I would have been the consummate actress, that Tucker never would have suspected a thing. But deep inside, I knew Martin had made the right call.

"You made it over there pretty fast," I said, "from Tucker's house to the doc's. What if you'd gotten stopped for speeding?"

"They'd have had to catch me first."

I imagined Martin on that big motorcycle, burning rubber, running lights, because of me. Because I'd been alone with a presumptive murderer. His concern sparked a warm little glow of satisfaction, immediately snuffed out by the bigger issue confronting us.

Tucker. Kari's besotted beau.

I love you, Kari. I'd do anything for you. Anything!

I groped for the door handle as that papaya-ginger smoothie I'd consumed hours earlier threatened to make a repeat appearance. I staggered away from the car and suddenly Martin's hands were on me, those solid, sturdy hands steering me around the car and onto the walkway flanking the waiting room, which at the moment was nearly deserted. I couldn't get air, I was drowning.

He held me and coached me through this strange new thing called breathing. I shook my head, trying to form words. I was not to talk, he instructed, my job was to breathe, to think about nothing else. So I did. I pulled air in and pushed it out. I did it again and then again. My head dropped to his hard shoulder and he smelled so good and I was trembling too badly to stand on my own. My heart banged and banged and I knew he had to feel it, he was holding me so close.

Gradually I registered his arm banded around my back, his other hand stroking my hair. My armpits were damp. I felt like I'd run a race. But my breathing had eased at last. The dizziness had abated. I closed my eyes and allowed myself simply to feel Martin's warmth, the enveloping security of his embrace, and tried to forget what had prompted it.

Finally I raised my head. He brushed strands of hair off my face. He searched my eyes. "Okay?"

"That wasn't a panic attack," I said.

"Of course not," he said, without a hint of a smirk, a kindness that made me want to kiss him.

"I don't get panic attacks. I don't know what that was."

"All right."

He seemed in no hurry to release me, so I gently pulled away, fearing the awkwardness of a lingering embrace more than the loss of his comforting warmth. Silly me.

Instead I hugged myself. "I guess I assumed we'd get together at Murray's later and you'd tell me he wears size twelve and he's in the clear."

"I wish it had worked out that way."

"Okay." I took a deep breath. "What's next?"

"Cullen."

I groaned. "Fine, but what do I say when he asks how I found out about Tucker's bloody shoes?"

"You're not going to talk to him, I am."

"Oh yeah, big improvement," I said. "He'll really listen to *you*. Where are you going?"

I followed Martin around the building to a secluded spot under the train trestle that housed a pay phone. Okay, I guess it made sense to call anonymously. But... "Won't he recognize your voice?" I asked.

He dug in his pocket for change, then lifted the handset and fed the phone. A few seconds later Sean Connery said, "Please put me through to Detective Cullen. It's urgent."

Now, I know what you're thinking. Everybody impersonates Connery's Scottish burr, it's no big deal. But trust me, they're all amateurs. A few rolled *r*'s, some mushy *s*'s, and they call it a day. Martin *was* Sean Connery. He *inhabited* Sean Connery. If I closed my eyes, I could convince myself James Bond had taken a break from dispatching supervillains to chat about Tucker Nearing's footwear.

"Detective Cullen! I have some information you will find shocking. Positively shocking."

11

World's Most Eligible Psychopath

"I LOVE HIM!" Kari screamed. "You don't care about me. I wish you weren't my father. *I hate you!*"

Okay, we were back to this. If only Dom's daughter could be constant, predictable, self-composed. Like other teenagers.

I'll wait for you to stop snickering.

It was Saturday afternoon and we were back in Dom's coldly elegant living room, the scene of the previous adolescent firestorm. I'd come by to see how Kari was dealing with Tucker's arrest. The answer: kind of how she'd dealt with Swing's death.

"While you're still a minor," Dom soberly intoned, "I'm responsible for your safety. I'm sorry if that makes you unhappy, but—"

"Shut up!" she screeched. "I don't want to hear anything you have to say. Tucker needs me, but you don't care about that. You don't care about anyone but *yourself!*" Which was her cue to sprint upstairs and slam her bedroom door.

I hadn't been altogether certain Cullen would act on the anonymous tip Sean Connery had provided yesterday. Cullen being Cullen, I figured it was fifty-fifty. He'd come through, though, and the end result was the arrest of Tucker Nearing on suspicion of murder. He'd been brought in too late to be arraigned the same day, so he'd had to spend the night in jail. This morning he'd been released on an exorbitant bail which his well-to-do parents had had no trouble posting. And of course, they'd hired an excellent criminal attorney.

Each new piece of information to emerge made me more and more depressed. A witness had seen Tucker enter the restaurant by the front door around ten-fifteen that morning, not long before I arrived and discovered Swing's body. Now that the cops had his fingerprints, they'd successfully matched them to the prints found on the handle of the knife Swing had been killed with.

As soon as I'd stepped through Dom's door, Kari had pulled me aside to beg me to sneak her over to Tucker's house. I mean, hey, I'm the cool stepmother, right? The one who lets the girl skip first-period gym and have Fruity Pebbles for breakfast. She could count on me.

She could not, as it turned out, count on me for that particular cool favor. And when her father refused yet again to let her visit or even communicate with the killer she claimed to be so passionately in love with—that's right, Dom confiscated her phone, brave man—the last hope for civil discourse in the Faso household evaporated.

Dom looked exhausted. "Glad you came?"

"She's been through a lot in the past couple of weeks," I said. "But then, so have you. Unfortunately, you get to be the grown-up."

He strolled into the humongous kitchen—black walls, floor, countertops, and island; white cabinets; acres of stainless steel—and poured a mug of coffee. He offered me some. I shook my head.

He leaned against the central work island, a slab of gleaming black quartz, rounded at one end. "So what I want to know is, why now?"

I leaned back against a counter and fiddled with a black-and-white checked dish towel. "Why *what* now?"

"Tucker's arrest." He looked at me steadily. "I've been wondering what prompted it."

"Um, I'd have to guess it would be the shoes they found in his closet," I said. "The ones that had tromped through Swing's blood. So I've heard."

He was still watching me closely. I looked away. "What *I* heard," he said, "is that Cullen received a phone tip. The person called from a pay phone and refused to identify himself, and Cullen didn't recognize the voice."

I straightened, astounded. "He didn't recognize the *voice*? How—" I clamped my mouth shut, too late. Dang!

Dom gave me that smug little smile that had been elevating my blood pressure for a quarter of a century. "I thought so. Martin? Had to be Martin. I doubt Victor could've concealed his accent."

"Oh, like I don't know any other men who could've done it?" I asked. "Just those two?"

"There's no one else you'd have trusted with it," he said. "How did you find out about the shoes?"

"Let's not… I don't even…"

"Oh, that's perfect," he said. "Breaking and entering. With your full knowledge and approval, I take it."

I wish the guy couldn't read my mind. It's one of his more irksome habits.

He wasn't finished. "I've told you before, Jane, Martin McAuliffe is trouble. One of these days you're going to find yourself behind bars because of him. Or worse."

I was groping for a response when we heard "Jane?" It was Kari, hurrying down the circular staircase. She sounded breathless. "Are you still here?"

I met her in the foyer. Dom wisely remained in the kitchen, although the open floor plan allowed him to eavesdrop. "What is it?" I asked.

If possible, she looked even more distressed than after Swing had died. "I get that I can't go over there myself. To see Tucker. But you could. Would you do that for me? I need… I need him to know that I still love him. That I believe in him." She teared up again. "Please, Jane."

"Oh, honey." I hugged her hard, feeling my own eyes fill. The last thing I wanted was to be face-to-face with Tucker, knowing I was responsible for his arrest. Not that I had anything to feel guilty about. On the contrary, I'd helped the police apprehend a dangerous criminal. A murderer. But between Kari and Dom and Victor, I was too emotionally involved. It was becoming increasingly difficult to maintain perspective.

"Of course I'll speak with him," I found myself saying.

"In person." She pulled back and stared at me, her dark brown eyes so like Dom's. "I need for you to see him, to see that he's okay."

"All right, sure." There went my cunning plan to phone him rather than visit.

"And come right back and tell me everything," she demanded.

I promised and she hugged me again, then fired a malevolent look over my shoulder, telling me her dad had entered the room. Up the stairs she went.

"Don't try to talk me out of it," I told him. "I promised her."

"You're not going there alone."

"I won't be alone," I said. "I'm sure his parents are home."

"I'm going with you."

"What? Dom, I don't need a bodyguard. I'm just going to drop in for a minute, relate Kari's message, and split."

"This is nonnegotiable."

"Really. Do the words 'You're not the boss of me' mean anything to you?"

"Jane, don't argue with me about this. You know as well as I do how dangerous that kid is." His gaze traveled up the curved staircase to where his daughter had retreated into her bedroom. "I can't believe that all this time she was dating someone capable of…"

"He certainly doesn't come off that way," I offered.

"I'm her father. I'm supposed to protect her. I should have seen something, suspected something."

I laid my hand on his arm. "Dom, don't do this to yourself. Tucker will go to prison and Kari will get over him— faster than you can imagine."

Now it was his turn to look me in the eye. "Please don't go alone, Jane. I won't attack him, I'll let you do the talking. I just need to know you're safe."

Dominic Faso, keeping all his loved ones safe. Was I still a loved one of his? He'd claimed so last spring when he'd tried so hard to convince me to remarry him. If nothing else, I was a permanent part of his family, this big extended family that he keeps expanding through divorce and remarriage.

The truth was, I was nervous about seeing Tucker and wouldn't mind backup. Perhaps if Dom had offered nicely instead of being so high-handed about it…

No, it had nothing at all to do with me being stubborn and ungrateful. How can you even think that?

"Well, you can't leave Kari alone here," I said. We both knew she'd bolt to be with Tucker first chance she got.

"I can't see her letting me drop her off at her mom's house." He pulled his phone out of his pocket. "I'll ask Lana to come stay with her."

"HOW'S KARI?" Tucker sat in his parents' den, slumped miserably in an ultramodern red armchair that looked like something out of *The Jetsons.*

Dom and I sat on the matching sofa. The boy's mother had let us into the house and, once she'd determined we weren't there to harass her son or cause trouble, left us alone with him.

"She's fine," I said. "She's worried about you."

He was pale, his eyes red-rimmed. I guessed he hadn't slept well in his jail cell last night. He gave an exhausted shake of the head, closed his eyes briefly. "I messed up."

I glanced at Dom. His sober expression didn't reveal much. I was about to deliver Kari's heartfelt message and skedaddle when Tucker added, "I heard you come in that morning."

"What?" I said.

"I heard you come into the restaurant and call Swing's name. I was still in the kitchen."

I had the absurd urge to grasp Dom's hand. Instead I took a slow, silent breath and said, "What did you do then? Slip out the back?"

He nodded. "I panicked. I should've stayed. It would have been the right thing to do. But now…" He lifted his hands and let them fall.

I didn't ask why he'd killed Swing. He'd thought his girlfriend had been sexually involved with the popular chef. He'd thought Swing had taken advantage of her youthful infatuation. Still, Dom had thought the same thing and he'd only beat up the dastardly seducer. There was a yawning gulf between fisticuffs and plunging a knife into someone's heart.

I wondered if the high-priced lawyer Tucker's folks had hired would have let him openly confess. "What did you tell the police?" I asked. "You know, yesterday after they took you in."

"The truth. I wanted Swing to leave her alone. She had this big crush on him." He shrugged. "Whatever, all the girls do. Did, I mean. He was on TV and everything, right? But then this girl from school, she works at the ice-cream place across from Dewatre, she told me she saw Kari going in there every Saturday morning when it was closed."

"Kari never told you she was meeting Swing?" I asked.

He shook his head. "He was teaching her to cook. I know that now. She wanted to surprise everyone with what she learned." He glanced at Dom. "Her family, me…"

"But you didn't know that then," I prompted.

"I thought they were…" He ran his fingers through his short black hair. "So I went there. To tell him to leave her alone."

"Wasn't it a school day?"

He shrugged. "I faked a stomachache and stayed home."

When he didn't continue, I quietly said, "I'm assuming things got out of hand? With Swing?"

Tucker looked at me. "Huh?"

"Well… what did he say when you confronted him?" I asked.

He scowled, perplexed by the question. "I never had a chance. He was dead when I got there." He flinched. "You think I did it?"

"I… Tucker, I'm just trying to—"

He jumped up. Next to me, I felt Dom tense. "I didn't kill him," Tucker said fiercely. "I never even *thought* about killing him. That's not—" He broke off and stalked away from us. I half expected him to break something, or put his fist through a wall, but he just stood there breathing hard. Finally he turned back to us, looking heartbreakingly vulnerable. "Is that what Kari thinks? That I killed Swing?"

"No," I quickly assured him. "No, she believes you're innocent. She asked me to come here and tell you that. And that she loves you very much."

Dom had promised to let me do the talking, but he spoke up now, his tone calm but firm. "Do not try to contact her, Tucker."

Tucker stared at him, making a conspicuous effort to govern his emotions. Dom never broke eye contact and eventually the youth gave a reluctant nod.

"Tucker." I gestured toward the chair he'd vacated. My tone was gentle. "Tell us what happened that morning."

He moved as if the past twenty-four hours had added fifty years to his body. He sat. "I knew Swing was there on Mondays when the place was closed. I knocked, but he didn't come to the door. I figured if he was in the kitchen he wouldn't hear. I was about to go away, but I tried the door and it was open."

I'd done the same thing a few minutes later, knocking before finding the door unlocked. "What did you do then?" I asked.

"I went through the dining room and knocked on those double doors to the kitchen. Then I felt stupid knocking and just went in. I didn't see him, but when I walked back behind that big horseshoe-shaped, you know…"

"The work station," I supplied.

"Yeah. I saw him on the floor. It was… the blood…" His gaze was directed inward as he recalled the hideous scene.

"Tucker." I leaned forward, urged him to focus on my voice, on me. "They found your fingerprints on the knife."

He swallowed hard. "I tried to pull it out. I didn't think about it, I just… It was, like, automatic, like maybe it wasn't too late and if I could just get the knife out—" His voice cracked. He cleared his throat. "But then I looked at his eyes and I knew."

"Then what?"

"Then I heard you in the dining room. I heard you calling for him. I knew you'd take one look and think I did it. So I ran out the back." He leaned his elbows on his knees and cradled his head. "I should've stayed. I should've called nine-one-one. The cops still would've thought I was guilty, but that's what I should've done."

"DO YOU BELIEVE HIM?" Dom asked as soon as we got into his BMW.

"I don't know," I said. "He seems sincere, but…"

"But he's had a couple of weeks to refine his story."

"Yup," I said. "I'll tell you who else is on my radar, though."

"It wouldn't by any chance be your houseguest?"

I groaned. "You heard about that stupid accusation?"

"Everyone's heard about it." He turned right at the corner and headed toward his house. "That woman, Swing's old business partner…"

"Leonora Romano," I said. "They call her Lee."

"Right. She's spreading it all over, claiming Victor killed his brother—well, *had* him killed—because Swing slept with his wife."

"Ex-wife," I corrected. "And he didn't do it. I mean yes, Swing slept with Emmie, but no, Victor didn't kill him."

Dom glanced at me. "How can you be certain?"

"Dom—"

"The man's living under your roof, Janey. You don't really know anything about him. You might not be worried, but I sure as hell am."

"And I appreciate it, but…" But what? Hadn't a niggling doubt wormed its way into my own mind when Cullen first questioned Victor as a suspect? How well *did* I know him?

Lee had likened him to Ted Bundy, which I'd considered laughable at the time. I thought about all those female fans who'd been obsessed with Bundy, obsessed with a handsome psychopath who'd beaten and strangled a bunch of young women. If Victor looked like Steve Buscemi, would I be so quick to defend a guy who, truth be told, I didn't actually know that well?

"In addition to revenge for the thing with his ex," Dom said, "Lee's also claiming greed as a motive. Swing was worth a fortune and it's all Victor's now."

"Okay, well, Lee has her own reasons for wanting to frame Victor." I told him about the TV show Swing had been offered and which she'd coveted, and her bizarre conviction that Victor had sabotaged her chances with the network. "And how badly did she want that show?" I added. "Badly enough to kill Swing so she could have a crack at it? She already hated him for supposedly tanking her restaurant when they parted ways three years ago."

"I don't know." Dom shook his head. "Does her behavior make sense if she's the murderer? I mean, she's making sure the whole world knows Victor's the killer. She's been quoted in news articles, podcasts, social media, everywhere. Why would she put herself out there that way, invite that kind of public scrutiny, if she's the guilty party? It doesn't make sense, it's not rational."

"You haven't met her, have you?" I said. "Trust me, we're not talking about the most rational individual here. The woman's a piece of work."

"What about the SEAR guy? Tooley," Dom asked. "Our friendly neighborhood firebomber. He has an alibi for the time of the murder. Out of the running, you think?"

I made a face. "Another paragon of mental stability. No, I wouldn't give him a pass quite yet. Try this on for size. Tooley gets one of his adoring disciples to do the deed while he's adding up columns of numbers in his day job, then Tucker comes along and messes up the evidence with his size thirteens and fingerprints."

Dom scooted into the right lane to bypass a left-turn

logjam. "And Tooley did it because…?"

"Same reason you and I almost became the charbroiled special of the day at Dewatre," I said. "Publicity for SEAR."

"That's one devoted animal-rights terrorist. Wonder if he owns a pet." He turned on to the long private drive leading to his mansion.

"I don't think they believe in the whole concept of keeping pets," I said. "For sure you're not supposed to 'own' animals. That's like slavery to them."

"So Sexy Beast is your slave?" Dom smiled for the first time that day. I returned it.

"If so," I said, "he's the laziest, most pampered slave in history."

He parked in front of the house where I'd left my car. Lana, Kari's mother, had parked behind me. Her car was red too, only it was a brand-new Lexus, not a preowned Mazda. But then, she'd divorced Dom after his income had soared and they'd produced two children. The confirmed nonreproducer I'd divorced didn't have a pot to you-know-what in—mainly because he was using it to cook up batches of bean soup and vegetarian chili so he could turn one little Janey's Place café into a certifiable health-food juggernaut.

Dom started to get out of the car. I stopped him with a hand on his arm. I sighed. "I wasn't going to do this."

He settled back in his seat. And waited.

"I was going to let it go," I said, "but it's been two months and I just can't. I just…" I made him meet my eyes. "Why did you get re-engaged so quickly to Bonnie? You wanted to marry me again, Dom. I told you I needed time. That's all I asked for, a little time to think it through. You agreed, but then you didn't wait. You didn't even do me the courtesy of telling me yourself. I learned about it when I saw that ring back on her finger."

He gave a weary sigh. "That was… the wrong way to handle it."

It was my turn to wait. My resentment had been brewing for two long months, and I had no desire to make this easy for him.

"Bonnie wanted us to get back together," he said.

"I know that. So?" As far as I was concerned, Bonnie Hernandez's desires had zip to do with Dom and me, although I could see how he might have viewed it differently back in July. On the one hand, here's this beautiful, smart, not to mention young police detective who wants to renew their engagement, who's saying their breakup was a mistake and she's ready for their happily ever after. On the other hand, there's the woman he divorced seventeen years ago, a divorce he now claims was a mistake, and she's dragging her heels and asking him to wait for her answer.

"You didn't know what you wanted," he said. "You couldn't seem to make up your mind."

I controlled my temper with an effort. "I asked for a few weeks to think about it. You said no problem. Seven days later she's wearing your ring again."

He stared through the windshield for a while, looking at nothing, then turned to me and said, "I'm sorry, Janey. You deserved better."

Tears scalded my eyes. I looked away. He took my hand. I let him.

Finally I said, "I… I was trying to get used to the idea. Of you and me together again. We were so young when we divorced. But still… so much history."

"I know." He brought my hand to his lips and kissed the knuckles.

"I'm not like you," I said. "I don't need a partner all the time. I can live on my own."

"You've done it for a long time," he said.

"I've had relationships."

"None that have lasted. I was so sure—Well, it's too late for all that."

"So sure of what?" I asked. "That you and I needed to be together again?"

He nodded unhappily. His espresso-dark gaze pinned me. "Could it have worked, do you think? Us?"

I was determined not to let one tear fall. I swiped at my eyes. "I think maybe it could have."

He didn't move. I watched his chest rise and fall, slowly. "I blew it, didn't I." It wasn't a question.

"This is… You're right, this is pointless."

"I didn't say that." He reached over and stroked my cheek.

"You said it's too late, and it is."

He hesitated. "Bonnie and I haven't set a date yet."

"For the wedding? So?"

"So…" He shrugged helplessly. "I don't know."

"I hope you're not thinking your engagement isn't official or something just because you haven't set a date. Trust me, to Bonnie it's official." I thought of her perusing those wedding books.

"Be that as it may," he said, "if it's not right, I'm not going through with it."

"When do you plan to decide whether it's right or not?"

He studied my face for long moments. His features softened even as his eyes grew darker still. Like I said, the man can read my mind. He leaned toward me, slowly, his familiar masculine scent making me weak.

Turning away from his kiss took every scrap of mental fortitude I possessed. It had been seventeen years since I'd felt Dom's mouth slide over mine, since I'd felt his arms tighten around me, his hands caress me, yet the memory was as mercilessly vivid as his daughter's tearful hug less than an hour before.

"No, Dom." He belonged to Bonnie. If and when he ended it with her—for good this time—a kiss would be possible between us. A kiss and more.

He sat back. He didn't ask why. He knew. He knew *me*, knew my sense of honor wouldn't permit it, no matter how much I wanted it. For that matter, Dom was no cheater. This almost-kiss was a testament to how conflicted he was, how strongly he felt about me.

He opened the car door, turning back briefly to say, "I'm serious about Victor, Janey. Send him to a hotel. You don't know a damn thing about the guy."

12

Shaken and Stirred

"I'M MIRANDA DANIELS and this is *Ramrod News*, where the truth comes to live free."

"The truth or something," Sophie muttered as she handed me an ice-cold bottle of beer.

Sophie Halperin, a plump, gregarious bundle of energy in her mid-fifties, was the mayor of Crystal Harbor. She was also one of my closest friends. We'd been through a lot together. We were in her homey, old-fashioned den, about to enjoy, if that word could be said to apply, Monday evening's episode of *Ramrod News*. The lofty catchphrase notwithstanding, I always thought of the sensationalist talk show as the place where the truth came to stumble, wheeze, and die an ignoble death.

Victor accepted a beer from his hostess. "Why do I suspect I'll need something stronger before this thing is over?"

Sophie jerked her thumb toward the fully stocked wet bar behind us. "Help yourself." She bestowed brisk scritches on Sexy Beast, who lay curled on my lap. I sat next to Victor on a massive leather sofa, which was adorned with colorful crocheted afghans and needlepoint pillows, the handiwork of Sophie's mother, long in her grave.

And okay, so no one in that room was what you'd call a

devoted *Ramrod News* fan, but this particular episode was required viewing for everyone in town. Hence our little three-humans-and-a-dog viewing party. Before leaving for the day, Sophie's housekeeper, Maria, had whipped up a giant bowl of her locally famous guacamole, along with homemade tortilla chips. I put up with SB's barely audible whining and soulful, gooey-eyed looks while I heaped guac and chips onto my plate, then informed him in the familiar singsong tone, "Not for puppy." It didn't take Kreskin to predict the spectacular results if I let the little guy fill up on this particular delicacy. He settled back down with a resigned snort.

"All right," Sophie grumbled as she settled in an overstuffed leather armchair and reached for a chip, "let's get this over with."

Miranda Daniels was nattering on in her usual bellicose way about the murder case that had transfixed not only the good citizens of little Crystal Harbor, New York, but the nation as well, thanks to the celebrity status of the victim. "Today marks two weeks since beloved chef and TV personality Pierre 'Swing' Dewatre was savagely butchered in the kitchen of his own restaurant," she announced, over silent video snippets of Swing doing a cooking demonstration on a morning news show and escorting a beautiful star at a movie premier.

"The Crystal Harbor Police Department has finally made an arrest. It took them long enough!" she went on, as more video filled the wide TV screen: Tucker Nearing and Romulus Tooley, surrounded by funeral picketers, yelling in each other's faces. "That's the suspect on the right of your screen. His name's Tucker Nearing and he's a junior at Crystal Harbor High School, and get this, the cops found blood-soaked sneakers in his closet—the very sneakers that tracked Swing's blood all over the ghastly murder scene!" This was accompanied by a shot of the exterior of Dewatre garlanded with yellow crime-scene tape.

I cringed inwardly. I'd suggested to Victor that he skip the show, but he refused to be kept in the dark about anything related to his brother's murder. I turned to Sophie, who for many years had worked as a paralegal in Sten Jakobsen's law firm. "Can they give out Tucker's name like that?" I asked. "And show his face? The kid's a minor."

"He's been charged as an adult," she said, "and that's when most news organizations take the gloves off. You're expecting a lot from the jackals at *Ramrod* if you think they'd hold back."

Close-up of Miranda's overly made-up face, her mean little smile. "Wait, it gets better. They found the kid's fingerprints—his *fingerprints*!—on the murder weapon. An open-and-shut case, right? Well, not everyone agrees. Of course, Tucker has an excuse, big surprise. He says he just happened to stroll into the restaurant, which was *closed* at the time, and found Swing lying in a pool of his own blood, and then he tried to save him—yeah, that's right, *save* him—by pulling out the knife." Miranda let her exaggerated smirk say what she thought of that bizarre scenario. "Good luck with that one, Tucker. Let's see what our panel has to say."

The camera zoomed out to reveal four other individuals sitting in the studio with Miranda, two on either side of her at a curved rectangular table crafted of some kind of thick, frosted glass with artfully jagged edges, by all appearances salvaged from the explosion of Planet Krypton. The *Ramrod News* studio is located in midtown Manhattan, just a hop, skip, and hour and a half from Crystal Harbor, making it a relatively simple task to assemble a panel of "knowledgeable" locals eager to spew their opinions on the subject of whodunit.

Sophie took one look at the show's guests and, even though she'd known what to expect, moaned, "Oy." She took a healthy slug of beer.

Miranda gestured to her right. "He's the spokesman for The Society for Endangered Animal Rights and had many dealings with Swing in that capacity. Romulus Tooley, welcome back to the show."

Tooley offered a lazy wave. His graying blond hair had been buzzed down to a crew cut, a style decision that might have had something to do with the fact that he'd singed the heck out of it during his failed attempt to incinerate Dewatre.

Miranda indicated the woman sitting to his right. "She's Swing's former business partner, Lenore Romano, and… a chef? Is that right, Lenore? You're a chef?"

Lee's bloodless smile froze in place. The woman who aspired to be a household name said, "It's Leonora and yes, I'm a chef."

"Well, that's great. And you've written a cookbook." Miranda reached under the table, displayed the book for about half a second, blurted, "*Lenore's Kitchen*, filled with delicious recipes," and moved on to the guest on her left. "We're happy to welcome Chloe Sleeper, Swing's agent, back to the show."

"Thank you, Miranda," Chloe said. "I'm glad to be back."

I happened to know that in fact Chloe had resisted a return to the *Ramrod News* studio. Her first appearance had apparently been more than enough for one lifetime, but Miranda had turned on the charm and managed to convince her that her input was crucial.

Miranda nodded toward the guest sitting to Chloe's left.

"She's Nina Wallace, a close friend of Swing's and a lifelong resident of Crystal Harbor—the current mayor, in fact."

Sophie and I jerked upright in unison. *"What?"*

"Well, not quite yet," Nina tittered. "The election isn't until March, but I'm confident I can unseat the current mayor." An upraised eyebrow hinted that the current mayor was not someone who merited reelection.

I won't repeat Sophie's next words. Suffice it to say Victor probably learned some interesting new Anglo Saxon vocabulary along with a couple of choice New York Yiddishisms.

I said, "Since when is Nina a close friend of Swing's? Did they even know each other?"

"In passing maybe." Sophie slumped back in her chair, scowling darkly at the screen. Sexy Beast, sensing a pack member in need—a member of his extended pack, anyway— hopped off my lap and onto hers. Absently she stroked him, and the unconditional doggie love appeared to do the trick. She began to visibly relax.

Nina looked adorable as always, elegant and stylish in a designer maternity dress, her dark hair cut short and feathery around her face.

"Well, good luck in the election, Ms. Almost Mayor!" Miranda said. "Sounds like they could use some fresh blood running the show there in Crystal Harbor." She turned to Tooley. "So what do you think, Romulus? Did Tucker do it?"

"He sure did," Tooley said.

I hollered at the TV, "Or here's a wild thought, just thinking outside the box here, Rom, maybe *you* did it."

"Tucker is a hero," Tooley continued, "a young man driven by passion for what he believes in. The animals. SEAR."

"You've got the passion part right," Miranda said, "but it

had nothing to do with endangered animals. It was about sex. Swing was messing around with Tucker's girlfriend."

I leaned forward and yelled, "No, he wasn't!" Victor reached around my shoulder and pulled me back. And left his arm there. Which made me kind of, you know, forget what I'd been yelling about.

Chloe flinched at the reference to her fiancé getting frisky with a local teen. For her sake, I was glad no one in that studio knew of her engagement to Swing, which she'd kept strictly private.

Miranda was on a roll. "It's the same reason the girl's dad beat the tar out of Swing a couple of days before the murder. Although I have to say, if both your boyfriend and your dad have to work so hard to defend your honor, maybe there's just not that much there to defend, you know what I mean?"

Will you be shocked if I tell you that Sophie had a few ripe words for that?

Victor shook his head. "The woman is shameless. Why do so many people watch this show?"

I shrugged. "Because the woman is shameless."

Sophie tossed her hand at the screen. "Tooley's full of it. Tucker, a passionate supporter of SEAR? They just showed video of the kid giving him hell."

Miranda must have heard her. "I was there when you guys picketed Swing's funeral reception, Romulus. I heard Tucker call you a shameless, publicity-hogging terrorist. And if he *is* the killer, he tried to *blame* it on you guys, remember? It was written right there on the floor!" She mimed writing in midair. "S-E-A-R!"

"Which only proves," Tooley said, "that he identifies with our organization in his heart even if he doesn't feel free to acknowledge it publicly."

"This nonsense is getting old," Victor groaned, "about Pierre and the animals. When will it stop?"

"Sooner than you might think," I said, with a mysterious little smile. "Stay tuned." I'd already informed Victor and Sophie that Lee Romano had instigated the rumor out of spite.

"Getting back to Tucker's girlfriend," Miranda said, "at first the cops thought that her dad, Dominic Faso, killed Swing. And why? Only because he did what any concerned father would do when his daughter's being taken advantage of by an older man who should know better. Rearrange his face."

Victor muttered something in French.

"Now, don't get me wrong," she continued, "we all loved Swing. But maybe that was part of the problem. He was like a kid in a candy shop." She mimed choosing from an assortment. "I'll have the blonde, the redhead, and oh, how about that juicy-looking brunette?"

I could hardly bear to look at Chloe, who managed to school her features but could do nothing about the angry flush scalding her face.

"We invited Mr. Faso on this panel, but he *declined*." Miranda said this in a way that implied ulterior motives. So what did that make Dom, then? A red-blooded American father who'd taken manly action to protect his unworthy hussy of a daughter, or a murder suspect with something to hide? She couldn't have it both ways. Or maybe she could. This was Miranda Daniels, after all, and *Ramrod News*. The network powers that be weren't about to quibble over a few mixed messages as long as the ratings remained in the stratosphere.

"Show of hands," I said. "How many of us here *declined* to be part of this farce?"

We all raised our hands. Yep, all three of us had received phone calls, first from a producer, then from Miranda herself, urging us to appear on the show and weigh in on the case. They even offered to send a car.

"What's that, SB?" I said, and watched his little head snap up at the sound of his name. Or rather, his nickname. My dog's smart, he answers to both. "No call from the network for you?"

Which was kind of unfair considering SB had in fact been the first to detect the presence of a corpse at the restaurant. *Ramrod News* thought that distinction belonged to me, which is why they'd wanted me on the panel.

Miranda said, "So, Romulus. You're out on bail, right?"

The change of subject appeared to catch him off guard. "So?"

"So you mind telling us what you were arrested for?"

I shouted, "Yeah, tell us, Rom, tell us all about it!" Victor's arm was still around my shoulders and he pulled me a little closer. I tried to think of what else I could yell at the TV.

"It was an act of defiance," Tooley said, "a political act on behalf of all of Swing's nonhuman victims, all those endangered animals he butchered and cooked over the years."

Sophie poked at an incisor. "'Scuse me, that darn gorilla meat always gets stuck between my teeth."

Onscreen, Tooley's self-righteous face was replaced with shaky amateur video, obviously taken by a bystander, showing him shrieking and writhing on the street outside Dewatre in a frantic effort to extinguish his flaming hair and jacket. And there, right on schedule, was Cheyenne O'Rourke abusing the heck out of him with those mile-high platform sneakers.

"Guess it didn't go quite the way you planned," Miranda

said, with that malignant little grin that never failed to raise the hair on my nape.

Tooley tried to salvage his pride. "It brought attention to our cause, and that's the important thing."

"Who's going to be spokesman for SEAR when you're behind bars for first-degree arson?" she asked. "There were *people* in the building you set on fire!"

"I didn't know that at the time," he huffed.

"Would it have stopped you if you had?"

He hesitated an instant too long. Before he could compose a response, Miranda said, "We have someone on the line who might offer a different take on your 'act of defiance.' Brett Griffith, thanks for joining us by phone."

I recognized the name. Griffith was one of the mental giants who'd helped Tooley firebomb Dewatre. Specifically, it was Griffith, wearing a rhino mask, who'd tossed the brick through the window. Tooley looked surly as a man's nasal voice said, "Yeah, hi, I love your show, Miranda. Never miss an episode. Keep up the good work."

"Thanks, Brett. Your pal Romulus here told the cops it was your idea to set fire to Dewatre. True?"

Most of Brett's response was bleeped. *Ramrod News* aired live, but clearly there was a profanity delay of a few seconds to allow for censoring. The truth might come to live free on the show, but naughty words got the snuff treatment.

"I think our audience at home got the gist of that," she snickered, "but try to express yourself in words we're allowed to air."

Tooley shouted, "Why are you listening to this loser? I don't appreciate being ambushed—"

"Yeah," Griffith hollered back, "and I don't appreciate

ending up arrested after you tell me and Billy it's gonna be a quick job with no risk. I'm glad you set yourself on fire, you stupid—" Cue the bleeps.

"Brett, I have to ask you," Miranda said, "since you're part of SEAR, did you have anything to do with Swing's murder?"

"Nah," he said, "that was another of Rom's brilliant ideas. I didn't want anything to do with it."

"*Whoa!*" Sophie straightened, causing SB to leap off her lap in alarm. "Did he just say what I think he said?"

I sat dumbfounded, staring at the screen. "I think so," I managed. I looked at Victor, who slowly leaned forward, a look of grim concentration on his handsome face.

"*That's a lie!*" Tooley was half out of his seat. "You're a lying sack of—" It was bleepity-bleep city for a while as the two devoted animal lovers screamed obscenities at each other.

"That's enough, guys!" Miranda barked. "Let's keep this discussion civil." Which should have been funny, Miranda Daniels demanding civility, but I wasn't in a laughing mood at the moment.

"Rom was all for taking out Swing," Griffith said. "He told everyone the guy was an animal murderer and needed killing."

"By 'everyone,'" Miranda said, "do you mean members of SEAR?"

"Yeah. One of our guys did it for sure," Brett said, "'cause Rom told us to."

"I can't believe you took all that seriously," Tooley cried. "It was hyperbole!"

Brett remained silent, probably because he had no idea what "hyperbole" meant.

Suddenly Leonora Romano broke in. "It wasn't Tucker *or* this idiot!" She flung her hand at Tooley, sitting to her left.

"Swing was murdered in cold blood by his brother, Victor Dewatre."

"Here we go," Sophie grumbled. Victor rose and headed for the wet bar. "Bring me a Scotch," she said.

Miranda started to interrupt, but Lee raised her voice, talking over her. "Swing was terrified of his brother. I know! We worked closely in my restaurant for eight years. He used to tell me how unstable Victor was, how scared he was of what he might do."

"Lenore—" Miranda started.

"He told me more than once, 'If anything happens to me, make sure they know it was Victor,'" Lee continued. "I have no intention of failing Swing. He deserves for his killer to be brought to justice."

Miranda tried to regain control of the discussion. "Lenore—"

"It's *Leonora!*" Lee shouted. "Not Lenore! For God's sake, is that so difficult to remember? Victor Dewatre hired a hit man to kill his brother while he stayed home in Paris, keeping his hands clean. And why?" She was staring right into the camera now, speaking directly to the viewers at home. "Revenge! Swing slept with his ex-wife, and his pride couldn't take it. I was there when Victor barged into my restaurant kitchen and threatened his brother's life. Also, and this is no small thing, Swing was a wealthy man and Victor was his sole heir. Is that enough motive for you?"

Lee paused for breath and Miranda jumped right in. "This is the tale you've been spreading all over, but if it's true, why are Tucker's footprints the only ones at the crime scene? His fingerprints too."

Lee gave the other woman a look of withering contempt.

"You can't figure that one out for yourself? It's because Tucker's story is true. He came upon the murder scene and inadvertently erased whatever evidence Victor's hit man left behind."

Victor handed Sophie her drink and resumed his seat next to me. He took a sip of whiskey. "Do you think Lee believes this?"

"No," I said. "She's still trying to punish you for supposedly nixing her chances with the Food Network."

"Plus it's a publicity grab," Sophie said. "She has a lot invested in her success, and she sees it all going down the tubes. Doesn't care who she takes down with her."

"Tooley's doing essentially the same thing," I said. "Using Tucker to boost publicity for SEAR." Not that I believed in Tucker's innocence, much as I wanted to. The physical evidence against him was hard to refute.

Miranda was talking about Lee's very public campaign to hold Victor responsible for his brother's death. Now she addressed the viewers. "Do you know what murder groupies are? They're women who develop a sexual obsession with a murderer. Ted Bundy had his share of groupies. So did Richard Ramirez, the so-called Night Stalker. Dahmer, Gacy, they all had these sick, pathetic females sending them letters, sending them money, wanting to marry them. You just want to shake these broads and yell, 'Get a life!'"

Another Bundy reference. I had a bad feeling about where Miranda was going with this.

"Leonora has made sure the whole world considers Victor a suspect," she went on, "so guess who now has not one but *two* Facebook fan pages! Here's a hint—it's not Leonora."

My head swiveled toward Victor as his swiveled toward

me. We gaped at each other in disbelief. Sophie cackled. Sexy Beast, once more ensconced on my lap, emitted what sounded like a snort of amusement.

"One of the fan pages," Miranda said, "presents Swing's brother as this drop-dead-gorgeous hunk with a sexy accent who's totally innocent and totally hot. The other page presents him as this drop-dead-gorgeous hunk with a sexy accent who's totally *guilty* and—spoiler alert!—totally hot. Either way, he needs the love and understanding of a good woman, poor thing."

Lee did not appear pleased by this turn of affairs. "You're right about one thing, Miranda—those women are pathetic. I only wish the police would take my allegations as seriously. There's a dangerous killer on the loose, living right in Crystal Harbor, and no one but me seems to care."

"Victor isn't the only one who had a run-in with Swing," Miranda said. "You two had a serious falling out, am I right?"

Lee was ready for this. "Oh please, that's all ancient history. Swing and I were both strong businesspeople with strong personalities. There was a little unpleasantness when we parted ways, but it was quickly forgotten."

"'A little unpleasantness'?" Miranda mocked. "More like World War Three, from what I've heard. You blamed him for destroying your precious restaurant. We just heard you claim Victor was motivated by revenge. The same could be said of you, couldn't it?" Without giving Lee a chance to respond, she added, "Still, something good came of all that free time you were left with. We're talking a serious transformation. Let's show the folks at home."

Miranda's smirking face was replaced by a pair of images on a split screen: on the left, a homely, obese, gray-haired woman wearing a tentlike chef's jacket and thick eyeglasses; on the right, the glamour shot from Lee's book jacket, showing her in all her sleek, blond, surgically enhanced glory.

Sophie said, "Wow. I didn't know medical science had advanced that far."

I cringed. Was I really feeling sorry for Leonora Romano? Yes. No one deserved this brand of public humiliation. But then, humiliation was Miranda's specialty. I'd been on the receiving end of it myself not too long before.

Just when I expected Lee to shrink into herself and admit that the bigger bitch had won, she gave an airy laugh and said, "Isn't it amazing? None of my friends recognized me! Thank goodness for talented plastic surgeons, that's all I can say."

I didn't buy her act for a moment. Her pride had to be crushed, but she refused to show it. I couldn't help feeling a grudging admiration.

Miranda seemed momentarily at a loss. She covered it by bringing Nina into the conversation. "As a Crystal Harbor insider, Nina, who do you think murdered your friend Swing? Was it Tucker?"

"I've known Tucker Nearing his entire life," Nina said. "I know the evidence is compelling, but I simply can't believe he's capable of such a horrific crime. Then again, young people nowadays, you never know what they're getting into, drugs and what-all."

I yelled, "Why do you have to bring drugs into it, Nina? Who said anything about drugs?"

Victor tucked me a little closer against him. Did he even realize he was doing it? And was it more romantic if he did realize it or didn't? I couldn't decide.

"I have two teenage daughters of my own," Nina

continued. "I know firsthand how challenging it is to keep them focused on healthy choices and wholesome values."

Miranda smiled. "With another on the way, I see."

"Another girl." Nina caressed her gently mounded belly. "Laura's due around Thanksgiving."

I wondered how deeply Miranda had dug into this particular guest's past. Deeply enough to have discovered that the baby Nina carried wasn't fathered by her husband? I mean, speaking of wholesome values and all. If Miranda knew that little Laura had been sired by a certain notorious individual from Crystal Harbor's recent past, she wouldn't hesitate to turn it into fodder for the *Ramrod News* meat grinder. I dreaded the possibility. It wasn't Nina I was thinking of, but her baby. No child deserved to come into the world under a stink-bomb cloud like that.

"I do want to make an important point," Nina said, "about my dear friend Swing and the irresponsible rumors that surrounded him."

"You mean about all the women he boffed?" Miranda said.

"Um, no, I'm talking about the endangered species," Nina said. "The stories about him cooking and serving exotic animals. None of that is true."

Tooley came back to life. "Yes it is! The man was a speciesist villain and got what was coming to him." He shot his fist at the camera. "Tucker, your brothers and sisters in the fight honor you."

Ever the lady, Nina maintained her composure. "That ridiculous rumor was cooked up by Leonora Romano after her restaurant went under. She was just trying to get back at Swing."

Lee wasn't expecting this, I could tell. Nevertheless, she

held her own. "Nonsense, I got wind of those allegations when everyone else did. Where on earth did you get the absurd idea I had anything to do with them?"

"Since you ask, I'll tell you," Nina said sweetly. "I got the 'absurd idea' from the media folks you used to get the word out three years ago. There was a certain restaurant reviewer for a slick food magazine, remember him? I believe he owed you a favor, something to do with a deeply discounted rehearsal dinner when his son got married. And then there's the influential food blogger who just happens to be an old sorority sister of yours. You were really sweet to introduce her to all the major players when she was just starting out."

The sangfroid so recently on display began to desert Lee. She stared unblinking at Nina, a mottled flush suffusing her throat.

"And let's not forget your nephew the entertainment reporter," Nina said, "the one you helped put through college and who's on radio and TV all the time now."

"I've been in the restaurant business a long time," Lee blustered. "I know a lot of people. So what? You're grasping at straws."

"I only mentioned the ones who've actually *admitted* to dropping hints about Swing at your request," Nina said.

Lee was, for once, speechless. Meanwhile Tooley sat silent and deflated, a man with much on his mind.

Victor was suddenly animated. "Is all this true? How does she know these things?"

"Because I fed Nina the information," I said, "once I learned she'd be on the show. She was happy to oblige. My only problem now, speaking of favors…" I made a face.

Sophie finished for me. "Is that now you owe *her* one." She gave a dramatic shudder.

Victor said, "But how did *you* find out about the blogger and the nephew and all that?"

"I called Ben Ralston," I said. "In less than an hour he came back with all these names, Lee's partners in rumormongering. Didn't even charge me." The PI had thought it great fun to investigate the origins of the rumor and to help prove that Swing had been no... how had Tooley put it?... speciesist villain.

Miranda was asking Nina how she knew all this. Nina responded that she wasn't at liberty to reveal her sources. Miranda turned to Lee. "How about it, Leonora? Is Nina telling the truth? Did you deliberately start that rumor?"

It would have been useless for Lee to persist in her denials. Without a doubt, millions of viewers, armed with smart phones and tablets, already had identified her accomplices.

As I watched, Lee straightened in her seat. Where moments earlier she'd looked trapped, all I saw now was self-righteous determination. She said, "You're not looking at some spineless doormat who takes all the crap the world has to offer and then whines, please, sir, I want some more! The restaurant industry—every industry, in fact—is filled with women who put their needs last because that's the way they were raised or because they don't have the *cojones* to stand up for themselves or, God help them, because they're afraid of upstaging their man!"

Miranda said, "I asked whether you—"

"I'm not finished!" Lee snapped in an imperious tone that made Sexy Beast come to attention with the obedient yip he reserved for those at the very top of the pack. "And don't even *think* about cutting my mic!" Again she spoke directly into the

camera, addressing the viewers glued to their screens. "No progress will be made until women become their own advocates, their own heroes. You're never going to get that wonderful career you want, or be paid what you're worth, or treated with the respect you deserve if you don't demand it and yes, when necessary, step on a few toes." In a sneering tone she added, "If that's too *hard* or makes you *unpopular*, well, boo-hoo, go back home and keep squirting out babies." Her stony gaze landed on the prettily pregnant Nina, who gaped in outrage.

"Well, whaddaya know," Sophie said, "someone's finally out-Miranda'd Miranda."

I said, "That'll be the last time Lee's invited on the show."

Miranda hesitated, clearly debating the wisdom of pressing Lee for an answer to her question, which had not been addressed except in the most roundabout way. She chose instead to move on to the one guest who had yet to be heard from.

"Chloe, you've been very patient," Miranda said. "Let me ask you, as someone who knew Swing better than most—was he afraid of his brother?"

"Absolutely not," Chloe said. "He never expressed anything but love and affection for Victor. I said it last time I was on this show and I'll say it again. If Swing wasn't murdered by Romulus Tooley himself, then the killer was a member of SEAR who took his instructions from Tooley. Now that the world knows what I've never doubted—that that hideous rumor had no basis in fact—it makes Swing's death even more—" She choked up for a moment, her eyes glistening. "It makes it even more pointless. He was killed by fanatics who believed a preposterous lie without bothering to verify it."

"When I said you knew Swing better than most," Miranda told Chloe, "I wasn't referring to the fact that you were his agent. Isn't it true you two were engaged to be married?"

Chloe froze. Lee Romano looked as surprised as the other guests.

I shivered. "Creeps me out when Miranda grins like that."

Sophie said, "Makes me want to reach for the shark repellant. So Chloe and Swing were getting hitched?"

Victor turned to me. "I thought you and I were the only ones who knew. That's what she told us, yes?"

"The only ones besides Cullen," I said. We exchanged a disgusted look. "Case closed."

"What?" Sophie said. "Chloe didn't even tell her family about the engagement? Her closest friends?"

"Apparently not," I said. "She asked us to keep quiet about it, said she didn't want the attention." Now I knew why Miranda had worked so hard to convince Chloe to come on the show. She had a nice juicy bombshell to drop.

Onscreen, Chloe was groping for a response. "I—I—" she stammered. "That's—How did you find that out?"

Instead of answering, Miranda said, "You had to know Swing was hooking up with all sorts of women, Chloe. You can't be *that* naïve. Did you two have some kind of *understanding*? Were you sleeping with other men? Were you into threesomes? Partner swapping?"

"Fair warning," I told Sophie. "I'm about to throw something big and heavy at your expensive television."

Sophie lifted the handmade pottery bowl full of guacamole and offered it to me. "Here. Miranda looks good in green."

"It wasn't..." Chloe said. "That's... That's degrading. How can you say something like that about Swing? Our love was pure, it was perfect."

"Chloe, Chloe…" I pleaded, "stop talking! You're walking right into it."

"I know how *I'd* feel if my man were slipping around on me all the time," Miranda said. "With actresses, underwear models…" Just in case the dimmer members of the viewing audience failed to grasp her meaning, she added, "Didn't you ever just want to…" She mimed strangulation.

Chloe fought back tears. "You don't know anything about him. About us. I'm not… I refuse to talk about this anymore."

Miranda had now succeeded in establishing three of her four guests as suspects in Swing's murder. I wouldn't have been surprised to see her go after Nina next. It was a sad day for law enforcement when Miranda Daniels's bellicose brand of investigative journalism managed to show up a police investigation.

"Fortunately," Miranda said, "we have someone on the line who *isn't* afraid to talk. For reasons that will become clear, he has requested anonymity. Thank you for joining us, sir. You're on the air."

"Thank you, Miranda," the voice said. "The name is Doe. John Doe."

Sophie said, "Since when does Sean Connery call in to *Ramrod News*?"

"I do not believe this," I muttered. "That's Martin."

"Martin McAuliffe?" Sophie chuckled and reached for her Scotch. "Well, of course it is."

Miranda said, "You have information about the police investigation, isn't that right, um, John?"

"About the detective *in charge* of the investigation," Martin said. "Paul Cullen, aka Paulie the Perv. That's how he's known by certain unfortunate members of the community he's supposed to be serving."

As Martin spoke in his spot-on Connery burr, I heard background noise: multiple voices, the clink of glassware, muted bluegrass music. "He's calling from Murray's Pub!" I said. "He's on the bar phone!"

"Paulie the *Perv?*" Miranda snickered. "What does a cop have to do to earn a nickname like that?"

"He has to abuse his position as a law-enforcement officer to sexually harass females suspected of minor crimes such as traffic violations. This has been going on since he was a patrolman."

"If that's true," Miranda said, "why has it been allowed to continue? Don't these women file complaints?"

"It is my understanding," Martin said, "that Cullen threatened retaliation if any of his victims came forward. A few brave women did, though, over the years. Those complaints were swept under the rug by Cullen's fishing buddy, Chief George Larsen."

"Larsen," Sophie growled. "That guy's always been a thorn in my side."

I asked, "Doesn't the mayor appoint the police chief?"

She nodded. "Larsen had been chief for about fifteen years before I was elected. Never did anything egregious enough to get fired, nothing I found out about, anyway. That might be about to change."

Victor said, "How long has Martin known about this?"

"Not long, I'm guessing," I said, "or we'd have heard about it before now."

"If your allegations are true," Miranda said, "then this Detective Cullen doesn't sound like someone I'd want investigating a high-profile murder."

"My thinking precisely," Martin said. I heard an unmistakable metallic racket and pictured him cradling the phone with his shoulder while wielding a martini shaker. Yeah, that's right, shaken, not stirred. "But you know what they say," he added, "a fish rots from the head down. I'd take a hard look at Chief Larsen, too."

13

#YouSlayMeVictor

"THIS IS SO NICE," Chloe said. "I don't think I've had anyone over since I moved here. Well, except for Swing, of course."

"Really? No one?" I set my white pastry box on her kitchen counter. It was a nondescript kitchen in a nondescript house, a 1970s cookie-cutter ranch on the not-so-swanky outskirts of Crystal Harbor.

She seemed embarrassed. "Well, I don't have any family and I haven't met too many of my neighbors yet. I just took the place a couple of months ago. It's a rental." She started measuring grounds into a French-press coffeemaker. "Once we were engaged, Swing wanted me to live closer to him."

I was kind of surprised she hadn't moved into his fancy house in the heart of the gold-plated section of town until I recalled that the couple had made a conscious effort to keep their relationship under wraps for the sake of Swing's career-boosting playboy image.

"I wasn't sure what you'd like," I said, "so I got an assortment." I lifted the lid of the box, adorned with Patisserie Susanne's gold-and-white label, to reveal a Napoleon, a chocolate éclair, opera cake, and a pair of chocolate croissants.

Yes, two of those, because it's my all-time favorite dessert and if I'd gotten just one and Chloe had made a grab for it, I'd have had to hurt her.

Chloe oohed and ahhed, made the obligatory references to empty calories and aren't we naughty, and pulled a couple of dessert plates from a cabinet. I had a reason for this visit, but now that I was there, I didn't know quite what to say. I wanted to let her know she wasn't alone and that others were thinking of her, stated a tad more diplomatically than: *I'm sorry your man was a cheating sack of dog poo and that Miranda Daniels chose to make your humiliation public.*

"How do you take your coffee?" she asked.

"Oh, just black, thanks."

Once she'd poured, we took our plates and cups into the potpourri-scented living room. I sat on a love seat upholstered in taupe velour, she on the matching sofa. A framed photograph sat on the lamp table next to me: Swing and Chloe standing close, smiling into the camera. It appeared to have been taken at some affair. They were in formal dress and held wineglasses. Swing looked ridiculously handsome in white tie with his arm around his lady.

The table had a lower shelf. I spied a stack of bridal magazines and couldn't help thinking that if my fiancé had been murdered, one of the first things I'd do is toss out such a painful reminder of the loss. However, if there's one thing I'd learned in my years as the one and only Death Diva, it's that people deal with grief in their own way.

"Okay," I said, "this has been bothering me. I hope you don't think I'm the one who spilled the beans to Miranda. About, you know, your engagement. It wasn't Victor either."

Chloe shook her head as if still coming to terms with the

way she'd been ambushed. "I should have known better than to let her talk me into going back on that horrible show."

"It's what she does," I said. "Anything for ratings."

"Well, never again," she said. "And don't worry, I know you two had nothing to do with it. Now that we know what sort of person Detective Cullen is, I think we can be pretty certain who blabbed."

"I don't think there can be any doubt." I pushed croissant crumbs around my plate. "Listen, I know how difficult it must be for you now, Chloe, with everyone knowing about your fiancé's, um…" *infidelity? cheating? shameless alley-catting?* "About his continuing to see other women."

She stiffened. Spots of color stained her cheeks. "People think they know Swing, even people who never met him. That's how it is with celebrities. Well, I'll tell you, no one knew him like I did. He wasn't… He wasn't… He was a good man. He loved me."

I leaned forward and reached for her hand, but drew back when she failed to respond. "I know he did," I said. "And I know he was a good man. I'm… I didn't express myself very well. What I'm trying to say is, I know you're hurting and I just… I'm here if you ever want to talk. Or maybe kick back a little, go for a walk, a drink at Murray's, whatever."

She avoided my eyes while she digested this, while she struggled to rein in her emotions. "Thank you," she said at last.

I sensed she had no intention of taking me up on my offer. I was glad I'd made it, anyway. "So, um, getting back to Cullen and that caller's allegations. The police department is conducting an internal investigation."

Chloe frowned. "But didn't the guy say Chief Larsen quashed the women's complaints? How can there be a fair probe with him in charge?"

"I have to agree with you there. I'm sure it's why Cullen hasn't been put on administrative leave and is still in charge of Swing's murder investigation." I didn't let her in on the identity of the anonymous caller. Sophie, Victor, and I were the only ones who knew, assuming none of the patrons at Murray's that night noticed their bartender talking funny on the phone. If word got around that he was the one who'd made that call, Martin would be subject to unwanted police attention. Or I should say, he'd be subject to more unwanted police attention than usual.

Turns out the padre had heard the occasional whisper about Paulie the Perv and decided now would be an auspicious time to dig a little deeper. What he'd found out last weekend had convinced him the nickname had been earned. And with Larsen covering for his fishing pal, Martin had concluded that a call to *Ramrod News* was in order. As much as I hated to agree that the smarmy talk show was good for anything, it certainly had shone a spotlight on the problem, forcing Larsen to at least put on a show of looking into the women's complaints.

Chloe set down her cup. "How can Swing's murder ever be solved by such a corrupt police department?"

"The whole department isn't corrupt." I lifted my cup, thinking of Bonnie Hernandez. Not my bestest gal-pal perhaps, but I'd bet serious bucks she's a clean cop. "The mayor's aware of the situation, so I'm hoping for a positive outcome. Oh!" I looked down at my pale-blue shirt, now sporting a coffee stain.

"You'd better take care of that before it sets." She pointed to the hallway. "There's a bathroom right through there on your left."

The john I found myself in was as boring and old-fashioned as the rest of the house. Green fixtures and tiles. Fake-wood paneling. I saturated a corner of a pink hand towel and dabbed at the spot on my shirt. It was a microfiber shirt, whatever that was, which meant I couldn't use bleach, right? If I didn't manage to get the stain out, this shirt would be added to my ever-growing pile of painting clothes. Ask me when I last painted a room, go ahead. I think it was the year before never.

Maybe Chloe had one of those handy little get-the-stain-out pens. I opened the medicine cabinet to check. It certainly wasn't because I'm one of those nosy guests who like to paw through other people's personal stuff.

Okay, I can hear you when you snort like that, so just knock it off.

Unlike me, Chloe kept her things neat and organized: deodorant, moisturizer, and so forth arranged just so. The part I could identify with was her preference for cheap drugstore brands. In that respect I could have been sneaking a peek at my own medicine cabinet—until I got to the shelf that had been set aside for men's deodorant, shaving cream, aftershave, hair pomade, a razor, nail clippers, and comb. Here were the snooty foreign brands advertised in snooty magazines for men who could afford to shell out forty bucks for a little tube of cream destined to be scraped off the chin of a multimillionaire celebrity chef.

I lifted a small prescription bottle containing a common sleeping aid, according to the label, on which was typed the patient's name: Pierre Dewatre. I'd already noticed the two toothbrushes in the ceramic holder and a man's burgundy silk bathrobe hanging on the back of the door. I assumed she'd kept a few items at his place, too. Just because they lived separately didn't mean there weren't sleepovers, although I couldn't picture Swing cooking in Chloe's sad little kitchen with the plastic-handled knife set I'd spied and the electric stove. Don't serious cooks prefer gas?

Back in the living room, I resumed my seat as Chloe refilled our cups and placed more pastries on our plates, followed by more of that we're-going-to-hell and I'm-going-to-pay-for-this talk. I mean really, why can't women ever just enjoy their darn food without making it sound like the moral equivalent of stomping baby ducks?

She forked up a bite of Napoleon. "By the way, I dumped Lee as a client."

"Now, there's a shock."

"I did it in the green room," she said, "right after the show. She actually seemed surprised."

"After essentially admitting she tried to ruin the man you loved by starting that awful rumor?" I said.

"And now she's going after Victor," Chloe said. "She's a very vindictive woman."

"You think?" I bit into my second chocolate croissant and had to restrain a carnal moan. Yeah, that's right, I *really* like these things. "Did you know Victor's been getting death threats?"

Her eyes bulged. "That's terrible! Because of Lee's accusation?"

I nodded. "From those nutty SEAR people, for starters."

"Wait, I thought they were happy that Swing was dead. Didn't Tooley call Tucker a hero?"

"That was before Swing was publicly cleared of that endangered-species nonsense," I said. "It embarrassed the whole organization. I mean, they lavished a lot of well-publicized venom on him over the past few years. And now here's Victor, who supposedly did in his brother and then blamed it on SEAR. They're not amused."

"But it was Lee who started the rumor that ended up making them look foolish," she said. "So why aren't they going after her?"

"My guess? They're scared of her. You saw her performance on *Ramrod*. I mean, you were sitting right there, for heaven's sake. She had the public hanging on her every word. If that fierce lady decided to go head to head with SEAR?"

"I get your point."

"But it's other people too, threatening Victor," I said. "All because Lee wanted to punish him for supposedly ruining her chance of getting that show."

"Right." Chloe's tone was arid. "It couldn't possibly have been her own fault. But Victor has the groupies, too, right? The ones Miranda mentioned."

I grimaced. "You see them around town, anywhere there's been a Victor sighting in the past—the pub, Janey's Place, the Harbor Room restaurant, even the dog park. But the worst is the women who show up at the house."

"Oh no," she said.

"Oh yes. I chased a few of them away, but you get these really determined ones who sneak around the house, spying in the windows. One even threw rocks at my bedroom window in the middle of the night."

"*Your* window?" she said.

"Must've thought it was Victor's. I'm not talking gravel here. These were *rock* rocks."

"That's scary," Chloe said. "Someone that obsessed, you

don't know what she's capable of."

"No kidding. 'Groupies' is too benign a term for these women. As far as I'm concerned, it's straight-up stalking. I called the police and now Howie Werker's handling it." At her puzzled look, I said, "He's a Crystal Harbor cop, a sergeant. And a friend of mine—nice guy. Howie's got patrol cars swinging by all the time. Now, when the loonies start sniffing around, I just call Howie and either he comes himself or he sends someone."

"Well, that's good," she said, "but I'm so sorry he has to go through that. You too."

"Thanks. He can't even go to the office anymore," I said. "You know he's been working at his firm's SoHo branch, right? Well, on Tuesday he was recognized at the station and the next day a whole bunch of women—teenage girls, really—swarmed his train car. They were all over him."

"What did the conductors do?" she asked.

"Stood there laughing. And taking pictures, natch. When the train finally stopped at Penn Station, he rode it right back to Crystal Harbor. Now he's working from home. No more commuting for Hashtag Swing'sSexyBro."

"I feel terrible for Victor," Chloe said, "having to rearrange his life like that, and after all he's been through. The idea of all these besotted females burning up Facebook and Twitter and Instagram and who knows what-all with posts about the poor guy. It's just too absurd."

"Hashtag VictorSighting," I said. "Have you seen that one? Hashtag TeamVicInnocent."

"I'm guessing there's also a Hashtag TeamVicGuilty."

"But of course," I said. "Oh, check this out. They started sexting him. Sending him naked pictures and pornographic messages."

Her jaw unhinged. "How on earth did they get his phone number?"

"Seems one of the groupies, a particularly resourceful one, phoned the Crystal Harbor Police Department and persuaded the dispatcher to share."

"Wait a minute," she said, "what kind of police dispatcher would release the phone number of a victim's family member to a random caller?"

"A drunk dispatcher," I said. "I got the lowdown from Howie. Seems the late-shift dispatcher is perennially inebriated."

"Next question," Chloe said. "How does a drunk keep a critical job like that? Who does he know?"

"*She* knows Chief Larsen," I said. "She knows him very, very well from what I've been told."

"Isn't the chief married?"

"Oh, you're such a stickler," I teased, and instantly regretted it. Chloe was understandably sensitive on the subject of infidelity. Before she could react to my words, I added, "Anyway, Victor changed his number after that, but the packages keep coming."

"Good grief, this just gets worse and worse," she said. "Dare I ask what's in these packages?"

"We don't open them, we just give them to Howie as they come in. I mean, they could contain anything."

She gave a disgusted nod. "Right. The death threats."

"A bomb, anthrax, who knows? So far, though, they've contained nothing like that." The suggestive look I gave her said the packages had contained nothing even remotely like that.

She stared. "Oh, don't tell me."

"Okay, I won't tell you." I brought the last bite of croissant to my mouth.

"What?" She leaned toward me. "What was in them?"

"Howie tells me the PD is amassing quite the collection of naughty undies. They could open their own Victoria's Secret outlet."

"Good grief."

"I'm telling you, Victor should feel honored," I said. "A one-off murderer with a fan base this huge? He's getting the full-on serial-killer treatment."

The doorbell rang, clearly surprising Chloe.

"Two visitors in one day," I said. "You're on a roll."

"Probably kids selling candy for their team or something," she said as she headed for the front door.

The eye-stinging fog of Leonora's perfume heralded her arrival even before she shoved past Chloe and marched into the living room. And to think, I actually used to covet that extravagant scent. Don't let anyone tell you aversion therapy doesn't work.

"I won't stay," she was saying, "I just wanted to get this back to you before you accuse me of stealing it." She tossed a pink cardigan on the sofa and then noticed me. Her unpleasant expression grew even more unpleasant. "Didn't mean to interrupt your little kaffeeklatsch."

Behind Lee, Chloe rolled her eyes. Through telepathic hoodoo I begged her not to invite the woman to join us. Chloe was inherently polite enough to do it, and Lee was inherently mean enough to accept, just to make us uncomfortable.

Message received. Instead of asking Lee how she took her coffee, Chloe offered me an explanation as she lifted the cardigan and folded it. "It was cold in the green room the other day. I lent this to Lee."

"Are you two having fun sitting here running me down?" Lee asked.

"A little," I said, "but mainly we have more interesting things to talk about." I was tired of this woman's bullying, and Chloe certainly didn't deserve it.

Lee acknowledged the gibe with a sneer worthy of the bitchiest girl in middle school. "Did Chloe tell you she abandoned me?"

"Seems to happen to you a lot." I lifted my cup. "Think it might be you?" I took a dainty sip.

She gave me a hard look and turned her attention to her former agent. "I didn't come by just to return your ugly sweater. I feel compelled to warn you, though don't ask me why."

Chloe frowned. "Warn me about what?"

"I know you think Romulus Tooley killed your precious Swing, but trust me, the guy couldn't skewer a marshmallow. He couldn't even toss a damn Molotov cocktail without setting *himself* on fire! Could you picture that bumbling fool running Swing through with a knife?"

I didn't bother reminding Lee that Tooley had an alibi for the morning of the murder. It was public knowledge by that point. If he'd killed Swing, it was by proxy. She just wanted to hear herself rant.

I said, "Get to the point, Lee."

She didn't so much as glance at me. "Victor Dewatre had his brother killed. It's taken long enough, but the police are finally beginning to put the pieces together. Meanwhile, guess who's trying to pull his cute little French butt out of the fire by shifting the blame to someone else who was very close to

Swing? Closer even than Victor himself, at least during the past year or so."

Chloe paled.

"Chloe, ignore her." I stood and joined them in the center of the room. "She's just trying to upset you because you 'abandoned' her. We already know how vindictive she is. If Victor thought you had anything to do with his brother's murder, he'd have told me."

"He *doesn't* think she had anything to do with it," Lee said, "because he did it himself. Try to keep up, Jane. But I must say…" She pressed a hand to her heart. "It is simply adorable that you think your live-in crush tells you everything, *shares* everything, because you're just so *attuned* to each other. Trust me, you have no idea what that man is capable of."

"This is priceless." I shook my head in wonder. "First you falsely accuse him of murder, in retaliation for an offense that exists only in your imagination. I mean, you *admitted* that to me, remember? In the bookstore?"

"I don't recall any such conversation," Lee said. "It seems like you're the one with the vivid imagination."

No surprise there. I didn't expect her to admit it in Chloe's presence. "And now," I said, "you claim he's doing the same thing to Chloe that *you're* doing to *him*."

Lee crossed her arms over her chest. "Tell me you never, not once, wondered if Victor might have murdered his brother."

After a second I managed to mumble, "Of course not," but her smug expression told me she heard my lie for what it was.

"You never mentioned who you *do* think did it," she said, "at least not to me."

"Well," I said pleasantly, "from where I stand, *you* look guilty as hell."

"Oh please," Lee said. "If I'd killed Swing, why on earth would I deliberately invite all this attention to myself by telling the world about Victor's guilt?"

Dom had asked that very same question the day I almost let him kiss me. My throwaway response had been that we weren't dealing with the most rational person here. But if I was being honest with myself, I did not in fact think of Lee Romano as mentally unsound. Vindictive? This has been established. Mean, catty, and blind to her own faults? You'll get no argument from me. But from what I could tell, the woman was sane, too sane to risk a murder rap for the vengeful pleasure of framing an innocent person.

Chloe's voice quavered. "Did he really do that, Lee? Did Victor tell the police I did it?"

"Oh, Chloe," I said, "can't you see what she's—"

"Yes he did," Lee said. "He's telling them it was out of revenge for Swing slipping around on you. The betrayal. The humiliation. You couldn't take it and you snapped. He's claiming he has evidence."

"But... But Victor's been so nice to me." Chloe's eyes glistened. "Why would he do something like that?"

"To protect himself. Why else?" Lee shrugged. "Remember, he's making the whole thing up, trying to deflect attention from his own guilt. He's doing it *now* because he knows the police are closing in."

"*She's* the one making it up, Chloe," I said, "and you're eating right out of her hand."

"He says he has evidence?" Chloe asked in a small voice. She must have thought the cops were about to break down the door and haul her away in handcuffs.

"Okay, let's just take a deep breath and think about it

logically," I told her. "If Victor really were guilty and he thought the police were 'closing in,' don't you think he'd be on the first flight back to Paris?"

"Maybe," Lee cut in. "The U.S. has an extradition agreement with France, but France doesn't always honor it. I checked."

Chloe was hugging herself, fighting tears. I wheeled on Lee. "Are you proud of yourself? You can never just let something go. What did she do that was so terrible? She stopped being your agent. And for a damn good reason—that evil rumor you started about Swing. Your vindictive acts just keep feeding on one another. I'd feel sorry for you if you weren't so reckless."

Lee made a show of haughty indifference, but a tic near her eye gave her away.

I got right in her face. "Fair warning, Lee. When you come for me, you'd better be ready for a fight. I'm not so easily bullied." I pointed to the door. "Get out! You've spread enough sunshine for one day."

14

Juggling Act

"YOU REALLY SAID that to her?" Victor slid a book off the shelf he was emptying. The carved mahogany bookcase took up an entire wall of Swing's den, floor to ceiling. Briefly he examined the book cover before adding it to one of the cardboard cartons at his feet, the one destined for his home in Paris. "This doesn't sound like you, Jane."

"You've never seen me when I'm really riled." I straightened the books in the other carton, one of those he planned to donate to charity. "When need be, I can throw down with the best of them. Right then I felt like I was channeling Nina Wallace."

He squinted at me. "Nina from that *Ramrod News* show? She has a temper? She seems too ladylike."

"That's because you've never gotten on her wrong side," I said. "Nina's great-grandfather was this notorious local gangster and bootlegger, Hank 'Hokum' Hannigan. Pals with Dutch Shultz. Nasty character, Hokum. Anyway, Nina definitely inherited the gene."

"About Lee." He plucked a thick volume from the shelf, its paper jacket in tatters. "Aren't you afraid of angering a murderer? It could be her, you know."

"I've been thinking about that. Something occurred to me yesterday at Chloe's. You know that perfume Lee wears?"

He made a face. "She bathes in it, I think. Should I keep this one? It's very old."

He handed me the book: *The New York Times Cookbook*, by Craig Claiborne. I flipped through it. Many of the recipes contained annotations in the margins, some in English—written by the book's first owner, I assumed—and some in French. I turned to the copyright page. It was published in 1961. A handwritten note inside the front cover, dated twelve years earlier, expressed the wish that Pierre would enjoy the book as much as the person gifting it had. It was signed, "Your Slave Driver." An old boss or mentor, perhaps.

"Your smile tells me everything." He took the book back and added it to the Paris-bound box. "At this rate my apartment will be overrun with Pierre's books."

I let my gaze roam over the remaining volumes in the bookcase. "They all meant something to him."

Victor looked sad. Distracted too. He'd put off this chore, going through his brother's house, deciding what to do with all of his things. I sensed he still wasn't ready, but it had to be done. I'd offered to help. I could think of more onerous ways to spend a Friday morning in early autumn than helping a sexy Frenchman sort through books in this rustic, high-ceilinged den. A humongous stone fireplace dominated one end of the room. Sunlight streamed through French doors set into the opposite wall. I recognized Swing's stamp in the solid furnishings and bold colors.

"So," Victor said. "What is this about Lee's perfume?"

"Well, every time I've been near that woman, she's reeked of the stuff. After she left Chloe's yesterday, the living room stank of it. We had to open windows and air the place out. Which got me thinking. The morning Swing was killed, I showed up at Dewatre around ten-thirty. No more than an hour had passed, according to the ME's estimated time of death."

"I think I see where you're taking this."

"If Lee had been there before me," I said, "and if she was wearing a gallon of perfume as usual, for sure I'd have smelled it, and I didn't."

"But if she stayed away and sent a hit man, then…" He let his shrug say the rest.

"Yeah, I know, but I just thought it was an interesting snippet to file away."

"That's it for the cookbooks." Victor twisted his torso this way and that, stretching his back, a stirring spectacle for the few seconds it lasted. He grabbed a handful of paperback science fiction novels and prepared to toss them into the donation box.

"Uh-uh-uh," I said, grabbing one and riffling the pages. "We have to check them all." So far we'd turned up six movie stubs, nine store receipts, twelve scraps of newspaper, and seventeen folded greenbacks—mostly dollar bills but plenty of other denominations, including a C-note—all of which Swing had pressed into service as bookmarks.

Victor seemed lost in thought as we commenced riffling and tossing.

"So let me ask you." I adopted a casual tone. "Lee says you told Cullen that Chloe's the murderer. You told him you have proof. She says."

It took him a moment to focus on my words. "How would she even know such a thing?"

This wasn't the response I'd anticipated. "Um, I don't know, she didn't say. I just assumed she made it up, like everything else that comes out of her mouth."

He gave a weary sigh and returned his attention to the books. "Then don't pay any attention to her."

"She said something else."

Clearly he didn't want to hear it. "What?"

"Well, she said the police—I mean, you know, Cullen—is looking more closely at you. As a suspect."

He didn't look at me, just continued to go through the paperbacks.

I tried to laugh it off. "I know, I know, you can tell when Lee's lying because her lips are moving."

"Cullen wants me to come down to the station for an interview," Victor said. "He's insistent."

My breath caught. "Are you going to do it?"

"I think I must."

"Don't you dare go without a lawyer," I said. "I'll talk to Sten Jakobsen. He'll recommend someone."

"Ben already did," he said.

"Oh." I was taken aback. "You've gotten that far."

He still wasn't looking at me. When he finally did, I saw a strange kind of sorrow I couldn't identify. I suppressed a shiver.

"I have to admit I'm surprised," I said. "I mean, that Cullen isn't just concentrating on Tucker. I'd pegged him as too lazy to keep working the case when he had this blatantly guilty—or guilty seeming—suspect basically fall into his lap."

"Tucker's parents are rich," he said. "They can afford the best, most aggressive legal defense. It would not be an easy case to prove, no matter how the evidence might look. Cullen knows this. The district attorney knows this."

"Well, that's true. Plus Cullen's kind of under a microscope at the moment. He's being investigated for that harassment business—okay, by his pal Chief Larsen, but still. Sophie and the Town Council are watching. He can't just blow off a credible suspect. One who might *look* credible," I hastily added, "to anyone who doesn't have all the facts. Obviously Sophie doesn't think you did it."

"Lee is making sure I look more than 'credible.'" He hurled a book into the carton with unnecessary force, making me jump.

"Victor." I placed my hand on his arm. "Come on, let's take a break."

His bleak gaze took in the room. "There's so much to do. I haven't even touched the upstairs."

"I'll get started upstairs. If that's okay with you? I can go through his clothes, get them ready to donate." It was a chore I'd done many times in my capacity as Death Diva. I could do it in a fraction of the time it would take an emotionally involved family member. "If I'm unsure about anything, I'll ask you."

"It seems wrong to be here without Pierre." He stared out the French doors to the expansive lawn, dotted with mature trees and bordered by a jolly profusion of freeform plantings. "He loved this house. He couldn't wait to show it to me. He bought it because it reminded him of our grandparents' stone farmhouse in Uzès."

"I can see that." I smiled. "The place definitely has a French country vibe. Where's Uzès?"

"Provence. It's a small town, not much bigger than Crystal Harbor. The house is large. It's been in our family for generations. Pierre and I own it with—That is, I own it along with my cousin Marie. We've turned it into a bed-and-breakfast, very successful. Marie is a talented baker and her husband, Serge, can fix anything. He keeps the old place running."

"I had no idea," I said. "It sounds wonderful."

"Pierre used to say he would retire there, perhaps add a real restaurant to the place. Nothing too ambitious, just..." He trailed off and met my gaze. "You should come visit, Jane. I'll show you the *Jardin Médiéval* in the center of Uzès—the Medieval Garden. We'll stay at the B and B. You'll love it."

We'll stay at his family's bed-and-breakfast? Victor and me? Of course you know the first thing that popped into my head. Was he thinking one room or two? I suppressed another shiver, the good kind this time.

His expression turned serious. "I would like it very much, Jane, if you would visit me after I return home."

I kept my voice steady, easier said than done with my heart slamming. "You make it sound like you're taking the next flight out."

"That would be the sensible thing, yes?" He pushed his fingers through his light brown hair, which had gotten appealingly shaggy during the past couple of weeks. "To go through Pierre's things this weekend, put the house and restaurant on the market, and leave. I can do nothing more for him here. I thought I could help keep the investigation on track, but the opposite has happened. I find myself a suspect."

I couldn't help remembering my words to Lee. If Victor were guilty, I'd told her, he'd be on the first flight back to Paris.

"Not to mention the death threats," he added, "and those

disturbed women who won't leave me alone. It's time for me to go home, get back to my life." He looked steadily at me as he said this, those silver-gray eyes like lasers.

I knew the response he hoped to receive, at least I thought I knew. *Don't go.* Of course I didn't want him to. I'd miss him like hell and would always wonder what might have been. But those warm feelings were tangled up with others, less warm, less benign. A small part of me wondered if I needed to fear this man.

I took a deep breath. "This is why you're finally going through Swing's stuff."

He nodded. "My lawyer told Cullen we would meet with him on Monday. I could be on a plane instead."

Monday. Three days from then. I thought of all that could happen in three days, including an arrest if Cullen got wind of Victor's plan to flee. Not *flee*! I admonished myself. He wasn't a criminal. He was simply going home. His work here was done and he was going home. Getting back to his life, as he'd put it. And as for an arrest, Cullen couldn't bring him in without probable cause, something more compelling than Lee Romano's squawking about a long-ago argument between brothers.

I avoided his eyes. "Okay, well, that sounds like a reasonable plan. I wish it were different. I mean, I wish you didn't have all this nonsense to deal with. Um, listen, I'm going to go upstairs and..." I pointed to the ceiling as if he needed help comprehending where upstairs was.

"Sure. Go," he said briskly. He scooped up a few more paperbacks. "Thanks for doing that."

I had no trouble locating the master bedroom. It was the largest room in the house, very much a man's room with ponderous dark furniture and a profusion of competing textures. The gargantuan en suite bathroom was tiled in stone and outfitted with ultramodern amenities—an exquisite blend of rustic and modern that took my breath away.

The his-and-hers walk-in closets were outfitted with all those organizational doodads you see in decorating magazines, prompting a serious case of closet envy. Swing hadn't come close to filling the "his" closet, and I swear the empty "hers" was bigger than the sad little basement apartment I'd moved out of when I'd inherited—all right, when a certain toy poodle had inherited—Irene McAuliffe's five-bedroom house in Crystal Harbor.

Doing a three-sixty in that huge, empty "hers," I thought of Chloe. There was no sign of her here or in the closet Swing had used. He'd kept a robe at her place, but here I saw no woman's robe, nightie, or change of clothes. I flipped through the garments on hangers, pulled open drawers. Well, that's what I was there for, right? To sort through his stuff? So it wasn't snooping.

All I saw was men's stuff—until I opened the built-in laundry hamper and noticed a flash of vivid fuchsia among the undershirts and boxer shorts. I pulled out a bra, an ooh-la-la concoction of lace and underwire. Here at last was evidence that Swing's fiancée had set foot in his house.

Or not, I mused as I held up the bodacious garment. Chloe was petite all over, a B-cup at best. I squinted at the bra's size label: 36DD. I gave poor dead Swing a mental shake. *Why get engaged in the first place if you can't keep it in your pants?* No one had forced him to put his great-grandmother's ring on her finger.

I felt for Chloe, having been on the receiving end of that

kind of pain myself. About ten years ago I'd been dating a guy I really liked. Alan. When I found out he was slipping around on me, I was devastated. The difference between Chloe and me? I'd lost no time kicking Alan's sorry butt to the curb. I can't identify with women who put up with a cheater, though I try not to judge.

I tossed the bra back into the hamper and shoved it closed. I'd gone up there for a reason. Time to get on with it. I started with Swing's suits. With the ease and speed of long practice, I checked all the pockets, depositing assorted change, a half-used roll of mints, and a concert stub in a ceramic valet tray sitting nearby. I recognized the artistry of the tray. Clearly it had come from the little pottery gallery located next to Janey's Place on Main Street, owned by a young couple whose names I never could recall. I made sure the suits sported no rips or stains, not that I'd expected to find any, then hauled them out of the closet and deposited them on the bed.

I left the bespoke tuxedo in the closet for now. It appeared brand-new and fiendishly expensive, and I thought it possible that Victor, who was the same height as his brother but a bit slimmer, might want to have it retailored for himself. He'd either think that a swell idea or consider me a ghoul for suggesting it. Either way, it was his call.

I performed the same routine on Swing's jeans, trousers, and sport jackets, piling them on the bed next to the suits. I sat and rested a moment. My gaze fell on the night table, which held a reading lamp, a coaster, a half-filled water glass, and a book. I leaned over and lifted the book, which turned out to be the French translation of a best-selling thriller. I could tell by the cover art and the author's name. Swing had used, what else, a folded five-dollar bill as a bookmark. He was two-thirds of the way through. He never got to find out the stepson did it. I'd bring this volume down to Victor, to add to one of the cartons he was filling.

The night table had a drawer. I had to check it because after all, Swing might have kept more clothes in there. Very tiny clothes. The drawer held a vial of prescription sleeping pills identical to the one in Chloe's medicine chest, reading glasses, a bottle of antacids, and a strip of condoms. My gut told me this last item had nothing whatsoever to do with his fiancée—a reasonable assumption based on what I'd found and, more to the point, hadn't found in Swing's home.

I cast my eyes heavenward and pleaded with my dead friend to stop trying to make me dislike him.

I took a break from my task and went back downstairs. I found Victor in the dining room, standing in front of the china cabinet. The glass doors were open. He held a porcelain soup tureen, turning it over in his hands, examining it lovingly. Hearing me enter, he returned the tureen to its shelf and closed the doors.

"*Maman*'s china," he said. I could have guessed.

"Victor, I have to ask you… have you found anything of Chloe's in the house?"

He frowned. "Is she missing something?"

"No, no, I just… well, your brother kept a few things at her place. Toiletries, a robe. I noticed them when I was there yesterday."

"You want to know if she kept anything here," he said.

"Well, it would make sense, right?" I said. "I mean, they were engaged."

He thought for a moment, then shook his head. "I haven't come across anything."

"And no photos of her," I said. "There was a photo of the two of them in her living room."

"Well, Pierre was not one to display personal photos."

"That's not strictly true. There's the one of your parents in the den," I said, "and another on his bedroom wall of the whole family. You guys are kids in it. Your grandparents are there, too."

"My father's parents." He smiled. "It was taken in Uzès at the farmhouse when they still lived there."

"Well, I guess I just thought he'd have a picture of his fiancée somewhere."

"That's because you think like a woman," he said with an impish smile. "A man would say, why should I hang a picture? I know what she looks like."

"Dang!" I snapped my fingers in mock frustration. "You guys are just so darn logical."

"Since you bring it up," he said, "it does seem odd that we see nothing of hers here. Usually one invites a girlfriend to leave a few belongings, yes? For convenience. And always there are items left by accident."

"Items?" I said.

A negligent shrug. "Makeup. Jewelry."

He was too gentlemanly to mention undergarments. I thought of Swing's 36DD friend who for some reason had waltzed out of here braless. Well, I could think of one reason she'd do it: to ensure she'd see him again. Had he been that good a lover? Did it run in the family?

Okay, I give you permission to tell me to get a grip. Bet you thought you'd never see the day.

"Perhaps he always slept over at her house," Victor said, "never the other way around."

"Why?" I leaned against the dining table and folded my arms over my chest. "I know you haven't seen Chloe's place, but you could fit three or four of her houses in this one. And she has this dinky little double bed."

What, didn't I mention that I peeked into her room on my way to the john? Well, who says I have to tell you everything?

"Again you are incapable of thinking like a man," he said.

One of my eyebrows rose. One finger might have done the same. "Oh, *do* enlighten me," I said.

"It makes sense that if Pierre entertained other women here, he might not want his fiancée to sleep over."

Entertained? I flashed on an image of Swing juggling condom packets. Come to think of it, isn't that what he was doing, with Chloe on the one hand and his assorted lovers on the other? A juggling act?

"I'm not talking about them staying over on the same night!" I said. Unless Swing was kinkier than I'd imagined.

"You know what I mean," Victor said. "It would be disrespectful. To Chloe. I'm thinking Pierre would see it this way."

"Oh, *that* would be disrespectful," I blurted, before I could wrangle my sarcastic tongue into silence.

"You know how I feel about Pierre's..." He sighed and looked away. "His dishonorable behavior."

"I'm sorry," I said, "I shouldn't have—" I flapped my hand as if that could erase the past thirty seconds. Victor had loved his brother. He didn't need to be reminded again of Swing's failings.

"Don't worry." He laid his hand on my shoulder. It felt absurdly comforting. "I brought it up, after all."

Time to change the subject. "Come upstairs with me, Victor."

His slow smile tugged at my insides in a most distracting way. "If you insist."

I answered his flirtatious teasing with a playful smack on the arm. He *was* teasing, right? I turned and led the way before he could see my face turn assorted shades of red. "There's a tux you need to look at."

15

A+ for Penmanship

"I USUALLY FIND moonlit walks on the beach to be pretty darn romantic," I said, "but tonight I'm just not feeling it."

"Moonlit?" Bonnie tightened the hood of her rain jacket and squinted through the icy mist at the impenetrable blackness overhead. If not for the meager glow from the parking-lot security lights some distance away, I wouldn't have been able to make out her form. "I don't see a moon."

"Are you always so literal?" Dom's fiancée had phoned earlier to ask me—more like order me—to meet her at the town beach at ten pm. I could have told her I had better things to do on a Friday night, particularly on what I had every reason to believe was Victor's last Friday night in Crystal Harbor.

Bonnie had warned me not to tell anyone about our little meeting tonight. Clearly she'd chosen the setting with privacy in mind. The beach was deserted on this wet and chilly autumn night. I'd left my houseguest at home watching a movie. He thought I was out picking up a late dinner. My favorite pizzeria doesn't deliver. Well, I *was* planning to bring home a Buffalo chicken pizza, along with some clever excuse to explain the delay.

"Where did you park?" I asked. My car was the only one in

the beach's lot.

"Near the playground. I didn't want to risk anyone spotting both our cars here."

The playground was way at the other end of Nevins Park, a sprawling recreation area bordered on the north by this beach, which faced the bay after which the town was named. Bonnie Hernandez, girl spy, had trekked a long way on a crummy night to make sure no one saw us together.

I stopped walking and waited for her to turn and face me. "I'd better leave here with some nuclear codes to peddle to China," I said, "or I'm unfriending you on Facebook."

"I'm not on Facebook."

See what I mean? Literal.

For someone who'd gone to great lengths to arrange a private tête-à-tête, Bonnie appeared awfully reluctant to reveal what was on her mind. Her troubled gaze scoured our surroundings.

Don't worry, I wanted to tell her, *we're the only numbskulls dumb enough to be out here.* The mist had turned into a light rain. The baseball cap I'd donned to keep my head dry was now saturated, as was my suede jacket. Yeah, poor choice, what can I tell you?

Finally she slid a white, business-size envelope out of her pocket, holding it close to keep it dry. "If you tell anyone I gave you this, you'll be very sorry."

My ex-husband's fiancée was threatening me. Nice. "You know what, Bonnie? I don't need this crap." I turned and strode briskly away. I'd made it to the edge of the parking lot when her iron grip on my arm jerked me to a stop. I tried to yank it away. She wasn't letting go.

She said, "That didn't come out the way I meant it."

My bark of laughter called her a liar.

"You wanted this." She released my arm and shoved the envelope at me. When I didn't move, she said, "Take it. Maybe you can do something with it."

I crossed my arms.

"Okay," she said, "I apologize for… for the way that sounded before. This whole thing has me…" She took a deep breath and pushed the envelope closer to me. "Burn it after you read it."

This spy stuff was getting old. On the other hand, I'd never before seen Detective Bonnie Hernandez so rattled.

Ultimately I let my curiosity make the decision. I reached out for the envelope and slipped it into my jacket pocket.

"It didn't come from me," she said. "If it turns out to be anything usable, I don't want to hear word one about it, I don't want to be associated with it in any way. Go through channels and keep me out of it. Is that clear?" Without waiting for an answer, she took off in the direction of the distant playground.

I got behind the wheel of my Mazda, tossed the sodden cap into the backseat, and turned on the map light. I ripped open the damp envelope and unfolded the single sheet of paper it contained. The first thing I noticed is that it was a photocopy. The second thing I noticed made my heart kick. It was a photocopy of a page in a notebook. A notebook that looked to be three by five inches and spiral-bound at the top.

The kind of notebook Detective Paulie Cullen carried.

What you're asking is not only unethical, Bonnie had said that day in the bookstore when I'd asked her to sneak a peek at his notes, *it would get me in serious trouble if I got caught. I won't do it.*

It would appear she'd had a change of heart. But why? One reason was obvious. Dom. He might no longer be the number-one suspect, but that status could change in a heartbeat, especially with a nitwit like Cullen at the helm. But I doubted that was the whole story. Whatever our differences, I never questioned Bonnie's commitment to the job, her bone-deep need to put away bad guys and see justice done—an unlikely outcome in this case if Cullen called all the shots.

Her integrity was something else I never questioned. She must have grappled with her conscience before making the decision to smuggle her colleague's notes to a civilian. I still didn't like her, but I'd be lying if I said I didn't respect her.

Before, if you'd asked me to guess, I'd have speculated that Cullen's handwriting would be close to illegible, the physical extension of a disorganized mind. Not so, as it turned out. The notes I was looking at were written in the precise penmanship of a second-grader intent on mastering cursive. The words never strayed from the lines. I was in no mood to ponder the psychological significance of this surprising discovery, but I invite you to give it a whirl.

"Phone tip" was written at the top of the page, along with the date and time: September 9, 7:12 pm. The day Swing died. Cullen had written the name "Meredith Dorn" and "Tolland, CT" along with several cryptic notations: "watched Ramrod News" and "hysterical" and "nutcase." No mention of what specific tip she was reporting or why he considered her a hysterical nutcase. The detective might have A+ penmanship, but as for attention to detail, we're talking D-, tops.

But there was more. Under that he'd written, "Followed up on tip, dead end." So whatever it was, at least he'd looked into it.

Below that was a second date and time: September 23, 7:01 pm. Last Monday. He'd written "Same caller," along with "Ramrod" and "still hysterical." Which is one of my least favorite words. I mean, when's the last time you heard it applied to a guy?

Cullen added the words "Told her I'd look into it blah blah." He actually wrote that. *Blah blah.* Our tax dollars at work. It was clear his only goal had been to pacify the caller and get her off the phone. No notation this time about following up.

The *Ramrod News* shows on those two dates had centered around Swing's murder. Chloe and Tooley had been the featured guests the first time. Then this past Monday it had been the two of them plus Leonora and Nina. Something about those two episodes had triggered Meredith Dorn's "hysteria." Clearly Bonnie had little faith in how her colleague had handled this particular phone tip. And with so few concrete details to go on, could you blame her?

When I finally walked through the doorway with the pizza, Victor was surprised to see me soaked to the skin. I babbled some lame excuse about making multiple stops trying to find orange soda, never mind that I have a case of the stuff in the pantry. I did not tell him about my side trip to the beach. For one thing, I had no intention of violating Bonnie's trust. And for another, well, Victor didn't need to know everything. And not because I considered him a suspect, because I didn't. Not really.

THE BIG WHITE colonial stood on a large, meticulously landscaped tract of land in Tolland, a charming town in northern Connecticut. The drive from Crystal Harbor had taken three long hours during which I berated myself for squandering a perfectly lovely Saturday chasing down a lead that had already been investigated.

By Paulie the Perv. It was his new nickname around town. I was still waiting for news regarding the investigation of his possible misconduct, but Sophie was keeping mum. Whatever actions she and the Town Council were taking behind the scenes, they weren't sharing until it was over.

The door swung open as I was making my way up the brick walkway to the wide, colonnaded front porch. Meredith Dorn appeared to be in her late forties. She had long auburn hair and wore little jewelry. Her well-nourished form was flatteringly displayed in a watercolor-patterned tunic and slim jeans.

From the bit of online snooping I'd done before leaving Crystal Harbor, I knew that Meredith was a widow with two college-age kids. She'd lived in Tolland for the past two decades and worked at Travelers Insurance in nearby Hartford.

We exchanged smiles and handshakes. "I'm sorry," Meredith said as she ushered me through the foyer and into a comfortable, traditional living room, "I don't recall your name. I should have written it down."

"Jane Delaney."

"You've had a long drive from the Island, Detective

Delaney. Can I get you some coffee? A cold drink?"

Okay, for the record, I had *not* claimed to be a police detective! How underhanded do you think I am? Don't answer that.

When I'd phoned her that morning I'd said simply that I'd gotten her name from Detective Cullen and could I ask her some questions concerning the Pierre Dewatre murder case. She'd agreed but said she was uncomfortable discussing it over the phone and could we meet in person. Hence the day trip.

"Um, I guess I wasn't very clear," I said. "I'm not with the police department."

Her eyes widened fractionally. "I don't understand. What's your connection to the case?"

I took a deep breath. "Well, the victim was a friend of mine, and another, um, friend was the initial suspect, and I, well, I don't have the utmost confidence in the investigation, so… I decided to see what I could find out on my own." *Please don't kick me out of your house.*

I watched her expression morph from suspicious to comprehending. She nodded. "Please. Have a seat." She indicated the pale-green sofa crowded with pretty throw pillows, and with relief, I obeyed. "Can I get you that drink?" she added. "A sandwich? You must be hungry."

"I had a soda and some snacks in the car," I said. "I'm fine for now."

Meredith sat facing me on an upholstered swivel chair. "I spoke with Cullen twice. I couldn't seem to get through his thick skull. Oh, he claimed he looked into it. Yeah, right. Probably made one phone call to the cops up here and concluded I was just some hysterical female. What?"

"It's nothing." I chewed back a grin, thinking of Cullen's

description of her. "You called him the day Swing died, after watching *Ramrod News?*"

She nodded. "And again after that second show. Nothing had been done! They have a killer on the loose, someone who's done it before, and it's like nobody gives a damn."

I'd had plenty of time during that long drive to ponder Cullen's cryptic jottings and what they might signify. I thought I had at least part of it figured out. But…

Someone who's done it before?

I said, "Are you telling me you think you saw this person, this killer, on both of those *Ramrod* episodes?"

"Yes!" She sat forward. An angry flush suffused her face. "What do I have to do to get someone to take action?"

"So he's killed before?"

"What?" She frowned. "Who?"

"Romulus Tooley. The SEAR spokesman. You said he's done it before." Tooley had appeared on both episodes.

As I watched her take in my words, a tremor coursed through me. I said, "You don't mean…" Could Meredith Dorn indeed be the hysterical nutcase Cullen had called her?

"Chloe Sleeper," Meredith spoke slowly and clearly, her gaze fixed on mine. "Chloe Sleeper murdered my husband eight years ago. She got away with it and now she's murdered again."

I swallowed hard, my throat suddenly dry, wishing I'd accepted a glass of water. "Can you… Can you tell me what happened? With your husband?"

"Tony was a professor at UConn," she said, meaning the nearby University of Connecticut. "English literature. Chloe was one of his students, a senior at the time. She fell in love with Tony. She was obsessed with him."

"I hate to ask, but were the two of them—"

"No. They weren't having an affair." Meredith's eyes glistened. "I thought they were, though. I mean, she visited me."

"Chloe did?" I asked.

She nodded. "She came over one day when Tony was at the campus and told me the two of them were lovers, that it had been going on for months. She said he was going to divorce me and that it would be best for everyone, including our kids, if I let him go without a fuss."

"How did you know she was lying?"

"I didn't at first," she said. "I'd never suspected him of cheating before, but you have to understand. Chloe was so sincere, so believable. Later, after everything, I realized it was because she actually believed her lies. She believed Tony was in love with her and that he was going to leave me and marry her."

My pulse whooshed in my ears. I took a deep, calming breath. "Let me ask you, what kind of man was Tony? I mean, was he introverted? Physically unassuming?" I pictured a literature professor from Central Casting.

"No, quite the opposite," Meredith said. "Tony was tall, handsome, outgoing. His students described him as charismatic."

Like a certain celebrity chef of my acquaintance. "Did you confront your husband? About what Chloe claimed?"

"Of course. He denied it. I wanted to believe him, but... well, I guess I'd been waiting for something like this to happen. His female students were always developing crushes on him. We joked about it. But Chloe... you would have had to be here. Listening to her. She'd convinced herself this mad love affair was real and not a figment of her sick mind, and to my shame, she convinced me too."

Gently I asked, "What happened then?"

A tear streaked down her face. She swiped it away. "I was going to divorce him. I tried to get him to move out. We had some ugly scenes. But a little part of me still thought… this is Tony. This is the man I love, the man I've always trusted. He insisted Chloe was mentally unhinged. What did I really know about her? He was determined to get her to admit the truth. He wasn't going to let this 'deranged freak'—his words—break up our family."

"What did he do?" I asked.

"He… He went over there. To Chloe's place. She lived in this house with a bunch of other students, but none of her housemates were there that day—it was just her. I'm assuming they argued. At some point they both left the house and she got into her car. She ran him over in her driveway. Killed him."

"Oh no… that's horrible." I shook my head. "How was she able to get away with a thing like that?"

"It was officially declared an accident." Meredith's eyes closed briefly. "She told the cops she was trying to get away from him and he leapt in front of her car. She said she was trying to break up with him, that they'd had an affair and her conscience bothered her. He was a married man with a family, after all. But he wouldn't let her go, she said. *He* was obsessed with *her*, she said."

"Did you tell the police about her visit to you?" I asked.

"Of course. She said she came to see me, but only out of desperation. She claims she tried to get me to help rein him in, to make him leave her alone."

"Kind of the opposite of what she really told you," I said. "And they just believed her?"

"When you've managed to convince *yourself* that you had this torrid relationship with one of your profs," she said, "then you're not really lying, are you? Others view you as credible. Including the authorities."

"Didn't the police interview her housemates?" I asked. "I mean, if they never saw Tony at the house, that has to count for something."

"Chloe told them she snuck him in and out of the house. She didn't want the others knowing about the affair."

I sighed. "Unfortunately, that sounds perfectly reasonable."

"That's the problem," Meredith said. "She always sounds perfectly reasonable, like the skilled little psycho she is."

"Let me ask you something. Did the police find any belongings of Tony's at her house?"

She hadn't been expecting the question, I could tell. But she said, "Yes, as a matter of fact. There was a comb of his, a toothbrush, that sort of thing."

"Stuff like that can belong to anyone—short of DNA testing, anyway."

"There were other things," Meredith said, "things that were definitely Tony's. A monogrammed shirt. An engraved watch that had belonged to his dad. I remember him telling me they'd gone missing from his office on campus. The shirt was the spare he kept there."

"When did this happen?" I asked.

"A couple of weeks before he died. She must have snuck into his office and made off with them."

I thought of Swing's silk robe at Chloe's. His razor and prescription bottle. I'd felt in my gut that something was wrong when Victor and I had failed to find anything of hers in his home, but what about the rest of it? The stack of bride magazines. The framed picture of her and Swing. The ring.

Good grief, the ring! If she and Swing had not in fact been engaged, how had she gotten hold of his great-grandmother's ring? Had she swiped it from his home, along with his toiletries? They were all small, concealable items. Even the silk robe could have been rolled into a compact bundle and shoved into a handbag.

I gave myself a mental shake. The thought of soft-spoken, levelheaded Chloe Sleeper shoving her client's personal belongings into her purse, then offing him and cooking up a fake engagement, was too bizarre to contemplate. Just like the story Meredith Dorn was telling about her husband and Chloe.

I'd just met this woman. She could very well be the nutcase Cullen had called her. Was I supposed to trust her word over Chloe's?

"What?" Meredith said, watching me closely. "What are you thinking?"

"It's just… a lot to take in," I said.

"Tony died thinking I believed Chloe." Meredith's chin wobbled. "Thinking I believed the worst about him. And everyone else, his friends and colleagues, they *did* believe the worst. I mean, the official verdict was that it was an accident following a lover's spat, that he was obsessed with her and caused his own death. They still think that."

"I assume that's what Detective Cullen was told when he followed up on your tip," I said.

"I tell you," Meredith said, "the first time I saw Chloe on *Ramrod News,* I almost had a heart attack. I knew right away that she'd done it again. And there she was, blaming it on that SEAR fellow."

16

One Big, Happy Ex-Family

BY THE TIME I got back from Connecticut, the parking lot of the Harbor Room was full to overflowing, forcing me to park on a side road two blocks away and walk back to the restaurant. Every year in late September the venerable eatery hosted the annual Friends of the Waterfront goods and services auction, and today was the day. Townspeople donated items to the cause, and the bidding was always lively.

My contribution was weekly flower delivery to a loved one's grave at Whispering Willows Cemetery for six months. My Death Diva duties regularly took me to the boneyard anyway, and it was no trouble making an extra stop. I collaborated with Russell Appell, a local florist, who donated the actual arrangements. The high bidder was always Celia Colvin, a snowbird who would be taking off for sunny Palm Beach in a few weeks and returning to Crystal Harbor in the spring. My texted photos of the lovely winter arrangements and wreaths I placed on her late husband's grave each week were a comfort to her.

I'd almost made it to the restaurant entrance when I heard my name being called. I looked around and spied a trio of girls leaning on the dock pilings, waving. As they sprinted toward me I recognized the teenage fan girls who'd fawned over Victor at Janey's Place last week. Compared with the weirdos who were sending lingerie to the house and pornographic texts to Victor's phone, these kids were refreshingly tame if a tad obsessed. *Haven't you ever heard of hobbies?*

"They won't let us *in*." Ariel shoved her glasses up her nose.

"'Cause we don't have *tickets*." Mandy rolled her eyes.

Phoebe said, "We just want to, like, help the, um, whales."

"Friends of the Waterfront," I corrected her. "Not the same thing. And that's not why you're here. You want to see Victor again." He was inside the restaurant. I'd texted him earlier saying I didn't think I'd make it to the auction but to save me a seat just in case. I was eager to share what I'd learned from Meredith Dorn. Together we'd decide what to do with the information.

"Can you help us get in?" Ariel pleaded.

"Sorry, you really do need tickets," I said, "but I'll tell Victor you said hi."

"We're gonna wait out here," Phoebe said. "Maybe we can catch him when he leaves."

"Suit yourselves." I pulled open the door. "But this thing won't wind down for a few hours."

A volunteer traded my ticket for a printed program. I squeezed into the back of the spacious dining room and surveyed the scene. The room was crammed with about two hundred people—far more than the legal maximum, I was certain. It didn't seem to bother Sergeant Howie Werker, who shared a nearby table with his wife and a bunch of their friends. I glimpsed many familiar faces, including Sophie and Martin, who shared a table with Porter and Lacey Vargas, a local couple who'd been at the center of some excitement a couple of months ago.

A wall of windows offered a view of the bay and the restaurant's marina, now jammed with boats. Depending on the season, almost as many patrons arrived by water as by car. Today the tables were laden with pitchers of soda and beer, carafes of wine, and bowls of nuts and chips.

"I have seventy-five, do I hear a hundred?" Kyle Kenneally, holding forth from a podium at the front of the room, displayed an old-fashioned fedora so everyone in the packed restaurant could see it. Never one to shun the limelight, he obviously relished his role as auctioneer.

Kyle, a self-important twit in his late twenties with red hair and a ruddy complexion, was the current owner of the Harbor Room. He'd hired me a few months earlier to find a place for his dead giant tortoise, Romeo, in a prominent museum. Romeo had lived to 180 and had an impressive history that included a Darwin connection, and in the end I'd found him a forever home at the Smithsonian, complete with a nice brass plaque bearing Kyle's name. Easiest five grand I ever made.

Few people seemed interested in the fedora, which had been donated to the auction by Nina Wallace. As I'd informed Victor, Nina's great-grandpa had been a legendary gangster. She was so proud of Hokum Hannigan, she'd created a Prohibition Museum in the basement of the Crystal Harbor Historical Society, of which she was the president. A onetime speakeasy, the space now housed a good portion of Nina's family heirlooms, including such questionable relics as a banged-up whiskey still and a Tommy gun.

Hokum had frequently held court in the room where I now stood. The Harbor Room restaurant dated from the 1840s and had played a significant role in the local economy during Prohibition, when Hokum's rumrunners bought booze from picket ships sitting three miles offshore in international waters. The crates entered the restaurant through a secret trapdoor behind the bar. Some was served there, but most found its way to New York City.

"A hundred?" Kyle repeated. He placed the fedora on his head and tilted it at what I suppose was meant to mimic a gangsterly style. "Come on, people, this is irreplaceable Crystal Harbor history here!"

"Irreplaceable" might not have been the best choice of words since this was the fourth Hokum fedora to be auctioned off in as many years. Not that I suspected Nina of donating fakes. Hokum had probably owned a bunch of them. I pictured a trunkful of her infamous great-granddad's chapeaux taking up space in her attic. Nina, sitting at a table up front with her husband and teenage daughters, looked none too happy at the anemic bidding.

Finally Kyle announced, "*Sold* for seventy-five bucks! Congratulations, Norman."

Norman Butterwick appeared enormously pleased with his win. Well into his nineties, with a full head of white hair, dapper duds dating from the Nixon administration, and a faulty short-term memory, Norman was no doubt blissfully unaware that he'd been the high bidder on this particular item the past three years as well. He could add this Hokum fedora to his growing collection.

The drive back to Long Island had seemed much quicker than the drive up to Connecticut, too quick to make sense of everything I'd heard and come to any logical conclusion.

No doubt Cullen had phoned the local authorities up there

in Connecticut and been told Meredith was in denial about her husband's extramarital affair and ignoble death, that the widow was out to make trouble for an innocent woman. Was it possible the cops were right? After all, they'd investigated Tony's death. Certainly they were privy to a lot more information than I had at my disposal. I knew nothing more than what the grieving widow had told me.

So let's say Tony and Chloe had indeed been engaged in a torrid affair. Let's say Chloe had tried to break it off and he wouldn't let her go. And let's say Meredith was either lying about the details or simply deluded, having spent the past eight years fixated on, and mentally massaging, the circumstances of her husband's death. She'd claimed Chloe believed her own lies. Perhaps she was describing herself.

Meredith's story was undeniably intriguing given the parallels with Swing's case, but what could I do with it? I knew what I *couldn't* do with it: take it to the detective in charge of Swing's murder investigation. Not only had Cullen already "followed up" on Meredith's phone tips, he would demand to know how I'd found out about them. So he was out.

Ditto for Chief Larsen, Cullen's fishing buddy and the subject himself of a corruption investigation.

As for Detective Bonnie Hernandez, she'd made it excruciatingly clear I was never to mention the purloined notebook page to her or even, I don't know, *think* about it in her presence. That woman was without a doubt too tightly wound for my good-natured, laid-back ex. This train of thought led to speculation about what kind of woman he did need, which led to speculation about what kind of woman needed him, which led to me administering a mental bitch slap and ordering myself to focus on where I was and what I was doing there.

As I scanned the auction program, I saw that I'd already missed a lot of it, including the auctioning of items donated by caterer Maia Armstrong (a dinner party for twelve), pub owner Maxine Baumgartner (one pitcher of beer per week for a year, with curly Cajun fries), bakery owner Susanne Travert (six dozen hand-decorated Halloween or Christmas cookies), and lawyer Sten Jakobsen (a pair of wills).

My breath caught when I came to item seven: a multi-course dinner for ten at Dewatre, including three kinds of wine, donated by Chef Pierre Dewatre. Clearly the program had been printed before his death.

I peered around the crowded room, looking for Victor, as Kyle auctioned off one hundred hours of personal training for next year's New York City marathon, donated by Howie Werker. Bidding was brisk on this one. Everyone in town knew that Howie routinely finished in the top ten percent of the pack. The winner was Porter Vargas, who owned a chain of sporting goods stores and could easily afford the three grand he'd just promised to shell out.

Porter's wife, Lacey, owned a lingerie shop called UnderStatements, located next door to Janey's Place. Lacey had donated a thousand-dollar shopping spree. Considering her store's prices, I figured that spree would cover a garter belt, a pair of naughty knickers, and a single silk stocking. Porter had contributed a shopping spree of the same value at Vargas Sporting Goods.

I spied Victor at last, sitting at a small table on the far side of the room with…

I muttered a bad word. He was sitting with Chloe. How was I supposed to fill him in on Meredith's tale with the subject of said tale sitting right there? Well, there was no help for it, that conversation would have to wait.

The two of them seemed to be getting along. Did Chloe still believe Lee's nonsense about Victor accusing Chloe of murder? It didn't appear so. Of course, now I was in the position of wondering how much of it *was* nonsense. Lee's vindictive taunt might have been closer to the truth than even she imagined.

As I made my slow way around the packed tables toward them, Kyle started the bidding on Dom's donation: a Janey's Place smoothie every day for a year, easily worth fifteen hundred vegetarian clams. Sophie Halperin trounced the other bidders to snag that one, a nice win for her which netted the Friends of the Waterfront eight hundred bucks.

Victor's smile when he saw me made me feel all warm and silly inside. He rose and pulled out the chair next to his, being kept warm by Sexy Beast, who greeted me as if I were a long-lost pack member. I knew Kyle wouldn't mind us bringing SB. Kyle liked me. I'm the reason there's a brass plaque with his name on it at the Smithsonian, for heaven's sake.

I greeted Chloe, who looked surprised to see me. She wore a green dress that complemented her red hair and was sipping white wine. "I thought you were tied up and couldn't make it," she said.

"I had an appointment in… New Jersey," I said as I settled SB on my lap. Best not to mention Connecticut, where Chloe had gone to college and might or might not have offed her prof. "It didn't go as long as I thought it would. Sorry I'm late."

"You were meeting with a client?" Victor sipped his red wine.

I nodded. "That's me, the tri-state Death Diva." I hadn't

told Victor about the info Bonnie had passed me since it had been illicitly obtained and was ultrasecret and not to be divulged on pain of death and all that. He knew nothing about Meredith Dorn's phone tips to Cullen.

At the podium, Kyle was in the process of auctioning Ben Ralston's donation: two thousand dollars' worth of investigative services. Lots of tittering and pointed comments for that one.

Chloe said, "If I had employees, I'd probably bid on that and use it for background checks. You can never be too careful."

"Some people do that when they start seeing someone, yes?" Victor said. "To make sure the person they're dating doesn't have a criminal record."

"Or a spouse," Chloe said. "It's sad, but people lie about that sort of thing all the time."

The little devil who lurks in a dark corner of my brainpan, where normally she just crouches there stroking her forked tail and snickering, decided to speak up. "Has that ever happened to you, Chloe? Where you, you know, were dating someone and found out he was married?"

She didn't hesitate. "No, thank goodness."

Victor said, "That probably means you're a good judge of character."

She smiled at the compliment. "I like to think so."

None of us mentioned what we all had to be thinking. Even if she'd never been involved with a married man—Meredith's accusations regarding her late husband notwithstanding—there was still the small matter of Swing's active social life, right up until the end. So it's not as if she'd never been deceived—*if* he and Chloe had actually been engaged, that is. As it stood now, that was a big *if.*

My brain hurt trying to sort through it all. I reached for the pitcher of beer, then thought better of it. I wanted my wits about me when I told Victor about the latest development. I reached for the cola instead and poured myself a glass. I tried to top off Chloe's wineglass, but she declined, explaining she was driving. Victor allowed me to refill his glass, although he already looked a tad bleary. I wondered how much he'd had before I'd arrived.

Sexy Beast was now standing on my lap, avidly hoovering all the enticing smells and entreating me with his eloquent gaze. "One chip. Make it last." I offered him a potato chip, which he sniffed and delicately took from my fingers before settling back down on my lap to dissect it.

"Sold!" Kyle announced. We joined the crowd in applauding Mal Wallace, Nina's husband and the high bidder for Ben's investigative services. Sure, Mal had two daughters of dating age, and a nervous dad might view background checks as a valuable tool for vetting their suitors. But he also had a pregnant wife—and little doubt as to the identity of the baby daddy. Sadly, it was not someone he greeted in the mirror every morning.

Nina managed to ignore the sly looks and whispered conversations rippling through the room, though her color spiked. Damn the woman, she even looked pretty blushing from embarrassment. Everyone present had to be thinking the same thing: With a wife like Nina, the investigative services of someone like Ben Ralston could come in handy.

Kyle announced the next item in the program: a dozen two-hour children's art or cooking lessons to be given in your own home. The donor? Kari Faso. I looked around the room and found her sitting with Dom and her mother, Lana, as well as Dom's third ex-wife, Meryl Hanover, the poet. Well, wasn't that cozy. The fact that my ex and all his exes got along so well—one big, happy ex-family—sometimes irked the heck out of me. I didn't know why that was, and chose not to explore those uncomfortable feelings. Does that make me immature?

Gee, thanks. I really didn't need you to answer that.

Kari looked blasé, but I knew that girl and didn't doubt she was nervous and excited as bidding commenced. A couple of well-heeled local matrons started it off, which prompted others to join in. Kari was well liked in the community, despite her association with a possible killer, her boyfriend Tucker Nearing. Most people who knew Tucker assumed he'd somehow been railroaded.

Suddenly Maia Armstrong joined the bidding, pushing the price for Kari's lessons into the high three digits and causing the other bidders to fall by the wayside, one by one. Gone was Kari's carefully cultivated façade of boredom. Her expression was a wide-eyed grin as she took in the action.

"*Sold* to Maia Armstrong!" Kyle hollered at last. The room erupted in applause as Kari accepted congratulatory backslaps and kisses. She was the youngest donor by far, and she'd managed to outshine most of the others.

"Good for her!" I turned to Victor, who appeared to be having trouble focusing on his surroundings. "Hey." I placed my palm on his back. "You okay?"

He offered a sleepy smile. "Too much wine on an empty stomach. I'm fine."

I pushed his wineglass away and shoved the bowl of chips in front of him. "Eat."

I watched Kari rise and make her way over to Maia, no

doubt to thank her. They hugged and chatted animatedly as Kyle introduced the next item on the agenda, this one donated by Martin McAuliffe: local chauffeuring on that big old Harley of his for a year or a thousand miles, whichever came first. The response was immediate and intense. Kyle had trouble controlling the bidding as women of all ages practically leapt out of their seats in their determination to snag this particular prize.

One of the bidders was sitting at the next table. Her perplexed husband asked, "What's the appeal of a few motorcycle rides? You have a brand-new Lamborghini sitting in the garage." Having personally clung to the padre's muscular torso while riding behind him on that big, sexy, rumbling machine, I could have told him what the appeal was. He probably didn't want to know.

The commotion was so lively and loud, it was impossible to conduct a conversation. Martin, shy and retiring as always, came to his feet and encouraged the ladies, winking and blowing kisses and driving the bidding skyward. For effect he wore his black leather motorcycle jacket over snug jeans and a black tee-shirt, with his helmet tucked under his arm.

"The man is shameless," I muttered. It wasn't a value judgment, it was more of, you know, an observation.

I glanced back over at Maia's table and saw that Kari was no longer there. She wasn't sitting with her parents either. I assumed she'd gone to the ladies' room. I stood and placed SB on my chair, grabbing my purse and admonishing him to lie down and behave. "I'll be right back."

Victor mumbled something in French. My confusion seemed to register and he said, "Is it over already?"

"No, I'm just going to the john. Sit tight, I'll be right

back." I met Chloe's gaze. She cut her eyes to the carafe of red wine. The level didn't look too low, but it might have been refilled. Victor wasn't a heavy drinker as far as I knew, but again I asked myself, how well did I really know him? And he'd been under a lot of stress lately.

"Think you could get hold of some coffee?" I asked her, nodding toward Victor. "I'm thinking that might be a good idea."

She got the message. "I'm on it."

In the ladies' room I found Kari washing her hands. We hugged and I congratulated her.

Her grin was a mile wide. "Maia's going to bring me in for children's birthday parties that she caters. I'll do cooking and art lessons as, like, a party activity. If it works out, she might hire me as a part-time assistant."

"You told me you want to be a chef," I reminded her. "This could be a great first step."

"I *know*," she squealed.

A stall door opened and Maxine Baumgartner emerged. "Hey, congrats, kiddo," she told Kari, her voice as rusty and grating as always. "You have the makings of a fine businesswoman. How old are you now?"

"Sixteen."

"Well, in a couple of years maybe you can work the kitchen at Murray's." She turned off the water and grabbed a paper towel. "You know, part time. How does that sound?"

"It sounds great. Thank you, Ms. Baumgartner."

She made a face as she lobbed the wadded towel into the trash. "It's Max. You make me feel a hundred years old with that 'Ms. Baumgartner' crap."

After Maxine departed, I checked that the stalls were

vacant and we were alone. Something had occurred to me, and I needed to find out whether I was on the right track. "Kari, I have to ask you something. It's about that party your dad gave last summer. When you met Swing. Remember? You told me you brought hors d'oeuvres and he said they were good?"

"He said they were great." She blushed, then sobered. "He was a nice person. He didn't have to say that. He didn't have to talk to me even, he was this big, famous chef. But he was just…" Her eyes glistened. "He was just really nice."

I sensed that Kari had moved past her adolescent crush and was viewing Swing from a more mature perspective. "It was a pool party, right?" I asked. "Do you happen to remember when it was?"

"Sure," she said. "The Fourth of July. Why?"

I thought I'd prepared myself for this possibility, but her answer still felt like a fist to the gut. I grabbed a sink to steady myself.

"Jane?" She touched my arm. "Are you all right?"

It was the same question I'd just asked Victor. My friend who'd had too much to drink. Only, I'd never seen him have too much to drink, and in the nearly three weeks he'd been living in my home, he'd had ample opportunity. I hauled in a deep breath and forced myself to *think*.

Swing had proposed to Chloe on July Fourth, according to her. He'd taken her to a fireworks display out east. Candles. White tablecloth. Champagne.

They'd toasted their engagement with Dom Perignon. His favorite. Only, she'd never actually mentioned the brand, had she? Victor had deduced it from Swing's cryptic calendar entry.

Dom p.

Shorthand for "Dom's party." My initial response to

Swing's calendar entry had been correct. "Dom" literally meant Dom, as in *my* Dom. It had nothing to do with any damn champagne.

"When?" I asked Kari.

"What?"

"When was the party?"

"July Fourth, like I said."

"No," I said, "I mean what time of day? Afternoon? Evening?"

"Evening," she said. "Well, all night. It went real late."

"How long did Swing stay?"

Her frown told me she knew this was important even though she didn't know why. "A long time. He got there around six—he brought ribs and beer brats—and he was still there when I went to bed about two in the morning. He and some others were horsing around in the pool, like, for hours."

So Swing hadn't been out east with Chloe that night, proposing to her during a fireworks display. The only accurate part was her calling the evening "magical," since magic is nothing but tricks and lies.

"I asked my dad why you weren't there," Kari said. "He told me you were out of town."

I nodded. "I didn't even know about the party. My aunt and uncle live in North Carolina. My folks and I were down there that whole week visiting them and my cousins."

On the drive back from Meredith's place in Connecticut I'd taken a fresh look at a few things, including Swing's texts. His emails. Not only had he and Chloe only talked business, there'd been not one reference to their engagement or anything romantic. I'd paid too little attention to the discrepancy. At the time I'd been more concerned with Victor's feelings, his dismay over the discovery that his brother had been a philandering jerk.

If Chloe's relationship with Swing, their engagement, was indeed a product of her demented imagination, then he had not in fact been a philandering jerk. He'd been what his friends and fans had believed at the time: a studly bachelor living it up with a variety of willing partners.

"I've got to get back." I yanked open the door and hurried back to the restaurant's dining room, where Kyle was directing the bidding for one of Norman Butterwick's landscape paintings, this one an exquisite rendition of a sun-spangled beaver pond in upstate New York.

"Three seventy-five," Kyle hollered. "Do I hear four hundred?"

Russell Appell bid four hundred, and immediately Nina shouted, "Four fifty!" I was pretty sure the painting would end up selling in the mid four figures. I also suspected that many of the folks bidding on it were counting on it increasing in value once Norman kicked the bucket. They might have a bit of a wait. Norman might be in his nineties, but his parents both lived well past one hundred.

I maneuvered around tables, bumping into people and apologizing, as I raced back toward my table. When I was almost there, I stopped short. The table was vacant. Victor and Chloe were gone.

17

"Nine-One-One, What's Your– Hiccup–Emergency?"

"WHERE ARE THEY?" I spun around, addressing everyone within earshot. "Where did they go?"

"Who?" asked the young woman who, along with her husband, owned the pottery studio on Main Street. We'd been introduced, but I could never recall their names, and I was always too embarrassed to ask.

"Are you looking for the couple you were sitting with?" Pottery Man said. "They left."

"He was acting funny," Pottery Lady said.

"Funny how?" I asked.

"Dizzy," Pottery Man said. "Stumbling. Hammered would be my guess. His wife said she was taking him home."

As I ran for the exit I heard Pottery Lady correct her husband. "She's not his wife. Didn't you recognize him? That's Swing's brother."

Outside, I shielded my eyes from the blinding sunshine and looked all around, hoping to spot Victor and Chloe. If I could stop them before she got him into her car…

They were nowhere to be seen. I ran around the side of the

building, scanning the cars parked alongside the dock.

"Jane!"

It was the trio of fan girls, leaning against the building. True to their word, they'd waited outside the restaurant. As they strolled toward me, I saw that Ariel was cuddling Sexy Beast.

"SB!" I took him from her and gratefully accepted his enthusiastic doggie kisses, though they did nothing to calm me.

"We didn't know who he belonged to," Phoebe said. "He was, like, wandering around out here all alone."

"Did you see him?" I demanded. "Did you see Victor? He was with a red-haired woman."

Mandy nodded. "Swing's agent, right? We saw her on TV."

"Victor was super drunk," Ariel said. "He could barely walk."

"He looked ready to face-plant," Phoebe said. "She had to, like, hold him up. We offered to help, but she said she had it under control."

"She's taking him home to sleep it off," Mandy said.

"Kind of depressing to see him so wasted," Ariel said. "I thought he had more, I don't know, class."

"It's worse than that," I said. "I think he's in danger."

All three came to attention at that, staring wide-eyed. Their beloved Victor, in danger?

"Did you see them leave?" I asked.

"Yeah, her car was right there." Ariel pointed to any empty spot in the middle of the parking lot. "They left, like, a couple of minutes ago."

"I'm parked—" impatiently I gestured down the street "—practically in the next town. Do you have a car here?"

"Come on." Ariel produced a key fob and beeped a bright blue Lexus parked a few feet away. The girls must have been among the first to arrive, in order to snag a spot so close.

Did I say something disparaging about girlish obsessions before? I take it back.

We piled in, with *Sexy Beast* and me riding shotgun next to Ariel. SB commenced his usual car-whining, which I ignored.

"Assuming she's taking him to her place, it's that way." I pointed toward the modest residential area on the edge of town where Chloe lived.

The girls shook their heads in unison. "That's not where they went." Ariel pulled out of the lot and drove in the opposite direction.

Mandy leaned in from the backseat. "They were headed toward the center of town, but that's all we know. Their car, like, disappeared around the corner."

Chloe could be taking him anywhere, I thought as I pulled out my phone and tried calling Victor. He didn't answer, and I didn't dare leave a message, not wanting to alert Chloe that I was on to her. As divorced from reality as she was, who knew what she might do if she felt cornered?

Now Phoebe leaned forward. "Shouldn't we, like, call nine-one-one?"

And waste time trying to explain the situation to a skeptical dispatcher—skeptical and tipsy if Chief Larson's mistress was on duty that day—then hope she'd eventually get around to sending someone?

"Damn!" I blurted, making the girls jump. Why hadn't I grabbed Sergeant Howie Werker? He was right there at the auction. Because I was rushing to catch up with Victor and

Chloe outside the restaurant, that's why.

"Should I turn here?" Ariel's voice was tight. "Where should I go, Jane?"

"I don't know. Phoebe, yeah, go ahead and try nine-one-one." While she did so, I called Howie's phone. No answer. I groaned. The raucous auction was in full swing. He probably couldn't hear his phone. I left a message, telling him it was a matter of life and death—trite but true—and begging him to call me back.

In the backseat, Phoebe was becoming increasingly frantic as she tried to communicate with the police dispatcher. "I don't *know* where she's taking him," she shrieked, "but she's driving a *green Mini Cooper with a white top*, which has to be super easy to spot. If you just—Ma'am, I—Would you just *listen*—" Phoebe put her hand over the mouthpiece and informed us, "This woman's either drunk or super high."

Where would Chloe take him? What would she be trying to accomplish?

"Oh!" I sat up straight, nearly pitching Sexy Beast off my lap. "I think I know where they're going. Turn left here. *Here!*"

Tires squealed and car horns honked as Ariel obeyed, bumping over the curb and nearly clipping Russell Appell's florist van.

"Phoebe, tell the dispatcher to send the cops to Dewatre!" I said.

"Too late, she hung up."

"Call her back! Keep trying!" To Ariel I said, "Dewatre is Swing's restaurant. You know how to get there?"

"Sure." She lead-footed it, swerving in and out of traffic, blowing through red lights, and almost turning us into a window display at Vargas Sporting Goods. Miraculously, Sexy

Beast stopped whining, whether from sheer terror or lack of oxygen due to my death grip, I couldn't say.

I tried Howie again. After the voice-mail beep, I screamed into the phone, *"Howie, I need you at Dewatre! Chloe killed Swing and now she's got Victor. Hurry!"*

As we neared Dewatre, I said, "I'm figuring Chloe would take him in through the alley in back, so let me out in front." I tossed my phone to Ariel. "Keep trying Howie. Also Detective Hernandez, she's in my contacts."

"How will you get in?" Ariel asked.

I jangled a keyring. I'd neglected to give it back to Victor after that day I'd let Denny into Dewatre. "Victor carries another set," I said. The restaurant's manager had recently returned it to him.

As we pulled up in front of the restaurant, I saw that the crime-scene tape had been removed. The broken window had been replaced and was now covered with brown paper.

Mandy touched my shoulder. "We'll go with you. You shouldn't go in there alone."

"No way, you guys keep trying to get help," I said as I let myself out of the car. If my hunch was right and Chloe and Victor were in the kitchen, I might be able to quietly sneak in through the front and surprise her. For sure I couldn't do that with this trio in tow. Also, there was no way I was going to expose teenage kids to that kind of danger.

Sexy Beast had picked up on my anxiety. He leaned on the car window, staring after me, making odd guttural sounds, the canine equivalent of the advice we yell at the screen during horror movies. *Are you nuts? Don't go in there alone! The crazed killer is going to get you!*

My fingers trembled as I turned the key in the lock. The

dining room was dim and sad looking. Victor had had it cleaned, but evidence of the firebombing and water damage remained, along with the lingering smell of scorched furniture. I heard nothing as I made my way toward the kitchen. Was my guess wrong? Had Chloe taken Victor somewhere else?

Light shone through the windows set into the double doors to the kitchen, just as on that terrible morning when I'd found Swing lying dead. My heart was a jackhammer. I approached from the side and took a peek inside. Nothing. Could the light have been left on by the cleaning crew?

Very slowly I pushed on the door, grateful for the silent, well-oiled hinges. The first thing I noticed was the rotten-egg smell of natural gas, the kind that fueled Dewatre's big commercial stove.

Someone was speaking. It was Chloe, her tone quiet and conversational. "...loved me to distraction. He wasn't very good at expressing it, though." A little laugh. "Well, you know Swing. He never wore his heart on his sleeve. I didn't mind. I always knew how he felt."

I still didn't see her as I eased the door closed and silently crossed, hunched over, to the U-shaped work station. She must be sitting on the floor somewhere behind it, but where was Victor?

The oven hissed. The smell of gas was getting stronger by the second.

"We only made love the one time," Chloe was saying, "but it was... oh, it was magical."

Magical. The same word she'd used to describe Swing's proposal. Which never happened. Had they actually had sex or was that, too, all in her head? Slowly, on all fours, I crept alongside the work island.

"I knew he wanted me to move to Crystal Harbor, to be closer to him," she said. "Oh, he didn't say it in so many words, but he didn't have to. The depth of our bond… well, words weren't necessary."

I looked around for a potential weapon and came up empty. The knife rack was on the other side of the kitchen. There were a few heavy pans, as well as a hefty stone mortar and pestle, but they were out of reach.

"It didn't have to end the way it did." Chloe's tone was wistful. "We were so *happy*. But then that ridiculous accusation. Some of his things had gone missing. I said, don't you remember? You left them at my house!" Her sigh was one of affectionate exasperation. "As if I have any use for his robe. His *deodorant*, for heaven's sake. Well, you and I both know how absentminded your brother could be."

Absentminded? Not the Swing I knew. I imagined Chloe relied on various fictions to help her rationalize anything that contradicted her demented worldview. I continued to silently crawl along the work island, wondering what would happen when she realized I was there.

"Swing demanded to know where his great-grandmother's ring was, can you imagine? So I told him—it's safe at home in my jewelry box, silly, just where I placed it the night you proposed." Her voice softened. "Well, except for when I'd take it out and try it on, of course. I understood why we couldn't make our engagement public, but I don't mind telling you, it sometimes stung that he had to keep pretending to be this big playboy."

I crept another couple of inches. Suddenly a foot came into view, clad in an elegantly casual lace-up shoe I recognized as Victor's. I swallowed hard. He was lying precisely where his brother had lain three weeks earlier, and he wasn't moving.

The floor beneath him was pristine. Denny and his team had done a superb clean-up job. Anyone viewing this room for the first time would have no inkling of the horror that had occurred here a few weeks earlier. I doubted any residual odor remained, but if so, it was masked by the sulfurous stink of the oven gas that was rapidly filling the room.

Chloe's voice cracked. "He fired me as his agent. I mean, we're engaged to be *married* and he tells me he no longer needs my services? I was obsessed with him, that's how he put it. He sounded so... so kind, like I was some kind of *underling* and he was trying to let me down easy." A watery, uncomprehending chuckle. "It made no sense. He's my fiancé and he... he thinks he can just *dismiss* me? Like some incompetent busboy?"

I leaned forward until I could see the lower part of Victor's legs. Still no movement. I hoped to God I wasn't too late.

"I didn't plan it," Chloe continued, "it just happened. One moment we're standing right here, in this exact spot, and I'm trying to make sense of all this... well, frankly, all this incomprehensible nonsense, and the next moment Swing is on the floor, and the blood... I don't remember grabbing the knife. I was just so upset. Well, you can understand, can't you?" Her tone hardened. "No, I guess you can't. Somehow you figured out what happened and you went straight to Detective Cullen. You told him I did it. Why did you do that, Victor? Don't you get it? Swing would have wanted me to protect myself, no matter what."

She'd said something similar at Murray's Pub the evening she turned the ring over to Victor, when she was trying to justify signing her fiancé's estranged former partner as a client before Swing was even in the ground. *I know for a fact he would have wanted me to take care of myself.*

"What's done is done." Chloe was weeping now. "Nothing can bring Swing back. But he loved me and he'd never want anything bad to happen to me. That's why I blamed it on SEAR. They're terrible people anyway. They might not have killed Swing, but you can't deny they deserve to be punished. It's why I called Swing's phone after I left here that day—to make it look like I had nothing to do with…" A sniffle, then her voice once more turned to steel. "It's why I have to do this to you, Victor. He would have wanted me to. Goodbye."

I took this as my cue, springing from my hiding place in the same instant that Chloe stood up and started for the back door. I took advantage of her momentary surprise to lunge at her, but she spun away and grabbed something from the steel counter behind her: one of those long butane lighters, the kind people use to light grills. I imagined Swing and his staff had employed it for flambés.

"I'll do it!" she warned, her finger on the lighter's trigger. "This place is filled with gas. If I light this, the explosion'll take out the whole building."

I knew she was right. I took a placating step back. Victor lay between us, pale and still. Thankfully, I could see his chest rise and fall with his breathing.

"We need to get out of here, Chloe," I said. "Even the oven's pilot light could set off that gas."

"I turned off the pilot light. That wasn't the plan."

"What," I said, "it's supposed to look like suicide by asphyxiation? Why would Victor do a thing like that?"

"Guilt," she said. "He killed his brother and could no longer live with himself. That's the conclusion the authorities will draw—or would have, before you butted in."

"You can't really believe that." I aimed for a calm, reasonable tone. "After a couple of hundred people witnessed you leaving the Harbor Room with him today? They saw the condition he was in. You really think they'd fail to do a tox screen and identify whatever you put into his wine?" I'd already decided she must have roofied him. The dizziness, the disorientation—he was under the influence of one of the so-called date-rape drugs.

"You've ruined everything." Her eyes were wide and panicked. A dark flush stained her face and throat. "I had it all under control and now you've ruined everything."

So much for calm and reasonable. I tried a different tack, forcing calm into my voice. "I want to help you, Chloe, really. Between the two of us, I think we can find a way out of this. You're right, Swing wouldn't have wanted anything bad to happen to you. He certainly wouldn't have wanted you to blow yourself up. I know that's not what you want either."

"What choice do I have?" she shrieked, gesturing with the lighter. "If I let you walk out of here, I spend the rest of my life behind bars. I'd rather die right here, right now. I don't have to light the gas. Just breathing it will kill us soon enough."

Victor muttered something in French. I looked down and saw that his eyes were half open. He was coming around.

I took one more stab at calm and reasonable. "Actually... and I know the gas smells poisonous, that's because of an additive they put in it for safety, because normally it's odorless. But the thing is, breathing it is not going to do us in all that quickly."

"You're lying. People commit suicide this way all the time."

"They used to," I said. "When's the last time you heard of

it happening? It's not the same gas they used back then." This is true, one of the countless, quirky, normally useless bits of trivia I acquire in my everyday role as Death Diva. The natural gas piped into today's stoves is far less lethal than the coal gas of yesteryear. Make no mistake, it's still plenty dangerous. Eventually you will expire from breathing it, if you don't die of boredom first.

Telling her that had been a gamble. Chloe could very well decide that, what the heck, since breathing the gas was unlikely to result in a swift and painless end, she might as well ignite it and end it all that way. As agitated as she was, I could see her impulsively flicking that lighter. After all, this was a woman with a history of losing control without warning, with deadly consequences.

Deadly for others, that is. I didn't doubt that if she could do it remotely, Victor and I would already be toast. Logically, her fierce self-protective instinct should keep her from blowing us all up.

However, the woman was nuts, and nutty people weren't known for logical decision making.

Victor struggled to sit up. "Jane…?" he mumbled. *"Où sommes-nous?"*

While I found this evidence of his being not dead comforting, Chloe apparently viewed it as proof that her cunning plan was well and truly doomed—and by extension, so was she. Judging by her expression of panicked horror, she could have been witnessing a zombie rising from its grave. While she stared at Victor, I focused on her right index finger, the one that was beginning to tighten on the lighter's trigger.

Chloe wasn't the only one with a healthy self-protective instinct. Acting on pure, dumb reflex, I launched myself at her.

As the two of us went down, I grasped her right wrist, twisting it for all I was worth. Her scream of pain and outrage bounced off all that steel and tile, making my ears ring. Her grip on the lighter slackened just enough to let me send it skidding across the floor tiles. It ricocheted off the massive refrigerator and landed a safe distance away.

For a relatively small woman, Chloe was surprisingly strong. I was having difficulty subduing her. I blamed it on all the adrenaline coursing through her system. That plus the element of surprise must explain how delicate little Chloe Sleeper had been able to plunge that big knife deep into the chest of a man much larger and stronger than she.

She liked surprises, did she? I hauled back and punched her in the jaw. Her head bounced against the tiles and she went limp. She wasn't unconscious, just dazed. In that instant the back door to the alley banged open and Ariel, Phoebe, and Mandy swarmed into the kitchen.

They took in the situation in a heartbeat. Ariel promptly grabbed a cast-iron griddle press and sat on Chloe, holding the heavy utensil inches from her noggin and daring her to make the teeniest move.

Meanwhile Mandy and Phoebe were all over Victor, checking him, with admirable thoroughness, for injuries and helping him to sit.

"Ew, what's that smell?" Phoebe said.

"Don't worry." I turned a valve on the oven, shutting off the flow of gas. I switched on the exhaust hood and opened the door wide. "It'll dissipate soon." As grateful as I was for the girls' intervention, the grownup in me felt compelled to add, "I thought I told you guys to wait outside."

"We heard you scream," Mandy said.

"That wasn't me, it was her." I jerked my chin toward Chloe.

Ariel said, "We were waiting in the alley in case you needed us."

"Is Victor going to be okay?" Phoebe half-supported him as he rubbed his face and blinked at his surroundings.

"I think so," I said. "He wasn't drunk, she roofied him."

The girls let Chloe know what they thought about that. They called her a bunch of bad names, several of them delightfully inventive. Meanwhile Chloe lay mute and defeated, glumly staring at the hefty griddle press poised to bash in her pretty cranium.

I said, "Any of you have your phone on you? We've got to—" I broke off at the sound of a siren. Correction, *sirens*, as in a whole screaming flock of them, getting louder by the second.

"Oh yeah," Ariel said. "That Howie guy finally called back."

18

The Elephants in the Backseat

"YOU SURE YOU have everything?" I asked as Victor descended the stairs with his leather duffel.

"If I forgot anything," he said, "I'll just have to come back for it."

"Anytime." I turned away so he wouldn't see the conflicted feelings chasing one another across my face. "Your flight is at six twenty-five?"

"Yes."

I'd only asked him the same question about a dozen times. It was three-thirty in the afternoon on October ninth, ten days since Chloe had nearly blown us up in the kitchen of Swing's restaurant and one month to the day since I'd walked into said kitchen and found Victor's brother lying in a pool of his own blood.

When had I stopped thinking of Swing as my late friend and started thinking of him as Victor's late brother? So much had happened during the past month. I hadn't mentally compartmentalized it all. I suspected it would be a long process, and wouldn't begin in earnest until Victor was back in Paris and I was once more alone in this big house. Well, not alone precisely. I had my pack-mate, Sexy Beast, for company.

SB stood yammering at us in the anxious tone he reserved for sightings of luggage. I said, "Don't worry, SB, I'm coming right back," while Victor knelt and treated him to plenty of farewell scritches.

Outside, it was overcast and chilly, with a brisk breeze: fall struggling to assert itself. I opened the car trunk. Victor tossed in his duffel and slammed the lid. Within moments we were negotiating the back roads of Crystal Harbor, headed for the parkway.

"Sophie called a little while ago," I said. "Are you ready for this?"

"I'm always ready for Crystal Harbor gossip," he said. "I'm going to miss it when I'm back in Paris. You'll have to keep me informed."

"No problem, I'll make sure you get daily updates. Well, you know the City Council investigated the police department and ended up firing Paul Cullen and his buddy Chief Larsen. Also Larsen's mistress, the drunk dispatcher."

He nodded. "Have they found replacements?"

"Yup. Howie Werker has been promoted to detective."

"This is excellent news." Victor grinned. "I like Howie. He deserves this. Do you think he and Bonnie will work well together?"

"Well, that's the other thing. She's no longer going to be a detective. They replaced her with someone from outside the department."

"They fired Bonnie?" He frowned. "Is there something I don't know about her?"

"They *promoted* Bonnie." I stopped at a red light. "She's Crystal Harbor's new police chief."

His eyebrows rose. "This is quite a shakeup. Do you think

she'll be a good chief?"

"I think so. She's a tough cop, does everything by the book." Well, almost everything. I hadn't told anyone, including Victor, about Bonnie's illicit sharing of Cullen's notes. I had no intention of doing so. Bonnie might not be my favorite person, but I'd given my word.

Speaking of said notes and the phone tips they contained, I'd been in touch with Meredith Dorn since Chloe's arrest. She'd gotten the authorities up there in Connecticut to take another look at the facts surrounding her husband Tony's supposedly accidental death. She was determined to rehabilitate his reputation.

"I hate leaving when it's all so uncertain," Victor said. "About Chloe."

"What's uncertain?" I said. "She's going to prison for a very long time."

"Unless her lawyer is successful."

"What, the insanity defense?" I asked. "Good luck with that. I don't know how it is in France, but over here, jurors aren't so quick to buy 'not responsible by reason of mental disease or defect.' Not that it's never legitimate, but in this case? Just look at the facts. Chloe tried to cover her tracks. She tried to implicate SEAR as soon as she did it, right there at the scene."

"And she called Pierre's phone a few minutes later to make herself look innocent, yes?" Victor said.

"Yes! So nobody can claim she didn't know she'd done a bad, bad thing and tried to get away with it. The prosecutor will use that to show she was sane. Well, sane enough to take responsibility for her actions. We both know the woman's a half bubble off plumb."

"There's no physical evidence that she did it," Victor said.

"Only because it was obliterated when Tucker showed up a few minutes later," I said. "He tried to pull out the knife, so that's whose fingerprints were found on it. And his big size-thirteen sneakers wiped out any shoe prints Chloe might have left." He still looked worried, so I added, "Don't forget, she *confessed*. She told you about how she killed him, and why."

"I don't recall any of that."

"Because she drugged you," I said. "But I heard it loud and clear, and unless this ends in some kind of plea bargain, I'll be on the stand helping to convict her."

Victor sighed. "Her lawyer, he's good, yes? Experienced. And juries are unpredictable."

"Okay, it's not going to happen, Victor. Chloe's going to find herself in an orange jumpsuit. Which for a redhead…" I shuddered. Talk about cruel and unusual punishment. "But if she *did* get off on insanity, they'd toss her into a secure state psychiatric institution."

"For how long?"

"Until she's deemed no longer, you know, dangerous." I merged onto the parkway.

"She can be very persuasive," he said. "She had us both fooled."

No way to deny that. "I thought Tooley was the unstable one. Well, he is. And Lee has her own wackadoodle issues. But Chloe just didn't emit those vibes—not at first anyway." Which might explain why I ignored that telltale uh-oh alarm when I found nothing but businesslike emails between Swing and Chloe. Not to mention the absence of evidence that Chloe had spent time at Swing's home.

"I believed her when she told us they were engaged," Victor said.

"Well, she did have your great-grandma's ring," I reminded him. "Swiped when his back was turned, no doubt. And she believed it, too, that's the thing. She believed the two of them were deeply in love and getting married. She came off as sincere because she *was* sincere."

"But still, she wanted the 'engagement' kept secret," he said.

"Supposedly because the attention would make her uncomfortable, but what I think? I think deep down she knew it was BS and she knew that if people started looking into it, her story would unravel."

"But she told *us*."

"Because she needed to return the ring," I said. "Her conscience wouldn't allow her to keep your family heirloom."

His tone was bitter. "No, it would only allow her to murder my brother, a man who'd shown her nothing but kindness."

I thought of something Chloe had said when we'd discussed Victor's lovestruck stalkers. *Someone that obsessed, you don't know what she's capable of.* She could have been describing herself.

We lapsed into silence while I drove at a sedate speed in the right lane. I was in no rush to see Victor step out of my car and out of my life.

At last I said, "So get this. Chloe told me she had no family. I believed it at the time. I mean, why not? Turns out, according to the cops, she has tons of family. Parents, four siblings, zillions of nieces and nephews and what-all. Two of her *grandparents* are still around, for heaven's sake. Most of them live in the Boston area."

"Why did she lie about that?"

"She was estranged from them," I said. "Seems she's been troubled for a long time and refused to get help. They've had no contact with her for years. Oh! You know I told you that Chloe had a picture of her and Swing at her place? The two of them looking all, you know, lovey-dovey?" When he nodded, I said, "Lee Romano, of all people, cleared that one up. She was at the charity event where that picture was taken. It was just Swing and his agent posing for a snapshot together—nothing romantic about it." Except in the agent's warped mind.

"What do you think of Lee's new venture?" Victor wore a crooked smile.

"I think she's finally found her calling. And if she gives Miranda Daniels a run for her money, I'm all for it."

Lee's combative performance on *Ramrod News* had snagged the attention of another network. They admired how she'd handled herself and floated the idea of her hosting a competing "news" show in the same time slot. Essentially they offered Lee a platform to take down any individual or organization she thought needed it. How could she resist? The result was *The Romano Files*, which had debuted three days earlier.

"She really did a job on Romulus Tooley and his pals." Victor, now grinning, shook his head at Lee's audacity. The Society for Endangered Animal Rights and its hapless spokesman had been the focus of her first show. She'd taken them apart with surgical precision, refusing to mince words, shedding light on little-known facts and assorted atrocities that the legitimate news outlets had been afraid to touch. No one else was willing to risk being sued or, worse, targeted for violence by terrorists posing as do-good animal-rights activists.

Lee Romano's attitude? *Bring it.* She refused to knuckle

under to people she described as cowardly thugs hiding behind pandas. The public uproar engendered by that episode had been instant and vocal, forcing the FBI to redouble their efforts to identify the worst ecoterrorists and bring them to justice.

"Well," I said, "Leonora Romano was determined to become a household name, and damn if she hasn't accomplished that."

"Except she wanted to be known as the finest *chef*," Victor said, "and this she has not accomplished."

"It's just a matter of time. I heard a rumor—"

"No! A rumor?" Victor teased. "In Crystal Harbor?"

I smirked. "Yeah, go figure. It's my understanding that Lee negotiated something else with the network in addition to *The Romano Files*. She kind of shoved it down their throats."

"Ah, this sounds like the Lee I know," he said.

"She's going to be doing these specials where she goes into a restaurant, rips into their signature dishes—you know, saying how disgusting they are, how no one there knows how to cook—and then teaches them how to do it right. Kind of like those shows where the mean chef helps turn around a failing restaurant. Only this isn't about saving a business, it's about the food itself."

"I don't know, it's a stretch," Victor said. "Lee being mean? Do you think she can pull it off?"

I pretended to mull that over. "Nah… it's just so out of character."

Despite my best efforts to drag out the trip, I couldn't simply drive past the parkway exit to JFK International Airport. The airport was huge, but unless I deliberately took wrong turns on the looping roads, we'd reach Terminal One in under five minutes. I steered onto the exit ramp.

"Well…" I glanced at Victor's handsome profile. "Next time you're in New York, you know you have a place to stay. Which should be pretty soon, right? I mean, you've listed Swing's house with an agent. The restaurant too. You'll have to come back for the closings."

"Not necessarily," he said. "My lawyer says I can do it remotely by granting him power of attorney."

"Oh. Um, well, your firm might want you back in New York at some point."

"Actually, my firm has an apartment near the SoHo office for the use of out-of-town staff."

"Oh." Then… "Wait a minute. All that time you were making that long, miserable commute from my place, you could have been staying, what, a couple of blocks from your office?"

"That's right."

I rolled that around my cranium. "Well, I suppose it would have been difficult for you to, you know, settle Swing's affairs from the city."

"Not that difficult. That's not why I accepted your hospitality these past few weeks."

He left it at that. I glanced over and found him gazing steadily at me, his expression one of unguarded longing. I nearly crashed into a light pole.

Victor pointed to the right. "Go in there. We have time." Obediently I turned and found myself in the cell phone lot. A handful of cars were parked near the entrance of the large lot. I drove to a relatively secluded spot and killed the engine.

Victor took my hand. Staring at it, he stroked the palm and entwined his fingers with mine. Finally he looked at me. "I wanted to be close to you."

I swallowed hard. I felt lightheaded.

"I still do," he continued. "I believe we have something special, Jane. I think you feel it too, yes?"

I took a deep breath, trying to corral my thoughts. I wouldn't lie. "Yes," I said, "but I don't know what it means, whether it's just… I don't know, a fleeting infatuation or…" I offered a helpless shrug.

His smile was gentle and understanding and ruthlessly sexy. "We don't have to label it."

"You know, we just went through a lot together." I was trying to be reasonable, not the easiest thing with Victor caressing my fingers. "I mean, this was an intense few weeks, what with your brother's murder and… the rest of it. That sort of thing creates a, um, an artificial closeness, you know? Like soldiers during battle."

"You think I'm saying these things because you saved my life." He shook his head. "Not so. I've felt this way for some time."

I emitted a ragged sigh and ordered myself to shut up. You'd think I had a steady stream of sexy Frenchman declaring their feelings for me, from the way I appeared so willing to blow this one off. Which I wasn't, not really. It was nerves, plus, if I was being honest with myself, a failure to know my own heart. I'd been without a significant other for so long, I wasn't entirely sure how to proceed. Or whether I even wanted to proceed.

I considered my words carefully. "This is why you were acting strange."

"Strange?"

I thought of that day at Swing's house when I helped Victor go through his brother's things. He'd spoken of leaving within a couple of days, bolting before his scheduled interview with Cullen—an interview that had never materialized since Chloe had been arrested the very next day. "You just seemed kind of, I don't know, subdued," I said. "Every time you talked about going back to Paris."

"I didn't want to leave you," he said. "It was eating me up."

Not guilt over Swing's death, as I'd feared at the time, but grief over our impending separation.

"What?" He turned my face toward his and brushed his thumb across the smile I was trying to suppress. "What does this mean?"

"Nothing. I'm an idiot. A clueless, self-defeating idiot."

"Well, I would like this clueless, self-defeating idiot to move to Paris with me."

I gaped at him, openmouthed.

"We don't have to completely understand what's happening between us, not yet," he said. "We just need to give it space to happen. And we can't do that when we're thousands of miles apart with an ocean between us."

"But… *Paris?*" Living in the City of Light. With Victor. I imagined strolling along the Champs-Élysées on his arm, Sexy Beast strutting along at our side, wearing a proudly raised tail and a snazzy little French beret.

I shook my head in an attempt to replace the seductive image with cold, immutable logic. "I can't move out of the house. Not while Sexy Beast is alive."

"Ah, yes." His tone was arid. "The house your dog owns."

"I'm his guardian and he has to remain in that house. It's the way Irene McAuliffe structured her will—Oh, you know all this." I'd explained the bizarre legal device to him. He was a smart man, I knew he got it.

"I like Sexy Beast. I'm hoping he lives a long, happy life." He tipped his head consideringly. "Maybe not too long."

I grinned, knowing he didn't mean it. Of course, there were no legal impediments to Victor uprooting his life in Paris, moving in with me, and working out of the SoHo office on a permanent basis. I wasn't even close to making such an offer, however, and I knew he didn't expect it.

And, too, I couldn't ignore the elephant in the backseat. Well, two elephants, though I doubted either my ex or the padre would appreciate the analogy. My feelings about them were too confused. I would need to unpack a lot of emotional baggage before I could even consider anything serious with my charming Frenchman.

"You know," I said, "there's nothing in Irene's will against Parisian vacations."

"*Long* Parisian vacations." He shifted closer and caressed the tender spot behind my ear, making me shiver. "With side trips to my bed-and-breakfast in Uzès." The way he said this left little doubt he was talking about one room, not two.

"Okay," I breathed. And then I stopped breathing because he was leaning closer, and his mouth was touching my mouth, and his hand was slipping around my neck and the kiss was turning so... *oh!* And if you ask was it a French kiss, I will slap you because it was so much sweeter and hotter and head-swimmingly perfect than I'd imagined his kiss would be. And I'd done a lot of imagining over the past month.

When it was over we sat with our foreheads touching, catching our breath, and somehow my arms had ended up around his neck, and his hands had ended up... well, wherever the heck they wanted to be, which was just fine with me. And that darn center console was playing chaperone, reminding us where we were and that Victor had a flight to catch.

"You said 'okay.'" He settled back in his seat, those silver-gray eyes crinkling at the corners. "That's a verbal agreement, Jane. Legally binding in the state of New York."

"Oh. Well." I turned the key in the engine, chewing back a grin. "If it's *legally binding*, then I guess I have no choice."

About the Author

Pamela Burford comes from a funny family. You may take that any way you want. She was raised in a household that valued laughter above all, so of course the first thing she looked for in a husband was a sense of humor. Is it any wonder their grown kids are into stand-up comedy and improv? Oh, and here's another fun fact: Pamela's identical twin sister, Patricia Ryan, aka P.B. Ryan, is also a published novelist. Patricia is the Good Twin, and yeah, Pamela knows what that makes her. But hey, Evil Twins have more fun!

It should come as no surprise that everything Pamela writes is infused with her own quirky brand of humor, from her feel-good contemporary romance and romantic suspense novels to her popular Jane Delaney mystery series, featuring snarky "Death Diva" Jane, her canine sidekick Sexy Beast, and a fun love-triangle subplot. Pamela's own beloved poodle, Murray, wants you to know that any similarities between himself and neurotic, high-strung Sexy Beast are purely coincidental.

Pamela is the proud founder and past president of Long Island Romance Writers. Her books have won awards and sold millions of copies, but what excites her most is hearing from readers. Swing by and say hi at pamelaburford.com.

www.ingramcontent.com/pod-product-compliance
Lightning Source LLC
Chambersburg PA
CBHW032110180726
48284CB00002B/526